Doctor Feel Good

Be Yours Series

Blue Saffire

Perceptive Illusions Publishing, Inc.
Bay Shore, New York

Blue Saffire/Perceptive Illusions Publishing, Inc.
PO Box 5253
Bay Shore, New York 11706
www.BlueSaffire.com

Publisher's Note: This is a work of fiction. Names, characters, places, and incidents are a product of the author's imagination. Locales and public names are sometimes used for atmospheric purposes. Any resemblance to actual people, living or dead, or to businesses, companies, events, institutions, or locales is completely coincidental.

Ordering Information:
Quantity sales. Special discounts are available on quantity purchases by corporations, associations, and others. For details, contact the "Special Sales Department" at the address above.

Doctor Feel Good: Be Yours Series / Blue Saffire. -- 1st ed.
ISBN 978-1-941924-54-9

Everything is in Divine timing. Find what's meant to be and run with it. Leave your mark on the world, don't let the world mark you.

—Blue Saffire

Online Love

Omid

"What are you doing?" my cousin, Ramses says as he walks into the room.

I jump, nearly knocking the laptop from my lap as I sit on the bed with my back to the wall behind me. I look up to find the twins both watching me with mischievous smiles on their faces. My parents would literally kill me if they knew about my online profiles.

Social media isn't allowed in Iran. My Persian parents are nothing but traditional. This...all of this would be frowned upon. Just the thought makes my chest hurt.

There are so many things I want to experience that my baba wouldn't approve of. I had to beg to stay this summer with my uncle and his sons. Uncle Jahan is the black sheep of the family to begin with.

If it weren't for Baba benefiting from my uncle's disinterest in the family's wealth and stature, I'm sure Baba would've disowned him by now. I still can't believe I'm here.

"Nothing," I mutter and try to close the laptop that my uncle gifted me upon arrival.

Remi, the other twin, rushes over and reaches out to keep me from closing the device. Plucking it from my lap, he sits on the bed beside me and begins to laugh. Ramses climbs onto the bed on the other side of me, sandwiching me in.

"Your father will never let you return if he finds out about this," Remi says as he starts to scroll through the laptop. "She's pretty."

"Let me see," Ramses says, reaching over me to grab the laptop from his brother. Pulling the device into his lap, he whistles. "Now that is a gorgeous girl. What do you plan to do with her?"

"Nothing," I mutter and rub my hands on my jeans.

"Is that the only word you know in English," Remi teases knowing that I speak English just fine.

My cousins are a few years older than me. They've been here in America since they were little toddlers. At eighteen, this is my first trip. I've looked up to them every time they've come to Shiraz to visit. I wanted to come spend time with them this summer to try to be as cool as they are.

"Ah, we can't have that. Let me help you," Ramses says and clicks to request the friendship of the beautiful girl I've spent the last two hours staring at.

"Wait, what are you doing?" My heavy Persian accent thickens.

"*Sakin ol, kuzen.*"

"How am I to relax? You just sent her a request. I…I don't even have a profile pic. Why would you do this?"

"Because it's time you got your dick wet," Remi laughs.

"What?"

Ramses laughs. "You heard him."

"It's a computer. How am I supposed to get my…How is this supposed to help with that?"

Remi bumps me with his shoulder. "You are a Vahid. She will drop her panties as soon as she sees your face."

"But that's my point. I can't put my face on there. Do you know what my father will do if he finds out?"

Ramses pauses as he already has his phone out to take my picture to load to the computer. "Okay. You have a point."

"He looks like us. His eyes are just different."

"*Doğru,*" Ramses says thoughtfully. "You shaved today. You take a picture."

"You want to put your face on…No, I want to be honest with her. I don't want to lie," I say firmly.

"Give him your Cavallis." Remi waves for Ramses to hand over his sunglasses.

I take the shades and place them on. Remi wraps an arm around my neck and snaps a picture. He then takes a few of himself. I fold my arms over my chest and frown at him.

"Have trust, Omid. We are looking out for you," Ramses says.

"We'll load this one of the two of us together. The shades will put off the snoops and if your father does see, I'll take the blame. When she sees it, she'll see two attractive guys and will accept your request. We'll put up these other photos to make it seem like it's my profile," Remi says as if it's so simple.

"We'll change the profile name too."

"Use Arman," Remi snorts.

"Ha! They won't know which. Nice."

Remi and I have the same middle name. This just may work. "Do you think it will work?" I say as hope starts to bloom.

I've been looking at this girl's profile since I got the laptop a week ago and started to browse the internet. She's gorgeous. Big brown eyes that are slanted and sparkle when she smiles. It's like she's looking at me in every picture. As if she's connecting to my soul through each image.

Her full lips must make kissing the most wonderful thing in the world. Her dark hair is in a different style in almost every picture. There's one picture of her in shorts and a bikini top. I've never been harder in my life than when I saw that image.

She's funny too. Her posts show her sense of humor. For a sixteen year old, she's extremely smart as well. I've been watching her debate on one of the sites. She has well-formed opinions and responses. I think her brain is more of a turn-on than her face and body.

"It will work. American girls are different. You will see," Remi's says.

"But…how am I going to…never mind," I say feeling like a fish out of water. She hasn't even accepted my request.

"Will you look at that? I told you we're too handsome to resist," Ramses snickers. "You're welcome."

I snatch the laptop back as my heart pounds. She accepted. She really accepted.

"What will you do now, Omid?"

Palms sweaty, I grin and send my first inbox to my new friend. I will not waste my time here in America. I want to know this girl.

Hello. My name is Arman. Can I have a minute of your time to tell you how beautiful you are?

I hit send and wait for the girl of my dreams to reply as my cousins sit teasing me. The wait seems to take forever. I roll my eyes at my cousins' antics, but on the inside I feel sick. I could've said something different. Something cool.

"You're a little smooth. We'll work on that," Ramses says.

"Shit, it worked," Remi says, "She's typing."

Divine

Lying on my stomach on my bed, I chew on my lip as I read the message again. I almost didn't accept the request. These thirsty dudes stay in my inbox. Still, there's something about ol' boy in the shades and the one without them is fine as hell too. I go to his profile and scroll through his pics.

I'm a little disappointed to find out that the one without the shades seems to be the owner of the profile. He's still fine and he got game. I shrug and click back on Messenger.

"Screw it," I whisper and start to type.

Boys at school never holler at me. I'm too dark, too outspoken, too whatever for them. I'm not butt hurt over it. I've gotten plenty of modeling gigs since my sixteenth birthday. I'm fine with the skin I'm in.

I bite my lip as I read over my message. I don't want to come off like I'm feigning or anything. It's simple enough. I hit send.

Hey, what's up? I'm Divine.

Clicking back to his profile, I look over the pictures again. "Arman," I test the name on my lips. He's Middle Eastern. I can tell that much. My dad would have a fit. I think for a minute that I could be talking to a terrorist but shake that stupid shit off. I hate the way one of my best friends at school gets treated. Dada is the coolest girl in my crew. People make assumptions from your looks in a heartbeat.

Your name is as beautiful as you are. Do you have a boyfriend, Divine?

I giggle and start to type back. "Oh shit." I startle when my cousin, Marica, flops down on the bed beside me. She falls onto her back giggling after almost scaring the bejesus out of me.

"You're not funny. I'm going to put my brother's dirty socks in your pillowcase tonight," I say and roll my eyes.

She knows I'm bluffing. I love Marica like my own sister. I hate that her family moved away. I miss her being here all the time. She's only here for the summer now.

"Whatcha doing?" she says, flipping over onto her stomach.

I chew on my lip again, deciding on whether or not to tell her. She knows how strict my parents are, but she wouldn't rat me out. I push the laptop between us and show her the profile pics of the guy that I'm talking to.

"He just requested me and popped up in my inbox," I explain.

"Oh, they're cute. Which are you talking to?"

"I think it's the one without the glasses," I say as I sit up and pull the laptop into my lap to finish typing.

"Oh, he got game," Marica laughs.

"Right!"

Thank you. No, I'm not seeing anyone. Why are you asking?

I hit send and laugh, falling into my cousin. She takes the computer and clicks to look at the pictures again. I think we are both drooling. He has such pretty eyes. They're a light amber color. Sort of hazel. His dark hair, thick brows, and lashes are arresting and sort of dangerous too.

"Does he look too old?" I muse as I knot my fingers in my T-shirt.

"A little. His profile says he's eighteen though. His birthday just passed." She gasps. "Oh, here. He replied."

Because you are now my princess. I have to go for now but we'll talk again soon. Later, gorgeous.

"Oh my God," Marica and I say at the same time.

Just like that. I fall in love with a boy I don't even know. Although, I can't stop looking at his friend with him in the picture. I shrug. Arman is just as fine and he sounds like everything.

CHAPTER ONE

Decisions of New

Omid

Lifting my head from the pillow, I look beside me. The bed is empty. Once again it was just a dream.

I turn and squint at the light coming through the open drapes. I groan. "Navid," I huff and lift an arm to cover my eyes.

It's my last day in Dubai before I head back to America. After Salat al-fajr, I thought I'd get a few more hours of sleep. I wanted to get some rest.

My family has been running me around since I got to Iran. So much has changed in the last few years. I'm here to make peace.

"You're the one that wanted to only come for two weeks. You should've known all of your mothers would want time with you. Your siblings as well. Your brother has been waiting for you. You promised him you would ride with him in the desert this morning," Navid says as he moves to my closet.

"Argh. Yeah, I told him I'd ride the ATVs. Okay, okay, *bana bir dakika ver*," I say and roll out of bed.

Knowing a minute is probably all I'll get before Navid starts nagging, I swing my legs off the bed. Standing nude, I stretch my six one frame upward before bending to drop into downward dog. Yoga has kept me centered over the years and helped me to keep fit, along with my four weekly workouts. Navid is accustomed to my routine.

My father may have been pissed when I left but he made sure the man I had by my side all my life followed me as I started my new life. At first, I thought it was to have a spy with me at all times.

Which was probably baba's intention, but Navid has become more like a father to me than the man whose seed I come from. He has been with me through all my greatest and most disappointing moments. He has watched me become the man I am today.

"Don't forget dinner with your parents before we leave. You have a lot of decisions to make, Omid," he says when I settle with my legs crossed.

I inhale and release a deep breath. I know what he's hinting at but play dumb for the time being. I don't want to think about what all of the changes mean. While my father has reached out, I'm not naïve enough to think it's without motive.

Uncle Jahan and the twins have made a major play. It's beginning to have a ripple effect. My father has no choice but to try to force me back into the fold. I grin as I think of the twins. They have turned into men to fear and love. They are still there for me to this day.

That summer I spent with them both broke and made me. My dream comes back to me. I often dream of her face. I will forever remember her, her face, and her name. She was my first love and her memory has stuck with me all these years.

Navid releases a heavy breath. I give up on the peace I'm trying to cultivate. It's clear he wants to get this off his chest.

"Go on. Say what you must," I breathe as I level my gaze on him.

"You have accepted his offer to come for this visit. That's as good as saying you want a run at the throne. Your parents are going to push themselves back into your life. This means you will have to protect everything you have built more than you have in years. Have you thought of this?"

"Yes, I have."

"Omid," he says sternly. Dropping into a whisper, he moves closer. "Do you plan to continue with your practice?"

"That I do." I stand and start for the bathroom.

"Men have been killed for less. Exile is the least of your worries," he says to my back.

Turning back to him, I glare and take a step forward. "I haven't feared my father since I was an eighteen year old boy. I'm here because Anne cried for me to come. If not for my mother I wouldn't be here," I bite out.

"Ah, but *your* mother will be the first to get behind your father to meddle in your life. It will not be just you against your father. Your family will not approve of this at all," he warns. "Sassa means well but she will not stop your father's wrath when he finds out about your lifestyle."

"Anne Sassa is the only mother that matters," I say and turn for the shower.

My father has three wives. His third wife and my birth mother, Hana. His second wife, Padma, and his first wife—the wife that has been a mother to me since I was a boy, Sassa. My Anne Sassa. I will always see her as my mother.

The burn of all those years ago comes back. I didn't expect my birth mother to go against my father but I did expect her to understand my love. She was the one who told me to experience life and follow my heart. As soon as I did she turned her back on me and allowed my father to take everything I cared about way.

I step into the shower and let the showerheads hit me from all angles. I want to forget. It's how I've pushed forward in my life. I've buried it away and forgotten as much as I can.

It was best.

Divine

"Is this really what you want to do?" Marica says through labored breaths as she runs on the treadmill next to me.

"Yeah, it's a part of my plan. Business is taking off well beyond my dreams. Next on my list is to be a mommy," I say with a smile.

"Yeah, but IUI?"

"Okay," I breathe, slowing my treadmill down to focus on my cousin. "Wait a moment. Don't tell me you're on this too. I thought you would support me. You're going to have the same procedure."

Marica stops the treadmill with tears in her eyes and I automatically want to kick myself. I know why my cousin has chosen this route. My heart breaks as I watch her lips tremble.

"He was my everything, Divine. I promised him I'd do this. I've put it off long enough. Honestly, I'm scared to death, but he was my best friend and the only promise he ever broke to me was the one he made the last time he left for a tour. He didn't come back home. I'm going to put on my big girl panties and I'm going to allow my husband to live on inside of me," she says and gasps like the wind has been knocked out of her.

I reach to cover her hand with mine as she bends over as if in pain. Keith was a good guy. He was a wonderful husband to my cousin.

My heart aches for her. I came out here to New Jersey to check on her. She ran from L.A. right after burying her husband. I think in reality she was running from this promise.

"We're going to do this together. We'll have our babies together. You're not doing this alone," I say softly.

Looking up at me through tear filled eyes she says, "I don't want you to do this because of me."

"I'm not. I want a baby. The fact that we're doing it around the same time is just a bonus," I say and smile.

"You're not fooling anyone, Divine. You're just as scared as I am," she gives a breathless laugh.

I shrug. "Maybe. Although, I'm more afraid of my kid not liking me than of doing this alone."

She pulls a face at me. "You're the cool aunt already. I know your baby will love you to the moon and back." She takes a pause and drops her eyes as if looking through her feelings. Then looks up at me. "I wish you would try to date first. You won't even try."

I pull my hand back as if I've been burned. I have been. Relationships are not for me. Trust me.

Once in my life, I loved so hard it took my breath away, just to have my heart broken with no explanation. That was enough for me. I've buried those memories so deep.

Since then I've had my heart torn out by a cruel college experience. Then I ended up in a two-year relationship with someone that was never mine to begin with. Yup, men are no good to me unless they're dropping their drawers to drop off some D and leave.

I'm selective about who I allow to make my special deliveries as well. While I've had some of the best pipe layers to keep me satisfied, not one of them has been a candidate for making a baby. I'd rather get me some sperm and have an anonymous contributor.

Yup, dating is not for me. Call me jaded. It is what it is.

"Most these dudes are intimidated by me to begin with. A black woman with a million dollar business that's growing like wild fire and I'm a popular influencer on social media.

"Girl please, these guys be looking for a pay check and free pussy when they find out who I am. I'm good," I reply.

Marica laughs and smiles at me. I can still see the pain in her eyes. It's been a year since she lost Keith. I wish there were something more I could do for her.

"I remember when we were sixteen and had it all planned out. We were going to get married first and then move to someplace exotic and live the life." She snorts. "None of that happened. I'm a crazy widow and you're a relationship phobic."

"Yeah, okay. You're not crazy and I'm going to pass on that other noise you're spewing. You can say all that if you want…Um…but ain't nobody broke around here. That means we're doing just fine," I say.

Marica laughs again and it reaches her eyes this time. Not only did Keith leave her with a healthy policy to take care of her. He invested some money and Marica being the hustler she is turned it into a future she can ride securely into.

"Facts. I'm going to miss you," she says.

"You'll be back in L.A. in no time. It's only three weeks. Then we can hold hands as we figure out what the hell we're in for." I give her a bright smile.

"I love you, girl. You don't know what this time with you has meant to me."

"I'd be right here with you until moving day if I didn't have meetings and a business to get back to," I reply. "Besides, you've been trying to make me fat. All this good eating. I'll be back to two a days when I get back home."

"Oh please. That body has been the envy of everyone since you turned fourteen. I'm so proud of you, Divine. You've been through some BS but you never let a closed door stop you. It's like all this shit eggs you on."

"The word *no* is some bullshit I'm not trying to hear. I'm always going to find a way."

"Yeah, I know. I'm going to find that again."

I give her a smile and reach to pull her into a hug over the handles of the treadmills between us. I love this woman. We're just as tight at thirty-five as we were at sixteen.

"You still have it. It will come out soon enough. You're a fighter, babe. You've got this."

"We're going to be mamas." She laughs. "I hope this Dr. Nobi guy is as good as they say. I'll be devastated if this doesn't work out."

"We've been waiting six months to get in to see him. I looked the place up. They're supposed to be the best. Keith did his research. I think we're going to be in great hands," I reassure her.

Her husband thought of everything. Freezing his sperm, finding her the best doctors. While this Dr. Nobi is a GYN and not a fertility specialist, he and his practice come highly recommended and have won awards and all types of accolades.

This will be just fine.

Omid

The ride with my brother was great. Bazar reminds me of how I'd been with the twins when I was younger. He looks up to me. Although he is my half-brother that has never made a difference to us. Not like it does with a few of my other siblings.

Even now as I sit at this table with the rest of my family, you can feel the tension in the room. The restaurant staff has picked up on it enough to give a wide breadth. I'll be happy to get on my flight and return home. I've never been one for the petty battle for my father's attention or chasing after ranks.

"Your father says you are a doctor."

I turn to the dark haired offering my parents think they're going to pass off on me. I'm not about to enter an arranged marriage. They've all bumped their fucking heads. When I left at nineteen, I left all of this behind. I haven't returned to pick back up where we left off.

The bright teal hijab brightens her light olive colored face and the dark strains of hair escaping are a note to her beauty, but she's not my type. I'm not falling for the shit. I've always been attracted to a certain type of woman and that's not what my family will allow.

So while very pretty, this woman will not entice me to change my mind and come around to what my family wants. I rolled my eyes the moment I saw her. She favors my mother with the light skin and the fair eyes.

No doubt my mother and father are hoping I'll recreate my odd colored eyes with this woman. Always looking to create fairer off springs. This isn't even the same girl I was supposed to marry before I left this life behind. No, her family accepted my brother as a replacement.

I look across the table at Paiman. He has let himself go and so has his wife that he gained from my absence. They both look miserable. This will not be my life.

"Yes, I am," I reply.

I can't even remember what they said her name is. I've looked at my watch numerous times praying for it to be my time to leave. I've been fuming since I arrived to find this woman and her family waiting to meet me. I should've seen it coming.

"He has done well for himself in America," my father says proudly.

I fight not to roll my eyes. He has no idea *what* I've been doing in America. I've made sure of it. My family in Shiraz knows what I allow. Uncle Jahan and the twins understood my decisions and connected me to the right people to help make my life happen.

"But you plan to return home?" The father of the woman next to me asks.

"I don't know where you're getting your information," I say tightly. "I have no such intentions."

"*Baban burada,*" my father says.

"Yes, my family is here but this hasn't been my home in almost two decades."

"Maybe that means it's time to come home. We've missed having you here," my mother says.

My jaw clenches. I will not disrespect my anne but this has her written all over it. I look to Anne Sassa and she gives me a small smile. I relax a little. I could never tell the people sitting at this table this but Sassa is the reason I became an OB/GYN with special interest in fertility.

Of all my father's wives, she is the only one without children. She's the best mother of them all but has never had her own. I was very small when she lost the only child she ever conceived. It's something that has stuck with me.

I shake the horrible memory away. "It was good to spend time with you all. Unfortunately, I must return home," I say and stand.

"My son, the busy doctor. You'll have to make more time for your family."

"Yes, Baba. I will," I say to my father and round the table to hug him and my mothers.

When I get to Anne Sassa, she pulls me into a tight hug and holds me for a long time. "I'm so proud of you. Keep becoming the man you love to be," she whispers into my ear.

"*Seni seviyorum, Anne,*" I whisper back.

"I love you too, Omid Arman."

I release her and reach to wipe at her tears. She gives me a big smile. I nod at her and move to hug the woman who give birth to me.

"If you don't like her we can find another. They're a good family. Nice match for you," she says into my ear.

"*Bir dahaki sefere kadar, Anne* Hana," I reply.

"Until next time, *oğlum.*" I don't miss the ways she says *my son* possessively. Her glare fixed behind me where Sassa sits.

Ignoring the exchange, I move on to my siblings. It takes me another half hour of goodbyes before I get out of the restaurant to head to the hotel to get my things and go home. I half expect my father to have me kidnapped before I get on the plane.

Navid looks like he's half expecting the same. I wouldn't put my father above it, no matter how much he knows I'd loathe him for it. I finally breathe when the plane lifts off headed back to California where I've built my life and my home.

The life I chose.

CHAPTER TWO

Opinions

Divine

The way this dude is looking at me across this baggage claim has me reconsidering the drought I'm on. He sucks his lip into his mouth as his eyes roll over me. You would think he could see right through my leggings and tank top the way they light up.

It's been over a year and a half since I've called on my special delivery dude. I've been too busy with my business to put in a call. Jamel was a god in the sheets which is why I may have shed just one tear when I heard he was getting married.

Whatever.

There's only one thing stopping me from ending this pussy vacation. The guy eye fucking me is Middle Eastern. That's a hard pass for me. While they're my greatest weakness—like I stalk several of my favs on the gram—they're also a hard limit for me. I refuse to date or fuck a dude that even comes close to being Persian. I prefer to drool from a distance.

My cellphone rings keeping me from flirting with the guy still making sexy eyes at me. I look down at the ringing device to see it's my father. He and my mother insisted that he be the one to pick me up from the airport today.

I normally use a car service. Sometimes, one of my brothers will come in my car. That's if they get to drive the car while I'm gone.

Knowing my parents they want to get in my business and hand over opinions I haven't asked for. I'm going through with having this baby. It was a courtesy for me to say something in the first place. I wasn't asking for input.

"Hey, Daddy. I'm at the baggage claim," I call into the phone after I answer.

"You know how much I hate this place. I told your mother I would've paid for the Uber or whatever. No, I had to be the one to come and get you. You've got ten minutes, Div. I'm not dealing with this shit all day. I'm missing a game," he grumbles.

I have to laugh to myself and roll my eyes. I didn't ask for him to come get me. Now I have to rush around because he will in fact leave my ass right here. This also tells me that my mother is the mastermind behind whatever they have planned—as usual.

"Daddy, I'm coming as soon as I get my bags," I huff and try to shift my carryon back up my shoulder. "Listen, I see my bags. I can't talk to you and get to all of them at the same time."

"All of them? Girl, you were out there for what? Three days."

"It was a week, Daddy. I'll talk to you when I get to the car."

"Spoiled ass women. I blame your mama. She put it on me and had me spoiling her and I lost my mind when I had little girls of my own to spoil. Made you all spoiled," he mumbles.

"Bye, Daddy," I laugh and hang up.

My father is an entire trip. He knows good and well he wouldn't have it any other way. Only reason he's not in here to help with my bags is because he's too cheap to pay for parking.

I rush to grab my two bags before they disappear. I laugh when I see the guy that was eye fucking me has moved on to his next conquest. I'm good with that.

Gathering my things I rush to exit the airport before my father leaves me and I have to find another way home. I think about it for a few minutes. Missing my ride may not be a bad thing. If he leaves me, I'm going home to my house.

Struggling with my bags, I stop and open the app on my phone, contemplating getting my own ride. When I see the wait time, I change my mind. I grab my things and start to rush toward the exit.

A woman with a carriage nearly runs me down. I side step her but run into the back of a man. "Excuse me, I'm sorry," I say, my phone beginning to vibrate just then.

"No problem," a deep voice says as I stumble to right myself.

A deep accented voice that rolls down my spine. I clench my jaw against the tightening of my nipples. Yup, my weakness. I don't even stop to see the owner of the voice. The accent alone sends up red flags.

We're not opening that kind of pain today.

Omid

"Did you see her?" I say to Navid.

"See who?"

I shake my head clear. I have to force myself not to run after the woman like a mad man. Her voice. I only got a small glimpse of her face but she looked just like….

"Nothing," I say balling my fists at my sides.

I dreamt of her on the plane. It's the reason I'm imagining things. I have no idea what she would look like now. Twenty years have passed. She would be thirty-five. Her birthday just passed a month ago.

"Are you all right? Maybe you should take a few more days off," he says as he watches me stare after the woman that just bumped into me.

"No, I'll be returning to work in the morning. Come, let's get home. I have a few case studies I want to read before bed," I say and rub my eyes.

"I'd suggest you take at least tomorrow off but I know you won't listen to me."

"Yet you just made the suggestion without making the suggestion," I say and grin to myself.

"You know me well, *şehzade*."

I snort and start out of the airport for our waiting car. Once out of the doors, I scan the area for the dark skinned beauty I had a small glance of inside. It's been a while since I've gotten laid. Even if she isn't who I want her to be, I could use a gorgeous woman in my bed. It's been a lonely place for quite some time.

I curse under my breath when I find not one woman that looks like the one I'm trying to find. If only I were so lucky. All of those curves would've been just what I needed. Climbing into the car, I adjust myself after I'm seated. I truly do need to get laid.

I grin as I think of Club Desire. Maybe a visit will be good for me. The place isn't as fun now that the twins don't come around as much. My smile falls.

I rub at my chest. I'm happy for my cousins. They deserve the happiness they've found. It's something I wish I had for myself. No, I don't want an arranged marriage, but I want a wife of my own. Someone I can go home to and talk to about my day. Someone to challenge me in thought and make me laugh.

No, not the club.

I'll go home as I originally planned.

Divine

"What your father and I are saying is that you're still young. There's time to meet a nice guy and get married. We don't understand why you feel you need to do this," My mother says.

I sink into the couch and clench my teeth. They've been at it for two hours now. First she started during dinner, ruining the taste of the cornbread, seasoned green beans, and roasted Cornish hen. Then my father jumped in, causing my ice cream to melt while I looked at him in awe. He never gets in the middle of my mother wanting to run all of our lives.

They can talk until they're blue in the face. My mind is made up. I'm not changing it. I wish they'd leave me alone. It's my body, my life, my decision.

"This is what I've decided on."

"You don't even know who's sperm you'll be getting. How can this be what you want?" My father says as he gives half of his attention to the game on the TV.

I'd escaped from the kitchen table to lure him into the living room, hoping he'd lose interest all together and get lost in the game. It's not working tonight as these two gang up on me.

"Daddy, in all seriousness. I can date and sleep with someone to get pregnant and still not know who I'm getting. Guys, I'm tired and you're not going to change my mind." I sigh and sag my shoulders.

It's like I've been in the boxing ring since I arrived. I want to go home and get into my bed. Thank god they didn't bring my siblings in for this intervention.

"The point is to get married and not be out here sleeping with random dicks," he mumbles under his breath. "Damn fouls better not let me find them sniffing around without intentions to put a ring on it."

I roll my eyes at him and rub my temples. These two are intent on giving me a migraine. Do I have any Tequila at home? I'm going to need it.

"Div, we just want what's best for you. Why haven't you taken your neighbor up on his offers to go on a date?" mom says.

I blink once at my mother so hard, my eyes hurt. She can't be serious. My father even has to cover his mouth and turn way.

"Okay, I'm not sure where in all this I give you the impression that I'm desperate. I'm thirty-five and I want a baby. I get plenty of male attention, I'm just not interested in a relationship." I stand and lean to kiss my mother's cheek. "You will get over it once your new grandbaby gets here."

"Divine," my mother calls sternly.

"Night, Mommy. Night, Daddy," I say hugging my father.

"We want to see you next weekend at the barbeque," my father calls to my back.

We get together as a family at least twice a month. If Daddy can barbeque during those get-togethers he's in heaven. I love watching him and my mother dance around the yard together.

I used to want that. Someone who I could have the soul deep connection with. Someone to grab me around the waist and not care who's around so he could dance me around and sing to me.

Yeah, I gave up on that bullshit dream a long time ago. My daddy is a one of a kind. I love him for that but I'm not going to put that type of pressure on myself to find another like him.

"Yup, I'll be here." I wave a hand over my shoulder. "I'll have the potato salad."

"That's my girl," my father shouts and claps his hands.

"You know you're no damn help," my mother chides.

I shake my head and leave out of the door. My older brother, Nashawn, used my car while I was out of town. I had him drop it off here since I knew my parents had plans to torture me and hold me captive. Daddy moved my things into my vehicle before we went into the house.

I hop in my car and turn it on. "Un-fucking-believable," I mutter. He left my shit on damn near E. I'm going to curse his ass out for not gassing up my car before returning it.

Good thing my house is so close by. I drive home and park, too tired to stop to fill the car up. Nashawn will be dropping off some gas with his trifling behind.

Turning off the car, I stare at my home. It looks too quiet and empty. I fell in love with the place when I first bought it. Although I don't live far from my parents, my neighborhood is still a few steps up from theirs. This house was the first move I made that caused my success to start to set in.

However, as I look at it I have to wonder what did I really accomplish. I'll get out of this car and walk into that empty house. This baby is something I truly want. Someone to share all the things I've built with.

My family may drive me crazy and get on my damn nerves but I love them. I loved growing up with so many siblings, three brothers and a sister. As horrible as I was treated as the baby, it gave me thick skin.

A part of me questions if I'm being selfish. I don't know if I'll go through with the IUI more than once after a successful conception and birth. If I only have one baby on the first try it will be just the two of us.

"You could find a man," I murmur to myself.

I frown in the same breath. Looking out of my passenger's side window I see my neighbor, Melvin, ducking to see into my car. Nope, I'll take my chances with the sperm donors.

CHAPTER THREE

Options

Omid

It's good to be back home and in the swing of things. It's been three weeks and I've fallen right back into my routine effortlessly. I love my job.

Keeping women healthy and helping them to have families brings me a joy I could never explain. I get to oversee the safe passage of their little ones. I'm there to watch tears of hopelessness turn to tears of joy. I think the other doctors in the firm have the same joy.

I met Dr. John Nobi a few years back at my cousins club during a party. We got to talking and found out we had a lot in common. I wanted to start a practice where I could research and work with fertility but some of the licensing and grants I wanted to go for would've been counterproductive to those that work to keep my life under the radar.

I'm okay with not having my name on display or on my research. Dr. Nobi has been someone I could trust with this fact. After running into each other at a few seminars and learning that we run in pretty much the same circle, we decided to work together.

John being a little older than me took me on as a little brother of sorts. Not when we're working. Dr. Nobi has the highest respect for me as a doctor. This practice was born of our mutual respect and we've been one of the top ten West Coast practices for the last five years.

"Ah, some of my favorite patients," I croon as I step into the examination room. "Johnathan, it's always good to see you."

"Omid," John pulls me in for a hug and slap on the back. "Good to see you."

"Always good to see a Black in my office. I think I have at least one birth from each of you under my belt now." I laugh.

"Don't be surprised if you see Wyatt or Noah's ass again soon," he laughs.

"You guys always make delivery interesting," I say with a smile. "How are we, mom? Ready to see this little one today?"

"I want pineapples, pretzels, and caramel. He promised them to me after we leave here. Let's make this quick," she snaps.

I grin some more. This isn't Nelly or Bean. I expected nothing more. This mother and father are two that intrigue me. I can see their love, but it's only because they can't hide it. Still, it's not because of their being overly affectionate. It's just something about them.

"We still don't want to know the sex," John says quickly.

"No problem, I enjoyed the bet you two had going last time," I say as I squirt gel onto my patients swollen belly. The tough exterior fades a bit as the worry of a mother sets in. "Let's find this little one and see what's new."

Silence fills the room until a tiny heartbeat breaks through. This is the part of my job that I love. Watching to see the love of a mother and father come to life as they see the little life that's growing inside.

"Everything looks great. I'll take a few images and you can go for your snacks."

"Thanks," she says softly.

John grins like a proud poppa, bending to kiss her lips. "How about we fly out to New York for the weekend. You can get some of that jerk chicken you love," he says lovingly.

"Oh, you're trying to butter me up. I told you I'm not doing this again," she says sternly, which I've come to know as her teasing.

"Sure," he says and bites his lip as he gives her a look that I'm sure I shouldn't be seeing.

But I do see it. I see what I've been longing for. I look back at the screen at the frozen image of their little one. I'm thirty-eight, my practice is booming, I have a great house and a few condos. I drive a Mercedes to work and own a Range Rover, Lamborghini, Aston Martin, and Porsche. Yet I don't have this, a family.

"Omid...Dr. Omid?" Johnathan's voice pulls me back to the room.

"Oh, sorry." I get the images from the printer. "Here you are. Pictures to take with you. Any questions for me?"

John looks at me with knitted brows. A few things cross his face before he speaks. "You okay? It's been awhile since you came over to hang out. Ryan's dragging us all out to some new place he can't shut up about next weekend. You in?"

I think about it. I always have a good time when I hang out with the Blacks. Their father has been such an important part of my life. Once the brothers joined the private investigation firm they have become entwined in my life as well.

They say we are all separated by six degrees. I'm inclined to believe that. From my cousins to my business partner to my circle of friends, we're all connected somehow.

The list goes on and on. When I hang with the Black brothers I'm surely in for a night of laughs and entertainment. For a minute, I get ready to say no. All of the guys are in relationships, married with children.

"Come on. It will be fun," he coaxes when I don't respond.

"Okay, I'll see if I can make it and send you a text."

He pats me on the shoulder and nods. I give a wave to them both and leave the room. Moving to the exam room down the hall closer to the reception desk, I pick up the file in the slot attached to the door. I place my hand on the knob just as I hear Dr. Nobi's voice at the front desk.

"You ladies have nothing to be worried about. You'll be in good hands."

The next voice I hear raises every hair on my body. I can't blame my dreams or imagination this time. I know it's her. All this time and that voice still tugs at my heart and sets my blood on fire.

"I can't wait," she says excitedly. "Do you think we'll be able to have the same due date?"

Dr. Nobi chuckles. "I think we can target the same date. It's going to depend on a few things, like each of your body's response to the treatments," he replies.

"Don't mind my cousin. She's a little crazy. Even if we have the same due dates that doesn't mean the babies will come on the same dates," someone else says.

"Thanks again." That voice wraps around me and squeezes. I can only see Nobi's back from here. He's blocking my view of the two women he's talking to.

"No problem. See you both next time," Dr. Nobi says.

Snapping out of it, I shake my head and start for the front desk. "Hi, Dr. Omid, are you coming inside?" I bite out a curse under my breath and debate pretending I don't hear the woman standing less than a foot away talking to me.

Turning, I put on a smile. "Yes, Ms. Oliver. I'll be right with you."

"Don't worry. I have to go to the little girls room for the third time. Bladder is brimming over again," she snickers.

"Take your time," I say and turn to head out front.

I don't make it there in time. When I step out the door into the waiting room, I don't see the familiar face I'm looking for. Dr. Nobi is leaning over the desk talking to our receptionist and medical assistants.

"Brenda, when you make appointments for the ladies they'd like to be together. Once their labs are in, I want to see both of their charts," he says.

"Yes, doctor," Brenda replies.

"New patients?" I ask coolly when I'm anything but.

"Hey, yeah. Come back to my office. I wanted to talk to you."

I follow him to his office holding my breath. All I need is her name. That's all I want to hear.

I can't even sit when we get behind the closed doors. I brace myself against the back of the chair. Due dates. She's here to have a baby. Is she gay? It wouldn't be the first time we had a lesbian couple come in with both partners wanting to experience the birth first hand.

If she's not gay, where's her man? Why wasn't he here for such a big step in their lives? Is she married? Does he pamper her the way she deserves?

"That was Marica Thompson. Maybe you remember her husband. My buddy from high school. He was a soldier—"

"I remember him. The guys that wanted his wife to have a baby if he didn't make it home. Shit, he didn't make it home," I say and move to take a seat.

Dr. Nobi's eyes take on the distant look. "No. He died about a year ago. I've been waiting for her to show up. "

"Damn," I say and pull a hand down my face. "Nice guy. He had a presence about him. I remember how happy he was that he could live on in this way. You know? I'd just hoped you wouldn't have to make good on this promise to him."

"Exactly. We have to make sure this is a success for her, for him."

I know John. He's a true friend. He will make it his mission to see this woman through this and keep his word to his friend. It's the way he's wired.

"What about the other patient? Does she have the same story?" I say not able to hold it in as my mind circles back to that voice.

"Oh no," he says shaking his head. "That one is an entirely different story. She's thirty-five and ready to become a mom and has no intention on waiting for a partner to do it with."

"Can I see her file?" He nods and slides it across the desk.

I pick it up and swear I can hear my own breathing above everything else. I open the folder and look at the name on the intake form. I close my eyes as I'm thrown back in time.

"Arman, when are we going to meet? I want to see you in person. You said you're staying with your family here in L.A. I can get away. I can come meet you," she said as I held the phone tightly to my ear.

"I don't know. I want to see you as well," I said. "It's just not as easy for me. My cousins have gone to New York for a bit. When they return I'm going to try my best to get to you."

"Will you tell me you love me again?"

"Seni seviyorum."

"It sounds so beautiful when you say it that way. I hope I get to see you before you have to go back home," she says. That sadness returning to her voice. I hated to hear her so sad.

I thought a million times of asking my father to allow me to stay in America. I want to study medicine here. Maybe he will be lenient if he knows I want to be a doctor.

However, I know he will never approve of the girl I've fallen in love with. I'm not a fool to think there isn't a wife waiting for me when I return to Shiraz. It's the reason I chose now to beg to come to America.

"We will make it happen," I replied.

"I love you, Arman. Promise me we'll figure out how to be together."

"I love you too, Divine. I will do everything in my power for us to be together."

And I did. I did everything I could. I walked away from my family, my home. The pain starts to dig in and take root.

"Are you okay?" Dr. Nobi asks.

"Yes, I will be now," I say and place the file down. "I should get to my next patient."

He nods and turns his attention back to the papers in front of him. I stand and leave his office. When I'm outside of the door, I bend over and place my hands on my knees.

"Divine Favors. I've found you."

Divine

"Girl, I don't know how you do it. You're always on," Marica says as I end the live I just recorded while she drives.

I have a new line of lipsticks coming out and I've been taking my followers though the entire process. Marica and I stopped at the office after our appointments. I just wanted to do a quick check-in before we had lunch and did some shopping.

"I don't let them into as much of my life as you think. I thought about sharing the pregnancy and the process but some things are just too personal," I reply.

"So true. I just don't have the patience to always have on makeup, always be high energy. I need my downtime and space. I need to be able to turn off. Even with what you don't share you seem like such an open book," she says.

"It's a part of my business now." I shrug. "I do what I need to do."

"Yeah, I hear you. What did you think of Dr. Nobi?"

"Other than the fact that the man is fine as fuck? Like seriously. The gray at the temples. He's fine as hell. I was praying I didn't embarrass myself in there," I say.

"You're crazy." She laughs.

"Whatever. You were thinking the same thing. It's okay, you can say it. I won't tell."

"Okay, he might have been cute. I wasn't focused on that."

I turn fully toward her in my seat. I know my cousin. She's lying her ass off. She was checking that man out just as much I was.

"Anyway. I'm excited. I can't wait until we can start shopping for the babies. This is going to be amazing."

"I am getting excited about it. I think Dr. Nobi's gentle bedside manor put me at ease a bit," she muses.

"Aw, Marica has a crush on the doctor that's going to be all up in her cat," I tease.

"You're such a fool," she giggles.

I lean over and kiss her cheek. "This is why you love me. Welcome home, cuz. You're stuck with me now."

CHAPTER FOUR

Meddling Moms

Divine

"No, I didn't like that color. I'm going to need you to revise that one," I say into the phone as I look in the mirror and turn side to side.

I'm getting dressed to head out to another barbeque at my parents' house. These jeans are hugging my curves right. I place a hand over my belly. My waist is snatched now but in a few months I'm going to have a little baby growing in there.

"Divine, we should be going to production. If we—"

"Hold on. I asked you to redo that color months ago. I remember being very clear that it wasn't the color or consistency that's up to par with my brand. Fix it," I snap.

There's a brief pause and I know it's because he's rolling his eyes and cursing me out on the other end. It's okay. I'll be leaving Darian and his attitude behind next quarter.

"I'll have them work on it. Can you come in next week to give your approval?"

"Let me know when and I'll be there," I say.

"Okay. Anything else?"

"Nope, you enjoy your weekend," I say and hang up.

Looking at the time, I frown and start out of my room. My heels click as I jog down the stairs. I head to get the potato salad from the refrigerator and grab the jug of Rum punch I promised my father. With my purse, keys, and my things for the cookout, I head out to my car.

A groan slips from my lips when I see Melvin outside trimming his rose brushes. He looks up and smiles that goofy smile of his. I still can't believe my mother suggested I give serious thought to going out on a date with this guy.

"Hey there neighbor," he says and waves at me like Forrest Gump.

"Hey, Melvin. How are you?" I say politely.

He crosses over my lawn to help me open my car door. Okay, he can be a sweet guy, but that's still a no. I get my things into the backseat and close the door.

"I'm even better now that I've seen you today," he says.

I open my door to make my quick escape. "That's so sweet of you. You enjoy your day."

"Hold on. I wanted to ask if you took any more thought about my offer for dinner. I know this great steakhouse."

The hope in his eyes makes me feel bad. He truly is nice. That's why I refuse to lead him on.

I would never go on a date with him. It's not just the fact that he's nerdy, and not the type of nerdy I can be about business. We have nothing in common. We hung out when I first moved in. I invited him over to my housewarming after he helped me move some things.

He lingered when my guests started to leave and we talked. I can tell you we're so far from being a match we'd be in the lost sock draw and still wouldn't be worn together. In this case opposites do not attract whatsoever.

"Melvin, you're a sweet guy, but I'm not looking to date or get into a relationship. I'm not going to lead you on and make you think I am," I say and give him an apologetic smile.

"Oh, well, I can't fault you for that. I...um...if you change your mind you know where to find me," he says.

"Sure do. Later," I say and climb into my car.

I turn the radio up and head to my parents' house. Looking in the rearview mirror, I see the poor guy standing staring after me. I hope he finds someone nice for him.

"Divine," my mother calls from in the house.

"Oh boy," I whine and stomp my foot. I was just about to sit down and dig into my second plate of ribs. I've been avoiding my mother all afternoon.

"You better get in that house," my brother Lance says.

My sister giggles as she pulls my plate toward her. "You didn't need this anyway."

I slap Patience's hand and take my plate with me. This could take a while and I'm not chancing my Daddy's barbeque running out. He smoked these ribs and made the sauce from scratch. Everyone out here has been licking their fingers and smacking their lips.

I step into the house to find my mother at the dining room table. I take a deep breath and sit down in the seat beside her. I know what's coming before she opens her mouth.

"How was the appointment?"

"Everything went well. It was mostly an initial exam and consultation so I'd know what to expect and they did some blood work. If everything goes as planned, I'll be expecting in a few months."

She twists her lips to the side. "A few months?"

"Yes. The doctor couldn't fit us both in at the same time for another two months. We had to wait a little bit to do this together," I say.

My mother watches me for a moment. I start to tuck into my plate while she figures out what she wants to say. If my mouth is full of food, I won't get my teeth knocked out by telling her to mind her damn business. Not that I would dare, I haven't lost my mind. Janise Favors is not the one.

"Baby, I understand things happened to put you off of men. You've never told me what but I know something happened before you dropped out of college," she pauses.

The concern in her eyes worries me that she thinks something much worse than the truth went down. I blow out a breath. This is her way of asking what happened.

I've avoided sharing this with my mom for years. My parents never knew why I dropped out. They just supported the decision. Not like my siblings. They made a big deal and tried to talk me into going back.

"Remember Gable?" I say softly.

"Yeah, the guy you were dating for a little while, Freshman year," she says.

I nod and push my plate away. "Yup, him. I looked up one day and realized I was wasting you guys' money. I knew more than most of my professors. I started to grow tired of listening to things I knew wouldn't benefit where I was headed.

"I always knew I had no plans of using a degree to get a job. I had other ideas. I was so excited about my epiphany, I ran right to Gable's dorm to tell him I planned to drop out and start my business." I take a moment as the pain slices in. "I was right outside his dorm room when I heard them."

I close my eyes as the memory comes back full force. My stomach twists with hurt and anger. A bitter taste fills my mouth.

"You still seeing that black girl?" A male voice drifted out into the hallway.

"Yeah."

"So have you closed the deal? You're the only one that hasn't completed this task."

"Shouldn't you be worried about your own score card?" Gable said.

"You guys totally cheated me on the Latina chick. I should've gotten an extra hundred points for her big ass. Dude, what are you waiting for? You get extra points for her being so fucking black. Damn, I wish I saw her first. All that dark ass skin."

"I didn't wait around for Gable's response. I was too hurt and disgusted. I came home that night. I was done with that place and him," I say to my mom. "I blocked his number too."

"Oh, honey. Not all men are assholes. I thought he was nice, but your father didn't like that boy. Although, I think we both picked up on something being off with him."

"Why didn't you say something?"

She reaches to cup my cheek. "Div, whenever we tell you, you can't or shouldn't do something you drive harder to do it. It was best to let you do your thing."

I give a shaky smile, she's right. I cover her hand with mine and look her in the eyes. "So why do you keep telling me not to have this baby?"

She gives a deep laugh and moves to brush a hand over my hair. "I keep asking myself the same thing. Your hardheaded ass will run face first into this. I've always thanked God that you land on your feet every time. Hell, my baby rises to the top with every challenge.

"I used to whip your brothers and sister's ass for telling you what you could and couldn't do. They were always goading you. You damn near broke your arm that one time." She scoffs and shakes her head. "However, somewhere along the way I noticed that you thrived off proving everyone wrong.

"I want to see you happy. I just feel it in my gut. This time you need to slow down. Think about this. Marica has been through so much. What she's doing…she and Keith agreed to that. I'm still not sure how I feel about it but I think that's her path. My sister has her hands full.

"You're my baby and I'm going to tell you straight like this…think about it. What some little dick pulled all those years ago shouldn't have left you jaded all this time. Do me a favor, Divine. Think about this."

She has no idea how right she is about that little dick. Gable had a lot of nerve. Okay, it was average. I shake that thought aside. Gable wasn't the one to put the nail in my dating coffin though.

I just won't be telling her that. I think I always knew Ben was no good. I never did introduce him to my family in the two years that we dated. That's saying a lot.

I take a moment to think over her words.

"I'll think about what you're saying, Mommy."

"Thank you. That's all I ask."

Omid

I pad barefoot to the balcony off my bedroom. I have a view that's to die for. I bought my Malibu home right out of college. I had no debts to be concerned with. My cousins spoiled me with my first car as a graduation gift. It only seemed right to treat myself with this home.

I inhale the night air catching a hint of sea salt. I bought this home thinking of her. The one regret I have in my life is not fighting harder, not standing up sooner. It all just got out of control so fast.

"She wants a baby," I murmur to myself and grin.

It's been a week and I still can't get over the fact that she was so close and I missed her. I've been thinking about going after her but it's been twenty years. I can't just pull her address from her file and show up on her doorstep no matter how tempted I am to do so. And I almost have, several times.

I take a sip from the bottle of water I'm holding, wondering what she looks like now. I've been kicking myself for not moving faster that morning. I look nothing like the scrawny kid that just came over from Iran all those years ago.

At two hundred pounds, I'm solid with a sculpted build. Not super bulky, but I stretch my shirtsleeves well enough. I've gotten looks from both my married and single patients. I have no shortage of women I can beckon to my bed.

I've also learned what to do in the bedroom. Having Divine in my arms will bring us both pleasure. A fumbling eighteen year old, I am not. Just thinking about showering her with my experience has me hard and I haven't seen her in years.

I pull out my phone to try to find her online profiles once again. I've been trying for years to find her online. The profile that led me to her had been erased. There hasn't been a trace of Divine Favors since…I close my eyes not wanting to travel down that road.

As I type her name in and fail to pull up a profile that matches, I get pissed. Just when I want to chuck my phone out into the ocean it rings. I groan when I see the number. Of all the times for my mother to call this is a horrible one.

"Shit," I mutter, but answer the call anyway. "Hello, Anne."

"Hello, Omid. I'm so happy I could reach you. I know you are a busy doctor," she says with pride.

"I have a little time," I reply as I turn to lean my butt against the railing.

"Have you taken time to think about Dilshad?"

I knit my brows. "Who?"

She mumbles to herself on the other end. "Your fiancée, Omid Arman," she says in exasperation.

"I have no fiancée. That would probably explain why I have no clue who you are speaking of."

"Maybe if we come to America and you get to know her you will warm to her. We can make a trip—"

"Absolutely not, Anne," I growl into the phone.

She huffs. "Why not? I don't understand why you wouldn't want to spend time with a pretty girl. You're not getting any younger. I come and you can show me your practice. What kind of medicine do you study? I realize you have never said—"

"Anne, the hospital is paging me. I have to go," I say and hang up.

I stare down at the phone and narrow my eyes. This may be a problem. My mother isn't going to let this rest. Knowing she and my father they're already planning the wedding.

"Damn it," I snarl.

I just found Divine. I'm not going to lose her again. I pull up Johnathan Black's number and accept his invitation to join him and his brothers tonight. I'll need to talk to Toby and Wyatt. I need to make sure my parents can't meddle in my life from Iran.

CHAPTER FIVE

Swing of Things

Divine

My mom did exactly what she set out to do. She planted the seed. I've been thinking about her words since I left my parents' house earlier.

I frown and signal the waitress for another drink. Marica and Dada would kill me if they knew I came out to drink alone. I just need some time to think to myself. Getting dressed up and coming out for drinks was a last minute decision.

"Here you go. Can I get you anything else?" the waitress asks.

"No, not at the moment."

"Okay, let me know if you need anything," she says with her bubbly personality.

I try to infuse some of that chipperness into my own mood. When that plan falls flat, I down the Cuervo she just set before me. Yup, it's one of those nights. Besides, when will I get to drink like this once I have a baby?

Bottoms up.

I laugh at myself as the tequila travels smoothly down my throat. Picking up my phone, my drunk mind tries to tell me it's a good idea to go live. I pull up the app getting ready to do something totally stupid.

"Excuse me." I look up and find the couple at the table next to me staring. It was the woman who spoke.

They arrived a little after I took my seat at my own high table. They look to be around my age. The woman is a perky looking blonde and the guy tall dark and handsome, with sparkling blue eyes and a pierced brow.

"Yes," I reply.

"I can't decide on what to drink. My husband is always teasing me about the fruity drinks I order. What's that you're drinking?"

"Tequila sliver, but this isn't for everyone," I say.

"A woman that can handle her liquor, nice," the husband says.

Um. She needs to check his ass.

I turn back to my phone to start recording, but it's clear these two aren't finished with our conservation. I refrain from rolling my eyes. This is what I get for coming out alone.

"Do you want to come sit with us?"

"Actually, I'm waiting for my friends," I say holding up my phone.

"Are you sure? You're such a pretty woman. You shouldn't be sitting all by yourself."

I lift a well-arched brow. I think this chick is hitting on me in front of her husband. Nah, it has to be the tequila. I'm tripping.

I fiddle with my phone like I'm sending a text. I mean, I sit here totally engrossed in my phone as if I'm reading and responding to a text. I turn my Hollywood ass all the way up.

"That's them right now," I say and start reading and replying again. "They should be here soon."

"Oh, okay," she says in disappointment.

I should get up and leave but I love this place and the vibe. Besides, their prices are the best on this side of town. I'm not calling an Uber just because of these two.

Deep laughter draws my attention to the doorway of the bar. At least ten fine ass guys just entered. When I say fine, I mean fine as fuck. I almost fall out of my seat. All six feet tall or over, red hair, dark hair, long hair, short hair, a man bun, and oh damn beards. I run my eyes over them but I don't make it through them all. I stop in my tracks.

What hits me in the chest and has me ready to throw in the towel is the tall, dark, and handsome Middle Eastern guy bringing up the rear. I don't even register the two guys with him. I can't take my eyes off of his pretty ass.

From his six foot and change height to his well-defined body under his black suit and navy shirt. Oh God, the bright white smile and that facial hair are just a bonus, and the swag coming off of him. The man is to die for gorgeous.

"I'm Jennifer, by the way," the woman from the table next to me interrupts my drooling.

I turn back to her and give a weak smile. In all honesty, it's better I talk to her than think a second more about the man across the bar. However, as I take in this couple and the way they're sizing me up, I start to become uneasy.

I fidget in my seat, reaching for my empty glass. Frowning at the lack of liquor, I lift the tumbler for the waitress to bring another. Suddenly, the atmosphere shifts. It's insane. It's as if the bar gains a pulse.

"And I'm Dan," the husband says as he leans in.

"Nice to meet you," I murmur.

"You really are stunning. My husband would have so much fun with you."

I whip my head back and lean away from them in my seat even with the four feet between us. Meanwhile, that feeling of being sucked in still grows and it's not coming from these two. The hairs on the back of my neck stand up.

I turn for the door again and my jaw drops. The same man I'd been drooling over has broken away from his friends and he's headed in my direction with a walk that has me weak in the knees.

I'm going to blame it on the Cuervo. Yup, it's the alcohol that has me licking my lips as my eyes roll over him. It's the tequila's fault my breasts are heaving damn near out of my dress.

Who the fuck is this man?

Omid

"Who invited this guy? He's seen almost all of our wives from the waist down," Braxton teases as we make our way to the entrance of the bar.

"Bro, glad to know I wasn't the only one thinking it," Ryan laughs.

"We brought him and Nobi because they're the only ones not married. They can take all the pussy that we'll be leaving behind," Wyatt laughs out.

We all join in the laughter as we file into the bar, me, Nobi and Nick bringing up the rear. "It's funny. I've never had to take anyone's leftovers. So I think you mean I'm here to distract all the pussy from you. None of you will matter until I leave for the night," I shoot back.

The group booms with more laughter. The Blacks, Nicholas Lincoln, Dr. Nobi and I make a crew of ten tonight. We turn heads from the moment we step into the place. Not just from our laughter. The good-looking men with me hold the attention of most in the bar.

"I'm not offended. I've told a girl or two we were cousins before," Ryan says.

"And they believed this?" I snort.

"It's the eyes. I can get away with it when yours are around this color." He points at his own.

I shake my head as we all laugh. While the Black brothers have golden colored eyes, mine can go from an almost colorless gray, to ranges of hazel or an extremely light gold. I'm told that my gaze can be startling. Before I left the house tonight, I found my eyes have settled on that light translucent gold color that I get most often.

I go to pat Ry on the shoulder and give him a retort, but my attention is grabbed by the gorgeous woman across the bar. She's sitting alone but there's a couple sitting at a table next to her who seem to have her attention. Something in her body language draws me in.

I squint, taking in her silky brown legs that are crossed as she sits at the highboy table. The black dress she has on hugs her curves, drawing attention to her thighs right where they meet. The sexy blue heels that strap over her feet and up her ankle have me darting my tongue out to wet my lips.

She lifts her glass to signal the waitress. I'm moving toward her before I can think better of it. I don't like the way she's pulling away from the two at the other table. Halfway to her, she turns in my direction and our eyes lock. The wind is knocked from me but I don't halt my steps—instead I move faster.

Allah is with me. Divine.

She's just steps away from me. For the first time in my life, I'm face to face in the flesh with the woman I've loved since I was eighteen. I know this is her. I can feel it in my bones.

She's more gorgeous than ever. Her face hasn't changed a bit. I like this thing she's done with her hair. One side is braided down to look as if it is shaven or not there. The other side boasts large curls that flip away from her face, cascading down her back and around her left shoulder.

Her lips are still full. So full you would think they'd take up most of her face, but they're perfect for her cute little nose and big brown eyes. I've dreamed of kissing those lips for years. Twenty to be exact.

"My wife and I would love to buy you a drink. Maybe we can go somewhere more private to get to know each other," the guy at the other table croons and licks his lips.

It takes the power of Allah and the prophet Muhmmad to keep me from grabbing him by his throat. Instead, I stop in front of Divine and stroke her cheek as she looks up at me. Her skin is softer than I ever imagined.

"Sorry I've taken so long," I say just before I capture her lips.

Divine

Oh my God, oh my God. Sweet baby Jesus.

Does he eat pussy like this? This man is kissing me like he knows me. No, correction. He's kissing me as if he owns me. Possessive isn't the word. We're so beyond that.

He's kissing me as if he waited his entire life to. I wrap my hands beyond his head, wishing my nails were shorter so I could claw at his soft hair and feel my fingers move through the short strands in the back. I move my ballerina tips to the tops of his hair where I can find better purchase.

"You taste of a thousand heavens," he says against my lips with a hint of an accent.

That voice. It's deep and sexy. I inhale and his cologne takes me over. I can't put together the nagging thoughts clouding my intoxicated head.

He pulls away with his gaze still fixed on my lips. I look into his eyes and my brain short circuits. I've seen some fine hazel eyed Middle Eastern men but his eyes…. They are so unreal it's almost scary. If he weren't so damn gorgeous I might be afraid.

That Instagram fitness guy and his brother come to mind. His name starts with a T, but I'm too gone to remember at the moment. This guy could pass for his twin, down to the facial hair and haircut. That guy is definitely on my stalk list. If this guy has an account, I plan to add him to my list as well.

"I…I. Um." I have no clue what to say.

This is so not me. Me, me would've slapped the shit out of him and left his ass to settle my bill. Believe me, I've tipped a waitress to make that happen for me before. The guy was livid, but he deserved it.

This guy leans in for one more kiss before he pulls the other stool at my table closer, and smoothly settles his sexy ass right next me. His leg brushes mine, causing me to uncross and recross my thighs as he flags the waitress. I try to pull it together. Maybe I did have too much to drink.

"We'll have two more of whatever she's having and can you bring me a few lemons," he says to the waitress after she rushes over with the drink I already ordered.

I take a long sip of the fresh drink hoping my sense is somewhere in the bottom of the glass. I don't do Middle Eastern men. Something in the back of my mind is telling me to run. My pussy on the other hand is screaming out the number of days since the last time I had sex.

627. SIX. TWO. SEVEN.

Yes, I get it. It's been a long time and from that kiss this guy will make it worth every stroke because I plan on counting those too. *Oh, Lordt.* I'm already letting him hit it in my head. *Run, Div, Run. He gonna set your soul on fire and ruin your pussy for everyone, including you.*

"What's that?" I ignore my inner warnings and lean into his words.

He grins and leans in closer. "How much have you had to drink without me?"

"I've had a few," I say as my cheeks heat.

The couple who had been trying to get me into their bed tonight stand to leave. My new date gives them both the glare of death as he places his hand on my back possessively.

Aww. He came to save me.

Could he see how uncomfortable they were making me? Did I send out an S.O.S with my body language? Wow, I might just let him break my back after all. I give a silly grin as that thought crosses my mind.

"What has that smile on your face, *prensesim*?"

I'm jolted by him calling me his princess. Painful memories push at my alcohol-laden mind. However, that all flies out the window when he buries his face in my neck and his silky beard caresses my skin as he nuzzles it.

"Shouldn't you tell me your name?"

He stiffens, lifting his head to look into my eyes. Something crosses his face briefly. He sits back in his seat and studies me.

"Okay. I'll tell you my name first." I snort and hold out my hand. "I'm Divine."

He takes my hand and caresses the back with his thumb. "I'm A…," he shakes his head. "Omid. Everyone calls me Omid."

He repositions our hands until our fingers are laced together. His lips are on mine again. I totally forget what I planned to say to him next.

"You're so beautiful, Divine," he says as he kisses his way down my neck. When he sucks the skin behind my ear into his mouth, I lift up out of my seat and squeeze my thighs together as a loud as moan escapes my lips. "*Sikme. Seni çok fena istiyorum*," he groans into my ear.

"Yes, please. I want you too."

He pulls back. His eyes blazing with desire and lit with surprise. I bite my lip and shrug my shoulders.

"I used to have a boyfriend who spoke Arabic, Farsi, French, and Turkish. I learned as much as I could to surprise him. I understand all four. I can speak at least two fluently," I babble drunkenly.

He places his fingers beneath my chin and looks deeply into my eyes. "I will make up for every day I've been without you in my life," he says.

I look at him curiously, my forehead creasing with the expression. He says the words with so much feeling and meaning in them as if there's history between us already. I wish I could sober up and focus.

I don't get a chance to try to clear my head enough to process or question his words. He has his tongue in my mouth making promises his ass better keep because there's no way I'm not having him in my bed tonight. Yup, he can get some thank you booty. That was real sweet of him to come save me.

If he's good, I might make him my new pipe boy.

CHAPTER SIX

Drunken Reward

Divine

After Omid rescued me from that swinging couple, we had a few drinks and talked for a little bit. Well, we talked when he wasn't taking my breath away with his addictive kisses. After thirty minutes of his gentle caresses and all-consuming kisses, I was ready to get out of that bar to give him a reward for coming to my rescue.

We stumble into my house after his driver drops us off. Yup, his driver. Navid he called him. I don't know what this guy does but he's not some fuck boy. I won't have to give him cab money when it's time to throw his ass out.

We've both had a lot to drink but I think I'm a little more gone than he is. I know that for sure when I almost fall over. He wraps his strong arms around me and tugs me into his chest. I lift my arms around his neck.

"We don't have to do this tonight," he says as his hands roam up and down my back.

I scoff. "Oh we're doing this tonight, honey."

He grins and shakes his head. "As you wish." His lips are on mine, devouring me in that possessive way again.

I push his jacket from his broad shoulders to the floor and start on the buttons of his dress shirt. I tug the shirt free from his slacks and relish in the feel of his hot skin against my palms. He releases the zipper on the back of my bodycon dress. The fabric falls to my feet revealing my strapless bra and matching black panties.

Now, let me be very clear in pointing out that I'm no small girl. Yes, this waist is snatched from waist trainers and dedication to hours in the gym for my brand, but I have hips, thighs, and ass for days to match a full triple D cup. I make an impression from every angle.

When he lifts my thick ass onto his waist, I know for a fact he's earned the spot as my new plumber. He breaks the kiss to explore my skin with his lips, teeth, and tongue. I'm so wet already.

He carries me over to my marble coffee table and lays me on the flat surface. I arch into him as the cool table greets me. He slips his hands to the clasp of my bra, taking advantage of the space I've just provided. My breasts bounce free and he groans.

Those eyes...he rolls them over my body as if looking at something rare and precious. I start to squirm feeling a little self-conscious. I have fans that would kill for this body, but I hold my own insecurities at times. No matter how hard I work at it, my legs never slim down the way I want them too. I've worn out several pairs of jeans from thigh rubbing.

It may not look like it but at five six, I still tip the scale at one ninety. I'm a solid girl. My brain doesn't always accept the disconnect between the mirror and the scale. Yet when he runs a strong hand up my thigh and gives a tight squeeze, I relax and melt into the table.

"You are perfection," he says with so much awe in his voice. "How do you like it? Should I be gentle with all of these sexy curves or do you think you can handle me fucking you breathless?"

"What did you just say?" I gasp.

He licks his full lips and gives me a wolfish grin. He dips his head to drag his tongue from my belly button up to my left breast and captures the peak into his mouth. I cry out and push my fingers into the front of his hair. It's just long enough for me to cling to.

He circles his tongue around my nipple while watching me with those ethereal eyes. He hooks his fingers into my soaked panties and starts to peel them down my hips. Slowly, he kisses his way back down my body.

"I want you to fuck the shit out of me. My question to you is can I do the same?"

I sit and stare at him. I'm too drunk to even lie and say that hasn't turned me on. I'm gushing and my nipples are so hard they hurt. He glides two fingers over my pussy lips, sucking his bottom lips into his mouth as he watches me for a reaction. I start to rock my hips, wanting desperately for him to push inside me.

"Please," I plea.

"Not until you answer my question."

I look at him in confusion for a few beats. I promise I'm not normally this slow. When I finally get it together I give him a saucy grin.

"Oh, baby, you don't have to ask to fuck me rough. I can take whatever you give. Just give it to me right," I purr.

Yeah, I should've kept my damn mouth shut. He grasps my waist with his long fingers and buries that handsome face between my thighs. With the hand he used to massage my weeping lips, he pushes inside my tight heat. His tongue massages my clit while his fingers work me from inside.

"You're nice and tight for me."

Again, for the second time tonight something in his voice tugs at me. My walls flex around his fingers. Not only am I tight, I'm aching for him.

"Oh yes, I deserve this," I cry out.

I can't remember the last time I met a dude that had serious head game. Not like this. His thick fingers are only serving to amplify the attention he's giving to my nub as he licks between it and my weeping folds.

It's like magic, the way his tongue and fingers are working together in perfect sync. He knows his way around the cookie box for sure. Scissoring his fingers to lick between them, beckoning my orgasms with each stroke.

He reaches up to pinch and roll my nipple with the hand he had been using to pin me to his face. I'm convulsing and crying out in three different languages. Stars burst behind my lids. I'm panting for air and trying to hold on to the little sanity I have left.

"You have an amazing response to me," he says, lifting to lean over my body to peck my lips.

I lazily suck my juices from his sexy mouth. I'm relieved when I feel him line up with my entrance. I don't suck dick. Period.

None of these dudes I've blessed with this body are my man. Head from me is a gift only for the one and since I'm never going to date or commit to a relationship head is off the menu. It is what it is.

Fair play my butt.

My drunk babbling thoughts are silenced when he slides into me. He's huge. Tears spring to my eyes as I stretch to accommodate him. I let out a breath, trying to remember how to breathe.

"Just relax," he says smoothly. "This pussy is mine. I'll fit."

Well excuse me, Mr. Confident.

He starts to rock his hips and I might just have to agree with him. At least for tonight I will. He's owning this pussy all right.

Omid

I start to move inside her with ease. She's so wet and tight, I have to clench my teeth to keep from losing my mind. I lift her brown legs over my forearms and push them back.

I want to lick every inch of her skin. I want to taste it all. Dragging my tongue across her collarbone, I groan in satisfaction as she shivers and clenches around me.

"Omid," she moans.

My heart swells as she calls my name. It hits hard. This is my Divine. I'm between her thick thighs, inside her sweet pussy. I take her lips again sipping from her gorgeous mouth. I need her flavor to ground me and to keep me from calling out something foolish.

I'm still in love with her. It's so intense I feel it in my chest, in my fingertips, in every cell within me. While I know I should've told her who I am, something stopped me. I can't say what.

Maybe it was the fact that she didn't know me right away. I've always had it in my head that she would know me the moment I found her. All of our talks on the phone Remi gave me...I wanted her to remember me. It stings to realize she had no clue that her man had found her and was the one consuming her lips.

If I have to fuck her sober, so be it. I need her to remember who I am. I need her to figure out who she's let into her body. I crave it as much as I crave her.

I lean into her ear. "I'm going to fuck you until you remember me every time you go to sit this pretty ass down."

"Yes," she whimpers and tightens around me.

Her long nails dig into my ass. I pump harder. Nuzzling her neck, I flick out my tongue against the soft sweaty flesh. Something savage takes over when she gushes like a geyser. I pull out to watch her soak the table and spray all over us both.

"Fuck. I can't believe it took me so long to find you."

"Me either," she says, clearly still not making the connection as to who I am.

I palm my cock and tap it against her sensitive button. She wiggles toward me and I reenter her heat. Reaching for her legs, I hold them in the air as I drive into her. I don't just move in and out. No, that's the action of a man only chasing his own release. I want her squirting all over me again. I thrust forward switching angles with each entrance as if doing a dance.

I'm only giving her just a little more than the tip and she's still going crazy. I power through another of her orgasms. Earning me another shower in her essence. If I would've gotten my hands on her when we were younger, I would've taken her and run away never to be found.

"You like that, you want more of that dick inside you? Tell me what you like? Can you handle more of my cock?"

"Baby, this is so good," she moans. "Don't stop, I need this so much."

My mind races. How many men have there been? I tighten my grip on her thighs as I hold them to my chest. My thrusts turn punishing as I think of others touching what's mine. I promised her we'd be together. Things got in the way, but I never lost sight of that promise.

"You are mine," I roar out above her screams of pleasure.

"Shit, Omid," she says breathlessly.

She was in my practice to have another man's seed planted into her womb. Jealousy and rage consume me. It will be over my dead body. My seed will be the only one she ever carries. I thrust deeper, this time intent on coming with her.

I don't listen to the reasoning my brain tries to offer. I listen to my heart that screams we've found the one woman that means everything to me. I'm more than aware I'm going about this the wrong way. The same threats that have kept me from her are alive and well. More so now that I've returned to the family.

Still, I come inside of her so hard, I dare my sperm not to implant itself inside her. "*Non ti perderò di Nuovo*," I say in Italian. A language I picked up from a few friends.

"What?" she says with a dreamy smile on her lips.

Thinking better of it, I don't give her the translation. She still doesn't know who I am. I won't scare her off by telling her I refuse to lose her again. Instead, I drop a kiss over her heart then say, "Show me to your bedroom."

CHAPTER SEVEN

Breakfast

Divine

When I start to gain consciousness the first three things I note are the banging in my head, the throbbing between my legs, and the heat against my back. I start to come fully awake and the heavy leg and arm are the next things that I register. Then there's the thick erection at my ass.

I try harder to push the fog from my brain. There's a man in my bed and I need him out. I don't do sleepovers. He should've been gone after I got what I needed. Now if only I could remember who I called over. Whoever he is, his ass knows the rules.

"Aç mısın?" he says in a deep accented voice. His minty fresh breath fanning the back of my neck as he asks if I'm hungry.

I stiffen. What the hell did I do last night? I *never* bring men to my home that I don't know. How drunk was I?

He slides his hand between my legs and starts to kiss my shoulder. His beard tickles my skin and it starts to come back to me. Me riding his face numerous times last night. Being twisted in so many different positions. Soaking the bed.

Oh shit, this dude had me squirting. That hasn't happened since that one dildo I refuse to use because that shit scared me when I made myself come so hard not only did I squirt but I passed out.

"Omid?" I test the name out hoping I didn't just call him by someone else's name.

"Yes," he says, not pausing in his soft kisses.

I race to think of something to say. I need to get him out of my bed and home. Those are my thoughts until he pushes two fingers into me and grinds his erection into my ass.

I turn to look over my shoulder and I'm met with light hazel eyes. Not the same odd clear from last night, but still unique. Everything comes flooding back to me. The couple who tried to pick me up. Omid coming to my rescue.

I gasp and my body coils tighter as images of me sucking the hell out of his dick hit me full force. I'm never drinking again. *Ever.*

"Um…I have to be in my office this morning. Do you need me to call you a cab?"

He pulls a face and his hand that's trying to scramble my mind through my pussy halts. I start to ease out of his hold to get out of the bed. I grab the sheet and pull it to my chest, clinging the fabric against my body.

"Navid is waiting for us. I want to take you to breakfast," he says calmer than his expression gives off.

"Oh…um…I don't know if I can fit that into my schedule."

"You need to eat and I need to eat. We'll do it together," he says with such finality, I have to raise a brow.

Before I can protest, he stands and walks his naked ass into my bathroom like he owns the place. I press a hand to my forehead. I should *not* be distracted by his chiseled back and tight ass. However, I'm standing here biting my lip as I marvel at the man to end all men in my fantasies.

Yes, I even love all the dark hair on his legs. Sue me, it's a weakness. It just screams man.

"Divine," he calls with that hint of an accent. Why on earth does he have to be Persian? I don't have to ask to know he is. I can tell. Many people don't know the difference between Arabs and Persians. I do. This man is Persian all day. "Come here. You will shower with me."

My mouth pops open. See now, when I was sixteen, I loved that shit. Ar…that boy, was always so bossy. I went along with it then and giggled about it like a fool. I'm not sixteen anymore and I refuse to think about how much the similarity stings.

When I don't budge, he reenters the bedroom heading straight for me. He snatches the sheet, tossing it back on the bed and lifts me into his arms. The sweet kiss he places on my temple takes a little of the heat out of my temper.

"What are you doing?"

"You said you have to be to the office. You're taking too long to come to me. We need to leave for breakfast so we can both start our day," he replies as if it's that simple.

Placing me on my feet in the bathroom, he reaches for my shower cap and covers my hair. I bite my lip to keep from melting at the gesture. He's a big guy. The care he's giving to something so simple seems to contrast the action.

I turn away to brush my teeth. Omid moves behind me and places his hands on my waist. My body reacts instantly. Butterflies take off in my stomach, my body seems to pulse with a new energy. I haven't felt like this in years. Not since that first call.

"Hello," I said nervously.

"Hello, gorgeous. Your voice is as beautiful as you are," he said.

"Thank you."

He paused for a moment. "I'm so glad we could talk. I wanted you to hear the first time I told you I love you."

My mouth fell open, my stomach dropped and butterflies took flight. I had this tingling sensation all over. I couldn't stop smiling.

"I love you, too," I replied shyly.

"You will call me at this time every day."

I giggled and bit my lip. "Okay."

Just then Marica rushed into the room with a box. I looked at her curiously. Her excitement rolled off of her.

"It's for you," she mouthed.

Placing the phone between my neck and shoulder, I reached for the box. I grabbed the scissors from my desk and opened it. Pulling the jewelry box from inside, I opened it and gasped.

"Arman?" I said into the phone. "Did you send me this necklace?"

He asked me for my address the day before. I gave it to him hesitantly. After all, we were moving at the end of the summer. If he turned out to be some crazy guy, I would be gone from this house soon.

"Yes, do you like it?"

I looked at the necklace and squinted at the heart pendant. Clasping it against my heart, I shook my head in disbelief. My face hurting from smiling so hard.

"Are these real diamonds?" I whispered.

"I will always give you the best. Put it on. Never take it off."

"Okay."

Omid's fingers dancing across my neck bring me back to the present. He's watching me in the mirror. Or should I say he's staring at my bare neck as if he just watched my memories play along with me. I move away from him as far as his body caging me in will allow and finish brushing my teeth.

When I'm done, he laces his fingers with mine and leads me into the shower. Why I follow without telling him he needs to go, I'll never know. Maybe it's the hangover.

We climb inside and again he cages me in with his body— his front to my back— as he turns on the water. I stand before him stiffly not knowing how I should react. I've never done something like this before.

My male encounters are usually so disconnected. I get what I need and they're gone. With my longest relationship, he was always in a rush to get home to his family I had no clue about.

Omid drops a kiss on my shoulder, before grasping my chin and tipping my head back. He hovers over me, kissing me deeply. I brace myself against the shower wall.

Oh, yeah. This is why I brought him home. Damn.

Too soon he breaks the kiss, leaving me dazed and frustrated. I want him, but I need to get him out of my home. I don't like the way I feel around him.

I'm too…comfortable. Oh, I cannot have that. Last time I allowed myself to fall for someone like him it broke my little heart in pieces.

When he begins to rub body wash into my skin—releasing the tension in my shoulders—I lose a little more of the battle within. I place my forehead against the shower wall and sag. I've only dreamed of being pampered like this.

Am I wrong to relish in this just a bit?

"There, that's better," he murmurs as he works magic with his hands. "Where would you like to go for breakfast?"

I let that question sink in while he lathers the rest of me then washes the soap from my body. He pulls me back against his chest and I'm wrapped in an unfamiliar secure feeling. Tipping my head back, he starts to target the pressure points on my face. I sigh in relief as the throbbing in my head subsides.

I start to question why I can't keep him. It's that thought that has me shaking myself out of bliss. I turn to face him and look up into his eyes.

"Listen, what I can remember of last night was amazing but I don't do sleepovers and I don't do breakfast. If you want to exchange numbers we can maybe do this again. All I ask is that you let me know if you're seeing someone else. I usually like for my sex buddy to be exclusive during our understanding," I say.

"Sex buddy?" he says in disgust. "I wouldn't reduce you to some woman I let warm my bed. Nor will you make me some breathing dildo."

He shakes his head and backs away as if I've drawn a knife on him. He looks pissed. I guess he won't be my next fuck buddy. I shouldn't feel so disappointed. I'm getting ready to have a baby. I'm sure that would be more of a turn off for him.

"I don't do relationships. I like my life the way it is. I haven't had a partner in almost two years. You broke my fast last night. If you're not interested then that's fine. I have a busy life as it is," I think I say the words more to convince myself than him.

He starts to mutter to himself in Farsi. I'm a little rusty, but I think he just said I lost my mind. He storms out of the shower snatching a towel to wrap around his waist, still fuming and muttering.

I blow out a breath and turn the shower off. I wanted him gone. So why do I feel like I just broke something vital to my own existence?

"Omid, wait," I call after him and begin to follow.

Omid

"Sex buddy?" I grumble as I tug on my pants.

She really doesn't know who the fuck I am. I'm no fuck buddy to anyone. Hearing my wife reduce me to a fucking fuck buddy burns right through me.

I don't care that she doesn't know that she's my future wife. I know and I'm not amused by this. My cell rings as her voice travels to the living room where I'm retrieving my clothes.

"Hello," I snap as I hold up a finger for Divine to quiet as I take the call.

"Hello, Dr. Omid. Mrs. Holiday has gone into labor. She's on her way to the hospital."

I look at my watch. Yesterday was my day off. Dr. Jennings was on call for me. She has officially been off for twenty minutes.

"Thank you. I'm on my way," I say sharply.

"You're welcome, Doctor." I hang up the phone and grab my shirt to pull on.

"I'm sorry. I think I offended you—"

I hold my hand up again. "We're not finished. We'll have to have a rain check on breakfast. One of my patients just went into labor."

I walk over to her and palm the back of her neck, dragging her to me to kiss her thoroughly. When I feel her melt into me I break the kiss and peck her forehead. "I will call you later, Divine. We can plan for dinner sometime this week."

With that, I turn and leave her standing, staring after me.

I'll show her a fuck buddy.

CHAPTER EIGHT

Who Are You?

Divine

My head is still spinning after Omid walked out of my home three days ago. Walking out to go deliver a baby. The irony. He's a doctor. An OB/GYN. Life sure does like to make fun of me.

After spending the morning remembering the night before in full, I decided to research the man that turned me out and had me doing everything I never do. I found nothing on the internet which is so damn odd. Granted all I have is a first name to work with. Still I thought I'd get at least one hit for an OB named Omid.

Nothing. That's what I've come up with. My curiosity grows with each day. I never gave him my number but he has sent me a text message every morning and night. Today, he sent one right in the middle of a little impromptu meeting with my team.

"Earth to Divine," Dada says.

I look up from my phone, placing it on my desk, I run a hand through my hair. That's a mistake. The gesture triggers memories of Omid tugging my hair while barking for me to *take this dick.*

I shake off the memory. "Sorry," I blow out. "Where were we?"

"The photo shoot. You were finalizing the looks," my assistant Terrance says.

"Right, I like these two outfits. This one can go. I think the makeup should be the focus for this set. This looks just too much," I say and slide the wardrobe photos around on top of my desk.

"I got you," Dada says.

I look at my childhood best friend. She's the only real one I have left in my life. All my other so called friends from growing up started to act funny when all of my success hit.

People are always surprised that she works for me. Whenever they see her wearing a Hijab they make all kinds of assumptions. All I see is my best friend that has rocked with me since junior high school.

"Can you give me an update on those sponsors? Am I still doing a video for that makeup remover?"

"Yup. I have you scheduled to do a few videos tomorrow. You have a few unboxings and two influencer requests," Dada says.

"I'll print out the schedule and bring it in. You have a few conference calls this week," Terrance says.

Terrance is another gift from above. He's a friend of my brothers. If you ask me they only wanted me to hire him for security.

However, Terrance has proven to be a great asset. He keeps this flowing and for the most part he doesn't run to tell my brothers my business. I respect that.

"Great—"

My phone buzzes on my desk. I suck my lip into my mouth. I know it's him before I look down.

Omid is annoyed with me. He asked me to go to dinner with him last night. I haven't replied since. I don't think it's a good idea. This dude has me all in my feelings. I don't even want to play myself and try to move this into the causal call zone.

After my head cleared, I realized how good the sex was and causal anything with him isn't going to fly. Not when he makes my heart flutter when he sends a text. Nope. I don't have time for that.

Glancing down at the text I suck harder on my lip.

Exactly how long do you think I'll let you get away with this?

And that would be the other reason I'm avoiding him. His high-handed, do as I say approach is not going to fly. Why? Oh, just because it's sexy as hell when he does it. I know my limits. Omid checks too many boxes for me. Boxes I forgot I once had.

"Div, who has your nose so wide open?" Terrance says.

"What are you talking about?"

"So we're going to ignore the glow you came in here with the last few days?" he says. "And what's with the look on your face each time that phone goes off?"

"What look?"

"Nothing," Terrance says and flattens his lips into a thin line.

"No, no," Dada says. "You're so right. I've noticed."

I stand from my desk and pretend I'm busy clearing it off. Neither of them gets the hint that this meeting is over. They sit watching me.

"It's getting late. We can touch on everything else in emails or tomorrow," I say to dismiss them.

A knock at my office door has me lifting my head. My mouth drops open. Omid is standing in the doorway, dressed in a tailor made charcoal gray suit. He has a large bouquet of flowers in his hand.

"What are you doing here?"

"I came to take you to dinner. Are you ready?"

"What...how...I never said I'd go," I spatter.

He moves into the office with all of that swag. He looks so good, better than I remember. The closer he gets the more I feel like I'm being pulled in.

Placing the roses on my desk, he reaches for my waist and pulls me into him. "I'm a resourceful man when necessary."

He leans in to nuzzle my neck and places a kiss behind my ear. I shiver in his hold, willing my hands not to lift to his waist or chest. He smells so damn good. My office will probably smell of him for weeks.

"You two are a beautiful couple," Terrance says.

"We're not a couple."

"Thank you," we respond in unison.

I narrow my eyes at Omid. He gives me a sexy grin and shrugs his shoulders. I drop my eyes to his lips. My body heats as I remember all they are capable of.

"Guys, can you excuse us?"

Terrance sucks his teeth. I turn and Dada is prying him out of his seat. I watch them leave before turning back to Omid.

He has his tongue down my throat as soon as we're alone. I moan into his mouth. He grabs a tight hold of my ass, pulling me into his growing erection.

"I've missed you, Divine," he says as he breaks the seal of our lips.

"You don't even know me. How are you here?"

"I told you. I have resources."

I roll my eyes. "I'd like to borrow those. I can't find a thing about you. Who are you?"

"Ah, you're curious about me. Come to dinner and you can ask me anything you like. I want you to know me." The way he says the last part seems to have a hidden meaning.

I search his eyes, knowing that I'm letting my curiosity get the best of me. I push out of his hold needing to put distance between us. Everything about his presence is overwhelming.

"I'm not dressed for dinner," I say looking over his immaculate suit.

His eyes roll over me in a heated gaze. I tug at the blue shark tail top I'm wearing over my tight acid wash jeans. He licks his damn teeth like a predator. A sexy predator, ready to devour my body where I stand.

"We can stop at your place for you to change," he says.

I cross my arms over my chest. The word no is shouted in my head but I can't get my mouth to follow suit. I don't know what it is about him. I narrow my eyes, trying to see something that's not there. It's more a feeling I have about him.

I'm not afraid of him. Yet, I get the feeling I need to be cautious with him. I can't quite explain it. There's also something familiar about him, beyond spending one night together.

"If I go to dinner with you that doesn't mean we're dating."

"Oh?" he lifts a brow.

"Omid, I told you I don't do relationships."

He tilts his head at me. Those ethereal eyes look through me. I take a step back as if that will shield me.

"Boys will be boys, Divine. I am a man. I've figured out the things I want in life. I want you. The past will not stop me from having you. No one or nothing in it has the power it will take to keep me from having you," he says in that confident way that both turns me on and annoys me to no end.

His words hit their mark. I'm stunned that he has read me so well. My knees nearly buckle.

His words spill out like sin and honey. I'm sticky between the legs as I try to catch my breath. He's not here to play. A trait that I know too well.

However, as he has just pointed out he's no eighteen-year old boy with an online summer crush. This is a real man standing right before me in the flesh. That's way more dangerous.

I lower my arms to wrap my middle. Marica tells me all the time it's just going to take the right man—one that's not going to back down from me—to win my heart. I'm just not sure I want my heart won.

I have a plan. I'm determined to stick to my plan. I've thought about my mother's words and I want to go through with having this baby more than ever.

Is it your mom or is it him?

I shudder at the thought. A part of me does want to go through with the IUI to keep myself from getting involved with this man. The next two months can't go by fast enough.

Against my better judgment, I square my shoulders and lift my chin. "Just dinner?" I say softly.

He waves a hand in the air. "It's a beautiful evening. We'll see where it ends."

Omid

As we wait to be seated in the restaurant, I can't keep my hands off of her. She looks stunning tonight. I thought she was fine in the blouse and jeans she had on in her office when I arrived, but now...I want to throw her up against the nearest wall and drive into her until both of our knees go weak.

I brush her hair from her face, causing her to tip her head up to look at me. "You're beautiful," I murmur and lean in to kiss her lips. I don't linger the way I want to.

"Thank you," she says ducking her head.

I reach to tip her head back. "I've never thought of you as shy."

Her brows crease. I kiss her with a little more passion this time. When I pull away she looks dazed. Settling a hand just above her lush ass, I guide her into my side where she belongs. Pressing my lips to her temple, I keep them there until the hostess greets us.

"If you will follow me, I'll take you right to your room, Doctor."

"Room?" Divine looks up at me and questions.

"I thought it would be better to have some privacy so we can talk. The chef is a friend. He has prepared a special menu for us tonight."

She takes a deep breath and nods. I can't know it for sure, but I believe I'm the cause of all of this reluctance she has for relationships and dating. I've been thinking about it since I left her home. My anger with myself and the circumstances around our parting have grown with each day. Knowing that I've scarred her life for twenty years makes me feel so unworthy.

I plan to spend the rest of my life making it right. After all this was meant to be. I've found her right when I have the right cards to play to keep her in my life. The threat may still be there but I have the power to silence it.

"Wow, this place is so…it's breathtaking," she says as we step into the private dining room of Nick and Kevin's restaurant. "I've heard about this place. I've just never gotten around to coming."

"Kevin Briggs himself will be cooking for us tonight," I inform her with a grin as I pull her chair.

"Um…I'd like to know what you do for a living. Who are you?"

I kiss the tip of her nose. "We have all night for you to figure that out."

I take my seat across from her as the hostess pours us two glasses of wine. Kevin's choice of the night. Everything will be paired perfectly for the meal he has designed.

When the hostess leaves, Divine takes a sip of her wine and gives a little moan. My eyes drop to the tops of her breasts on display in her figure hanging red dress. If not for my plans to have her alone tonight, I don't think she would have made it out of her home in that thing.

"You might want to bring those pretty eyes up here," she says.

I lift my gaze to hers and smile. "Can you blame me? That dress doesn't stand a chance of surviving tonight in one piece," I say in a subtle warning.

A little grin graces her lips. "You're sure one that's full of himself."

"Not full of myself. I just know when I plan to have what's mine."

She sits back in her seat. "What's yours?"

"You were born to be mine," I say reaching across the table to cover her hand. "Do you not feel that? I'm drawn to you. Even when I'm not with you, my thoughts are pulled to you."

"Who are you?"

I give a short laugh. "I'm Dr. Omid V-Shah. I'm an OB-GYN. I own a practice with a friend and a few other doctors. Dr. Nobi and I also specialize in fertility."

She jerks her head back. I narrow my eyes as I watch her connect the dots. Her lips part.

"You're Dr. O.V. Shah. I was searching for you wrong. Marica and I found it odd that your name was in initials at the practice when everyone else has full names. We spent a good five minutes joking about it in the waiting room," she says.

When I came back to America to study, I became Omid V-Shah. Most places I dropped my first name and used O.V. when I could. With the sizeable donation my uncle provided it was never questioned.

"I have reasons for it," I say simply.

"Reasons you don't plan to share." She gives me a side-long glance.

I stroke the hand I'm still holding. "You will learn that in time. There are other things you should want to know first."

"Such as?"

I don't get to reply. Kevin Briggs enters the room with a broad smile and two salad plates. He sets them down in front of us, then turns to me to pull me from my seat into a bear hug.

"It's good to see you," he says.

"Likewise, how's Mariah and children?"

"They're great. My boy is getting so big so fast. Sometimes, I wish I could freeze time to watch them be this small and cute forever," he laughs.

"Send your lovely wife a hello."

"Yeah, I'll think about that one. I mention you, she may think I want another baby. While I love and adore the ones I have. I only want to freeze them sometimes. Other times I'm counting down the days until they're off to college."

I laugh and pat him on the shoulder. "Kevin. This is Divine. *Aşkım*, this is Kevin Briggs."

She sits stunned for moment before shaking it off and reaching out a hand. "Nice to meet you."

"It's a pleasure to meet you. The good doctor has never brought anyone here. Tonight, I plan to pull out all the stops to celebrate this occasion. Great guy," Kevin says, patting at my chest. "Delivered my girls when Dr. Nobi had to go out of town for a seminar and those two couldn't wait for him to get back."

"Oh, wow and you two are also friends?"

"Yes, we have a big family of friends. We adopted this one a ways back," he replies. "I better get back to the kitchen. Please enjoy the salads. They have fresh tangerines and a little something spicy in them for a mixture of heat and freshness."

"Thank you," I say as I return to my seat.

Kevin nods and leaves out as fast as he entered. Divine sits staring at me. The wheels turning behind her eyes. I start on my salad, waiting for whatever words will come next from her pretty mouth.

Instead of asking a question, she starts on the plate before her as well. I watch her lips growing hard as they move. I plan to suck and fuck that mouth before the night is done. I've been distracted with thoughts of her for the last three days.

"This is so good. He's right, it's fresh with a kick but there's an acidic note too."

"Very nice flavor pairing. The right note of sour," I nod.

She looks at me and grins. "Yes, I think I remember you sucking down lemons at the bar."

"What don't you remember about the other night?"

Her cheeks glow and she turns her focus back to the plate before her. I can't help the smile that comes to my lips. I enjoy watching her blush and fidget.

The girl I remember had so much sass and personality. The old Divine was so quick to respond. This is a different woman sitting before me—older, more cautious. I think I like this new mix of old and new.

"I think I remember it all," she says in almost a whisper.

"I certainly do. Every single moment."

She inhales deeply. "I'm a patient at your practice. I...I've been in to see Dr. Nobi for my consultation so far. I'll be returning in two months for my next appointment," she rushes out. "This is a conflict of interest. I don't think we can see each other again."

"You are John's patient. Not mine."

"I'm going to him to have the IUI procedure done. It's probably not the best idea for us to be having a sexual relationship."

"You are allowed intercourse. We usually strongly suggest you don't have intercourse between the day of your trigger shot and the IUI. In fact, we could have sex the day after your IUI to increase the sperm count and your chance of becoming pregnant," I reply coolly.

Her eyes round in her pretty head. I have no intentions of her having another man's sperm inseminated inside of her, but I still give her the information. She will not use this to pull away from me.

"I'll be having a baby implanted in me in two months. This doesn't bother you?"

"A lot can change in two months."

"Which is why this won't work. I'm not changing my mind. I want a baby," she says, her eyes hardening in her resolve.

"I'm not trying to take that from you, Divine. You will have your baby."

"And you? What am I to do with you?"

"Enjoy me, as I plan to enjoy you. Things will work themselves out. They always do. Allah provides us with all we need."

"You practice Islam?" she says with alarm, placing her fork down. "Oh my God, Omid. Did we use condoms the other night? Shit, I didn't see a single wrapper in my house."

She shoves a hand in her hair and tugs. Alarm covering her face. I understand the reason for her alarm it was the same fear she had when we were teens.

Divine had questions about my religion then. What I never told her was that I had plans to marry her then. Because she was my wife in my mind, I never explained things to her fully.

Over the years, I've practiced Islam loosely, being manipulated in the name of Allah will do that. Remi and Ramses had their way of distracting me from the love I lost. Now that she's back in my life. I thank Allah and wish for forgiveness in being impatient. I stand to round the table and squat next to her.

"I am Muslim, yes. So you already know the answer to your question. No, you and I did not use condoms and never will," I say, reaching to pinch her chin and turn her face toward me. "You were my first partner in over a year. I can provide you with my last test results which were a month ago."

"I can't believe I was so stupid."

"I would never put you in danger—"

"No, because I'm doing a damn good job of it myself. I took you to my home, I had sex with you without protection. I know nothing about you. Maybe my parents are right. I'm not showing enough responsibility for a baby."

I capture her lips to calm her. It takes a second or two before she yields to my kiss. My need to claim her drives me to deepen the kiss and take more than I intended to. I release her mouth and press my head to hers, smashing her nose with mine.

"For now, we get to know each other. We will revisit sex later. It will kill me but I will wait to have you again."

"I'm not changing my plans. I'm having this baby."

I snort. "Do you always have a one track mind?"

"When it's something I want, yes."

"Then we have a lot in common. You are mine."

"We'll see."

Yes, we will.

CHAPTER NINE

Nightcap

Divine

"Do you visit home much?" I ask while sitting in Omid's lap.

We're back at my house again. He insisted I sit in his lap when I tried to take my own place on the couch. I've been warring with the comfort I feel in his arms, as well as the curiosity I have to know more about him.

"This year was my first visit in nineteen years. I spent some time home before a little family trip to Dubai," he replies.

I smile as I remember planning my own trip to Dubai. It was on my bucket list. I remember wanting to know all about it when I was sixteen.

I was promised a trip there. Just one more promise broken. I shake off that thought as my smile slips a little.

"Dada and I went to Dubai two years ago. That was an experience." I laugh to get my mind off the course it's started to travel.

"Good, I hope," he says with concern in his voice.

"Interesting. I was proposed to twice." I laugh at the memory.

His arms tighten around my waist possessively. I close my eyes as his facial hair tickles my neck. I'm getting used to him nuzzling my neck as much as I think he is.

My nipples tighten and moisture starts between my legs. I ignore my body's response to him. There will be no sex.

My father would kill me if he found out I was on the verge of converting to Islam when I was sixteen. I was that in love. I studied everything I could to know more about my boyfriend.

What I didn't learn on my own, I asked him about. I wanted to fit into his world. We had planned to make love and safe sex was my biggest concern.

"Arman, what about condoms? You can't use them, right?"

He sat silent for a moment. I could almost hear him thinking through the phone. I held my breath until he gave his response.

"It is against my beliefs. I will take care of you. You don't have to worry about that."

I bit my lip and twisted my fingers in my shirt. He said I didn't have to worry but I was.

"What if I get pregnant?"

"It would be Allah's will and I would be the happiest man on earth to have you carrying my child. I love you. It will be fine."

"Okay, I trust you. I love you too. Will your cousins return soon?"

He groaned and blew out a breath. "I hope so. I want to have you in my arms soon."

"Where have you gone?" Omid says in my ear.

I shiver. His voice is so similar to Arman's in this moment. Just a bit deeper. It's almost eerie.

"Just thinking."

My thoughts travel back to dinner. He called me his love when he introduced me to Kevin Briggs. I was thrown by the endearment at first.

"Tell me about your business," he says.

My smile takes over my face. I love what I do. Makeup, fashion, connecting with people and inspiring them. I'm so grateful that I've been able to build this life I have.

"My makeup line is called Gossip. It's so hard to find makeup pigmented for women as dark as I am. I started playing with different brands and looks and posting them online. One thing led to another and I've become an influencer and launched my own makeup line.

"I just launched my first fashion line and we're getting ready to launch a line of fitness products, hair and lash products, as well as, my second line of makeup in the next few months," I say happily.

"That's amazing. This is a beautiful home in a very nice neighborhood so you have done well. I'm very proud of you," he says.

I turn to look at him. "Thank you."

He pecks my lips. "You don't have to thank me. You're a brilliant woman. I think it's very sexy."

I turn, clearing my throat. He's the sexy one here. The man oozes sex.

Starting with his strong arms around me, the bulge of muscle beneath his shirtsleeves. The scent of his cologne that has wrapped around me. I've been wanting to bury my face in his neck and inhale him all night.

"What are you wearing? What scent is that?"

"YSL, L'Homme."

"Oh my God. I should've known."

"Do you like it?"

I ignore his question. "Where did you say you're from?"

He stiffens. It's brief but I sense it. It stokes my curiosity. Omid has secrets, that much I'm sure of.

"A city within Iran…Shiraz," he says.

This time I stiffen and turn to look him in the eyes. My heart hurts. Arman was from Shiraz. This is too much. Just the thought of his name cuts me so deep. I can't do this.

"I think we should call it a night," I say and go to stand.

He shakes his head at me, pulling me into a kiss. I have to fight the tears back as he devours me in that all-possessive way. Hurt and anger mix.

Arman was always so concerned with me not talking to other boys. On every call he would demand the same. I was his. I wasn't to give any other boy my attention.

I tell myself he would be pissed to know I'm in the arms of another man. Even if that's a lie, I want him to hurt for lying to me, for making me fall in love with him then breaking my heart. I turn, hiking my dress up and straddle his lap. He groans when I suck his tongue into my mouth.

"Divine," he says in warning.

"Yes?"

"Shit," he growls flipping me onto my back on the couch.

He moves swiftly down my body and tears my panties right off. I gasp and lift my hips toward his face. When he latches onto my nub, I cry out into the room.

"No penetration, but I'm going to feast on you all night," he says huskily.

I push his head back between my thighs. My main goal is revenge on a man who doesn't care about me. A man I've never met and haven't spoken to in years.

I don't have to think as he eats my pussy as if he's making up for all the wrongs I've ever encountered. All I do is feel. Orgasm after orgasm, feeling is all I do. Eventually, I think I begin to feel too much.

Omid

I brush her hair from her face as she gives me a sleepy smile. I'm in her bed again but I've kept my word. I will not sink into her warm heat no matter how much I want to and I want to with everything I am.

I ache for her. I want nothing more than to have those thick thighs wrapped around me while I rock into her tight pussy. I lick my lips and smile as her essence still flavors my mouth.

"You do know this is the point when you're supposed to leave?" she says, the teasing tilt of her lips stilling my annoyance.

I brush my fingers over her cheek. "I have walked through hell to lie in this very spot. I'm not leaving tonight."

She gives me a questioning look before shaking her head. "I'm too tired to get up and kick you out so you can stay this time," she murmurs sleepily.

I scoff and kiss her forehead. "Right."

"You're going to stop ignoring what I say. I'll kick your ass, Omid."

"I'd rather take a bite of yours," I croon in her ear and squeeze her back side.

"Shh," she whispers. "I'm trying to sleep. Don't make me put you out."

I chuckle and kiss her collarbone. I go to settle in to get some sleep, but my phone vibrates. I frown. Just my luck. One of my patients would go into labor tonight.

I lift my phone from the nightstand and it's Navid. Concerned, I look at a sleeping Divine before slipping from the bed and leaving the room to take the call.

"Hello, what's wrong?"

"I believe you should call your Anne Sassa. She has interesting news you will want to know."

I close my eyes and groan. It has to be my mother. I get the feeling she plans to make my life more difficult. I don't need to call Sassa. I know what she will tell me.

I got sidetracked the night I went to the bar. I had planned to talk to the Blacks about my situation. Joe Black handed my case to his sons a few years back.

I need them to make sure my family can't find out about my life. "I will talk to Wyatt," I say. "I will also give my uncle a call. I'm sure he can find a way to keep his brother in Iran."

"Yes, but for how long? They want you to marry Dilshad. Her family will pressure your parents with your known history," Navid says nervously.

I sigh and rub my eyes. "It's in my uncle's best interest to keep them where they are, but I'll call my mother and see if I can do something as well."

"Hurry, they're packed and ready to make their trip."

I clench my teeth and end the call. Looking at the time it's 9:41 a.m. in Iran. My parents are up and about their day already. I inhale and dial my mother.

"Omid!"

"Hello, Anne."

"I'm so happy you have called. We have so much to do. I think it will be good for you to spend time with Dilshad. You need to get to know her," she rambles.

"No. I don't. I will not be getting to know Dilshad. I am busy with a study," I say thinking quickly. It isn't a complete lie. However, it's not the full truth. I ask Allah for forgiveness as I continue. "I will not be around to entertain. I have travel."

"Oh. I didn't think of your busy schedule as doctor. When will this study be over?"

"In a year or so," I say.

The excitement falls from her voice. "That's so long. Dilshad will have to wait a year for the wedding?"

"If it takes her parents that long to find a match. Yes. She's not the one for me. Do not lead that woman into thinking otherwise."

"She will be just the first of your wives. She's pretty. She's very smart—"

"She will not be the first of anything for me. I need rest. I will call you another time."

She sighs on the other end. I can hear the hesitation. One thing I know, as much as my parents will meddle they both respect the work they believe I do. My being a doctor is important to them.

"I will let her family know. I hope that we get to see you during the next year."

"I doubt it. I'll be very busy. I don't know when I'll have free time," I say.

I run a hand through my hair. I'm skirting so much of the truth. Yes, I'm working on a study. Yes, I will have to travel a bit. However, that traveling will be done within California and maybe as far as Nevada.

"Oh, okay. Well, call me when you can. Rest well."

"Thank you."

I end the call before she can hatch another plan. I will still be making those other calls in the morning. I don't put it past my parents to still try to make their way here to the States. That I can't have.

I return to the bedroom and climb into bed. Gently, I tug Divine into my arms. When she snuggles into my chest, I sag into the bed in relief. This is where I need to be.

I finally have what I want. No, I can't have my parents anywhere near my life. By any means, I will keep that from happening.

CHAPTER TEN

Dropping in

Divine

Laughter rings through the office as my team sits around teasing and joking while we work. I love the chill atmosphere we have. I usually come out of my office, when I'm here, and hang with them while we work, even if it's just Dada and Terrance.

Dada has been roasting Terrance while I get some new footage ready to post. My stomach hurts from laughing so hard. I swipe at tears in the corners of my eyes.

"Come on dude. Our girl is launching a clothing line. You have to rep the brand. You come in here some days looking like you rolled out of bed. You have Div's back and you can keep a schedule tight, but fashionable you are not," she says.

"Wow, you're just coming for my neck. All I said was them shoes aren't your usual style. I didn't say that was a bad thing," Terrance retorts.

"I saw it in your eyes. You were coming for me," Dada says and huffs, placing her hands on her hips as she stands up at her desk.

"It sounds like I'm missing all the fun." That voice. I close my eyes and try not to shiver as it rolls down my spine.

I turn to find Omid in a pair of scrubs holding a tray of frappés. He puts a hurting on a suit. What he does to these here scrubs should be illegal. He hands Terrance the tray of drinks, pulling two out before walking over to where I'm sitting.

"I'm getting used to you having a man," Terrance says. "He gets our drinks right too. Don't mess this up for us."

"Shut up," Dada and I say at the same time.

Omid just smiles, carefully placing a drink down next to me. He then leans over me to capture my lips. I try my best not to moan, but when he nips my lips I lose the fight. When he pulls away looking down at me with lust in his eyes, my cheeks heat.

"Good afternoon, gorgeous."

"Hey, what are you doing here?"

It's not like he hasn't found random reasons to show up at my office. If it's not my office then it's my house. For the last few days, we've fallen into a routine that he has set. I feel like I'm in a relationship and I'm not even sure how.

"Wanted to see you before I have to head to the hospital. I have two scheduled C-sections," he says.

"That's so sweet. I adore you two," Dada says.

I stand and grab my drink in one hand and Omid's hand in the other. Once in my office, I close the door behind us. He plucks the drink from my grasp and places it on my desk. In the next motion he has me on his waist, pressed to the wall beside the door as he kisses me senseless.

I wrap my arms around his neck, getting lost in the moment. When he slides his hand into my leggings, I jerk back and try to wiggle free. He bites down gently on my neck, pressing his erection into me.

"I just want to make you come. I've been thinking about it all morning," he says in my ear.

He knows that drives me crazy. Whenever he talks in my ear, I nearly come from just his voice. Cupping his handsome face, I bring his lips to mine.

"You made me come this morning in the shower. We're not doing that with my employees right outside the door," I say then complete the kiss.

He sucks his teeth, turning to place me on the edge of my desk and stands between my legs. This time he cups my face, mirroring the gesture I'd done just seconds ago. He kisses me briefly before pulling away and planting his palms on either side of me against the desk.

"What should we have for dinner tonight?"

"I can't keep eating takeout every night."

He furrows his brows, looking at me questioningly. "When have we had takeout?"

It's my turn to look at him strange. He's been bringing dinner to my house every night when he arrives. It's all been delicious. Always something different and from a different culture.

"When you bring dinner that's not takeout?"

He gives a deep laugh. "No. We've never had takeout. Navid loves to cook. He prepares all my meals. It's safest that way."

"Safest?"

His smile falls and his thoughts race across his face. "I don't tolerate food from everyone well. Navid knows me best. He protects my tummy," he says, reaching for my hand and placing it against his tight abs beneath his scrubs.

The look on his face is sexy and adorable. The thought of him needing protection from anyone is laughable. I'm the one that needs help. He leans in for another kiss and I forget what we were initially talking about.

"Navid makes great Thai food or Moroccan cuisine. He makes the best Khubz. You will love it," he says with his lips pressed to my cheek.

"Sounds good."

"I will be at your place around six, unless a little one decides they need a date with me more."

We're not dating.

I've been trying my best to tell myself this. I've never lied this much in my life. He reaches to brush a lock of hair from my eyes and the expression on his face as he does is one of the things that has drawn me to him.

I've had men look at me with want, desire, lust. The way he looks at me is more like I'm someone to cherish, hold, worship. I almost burst into tears from the intensity of it. However, my mind won't allow me to push aside the warning bells.

"How long can you stay?" I end up blurting out.

On the inside, I know I'm not talking about today. I want to know how long I have before this is just a memory, before he turns into some asshole I never should've let in. I need to know the expiration date on these feelings that are growing.

"Let's order some lunch. Navid can make us something light," he says with a smile.

Omid

"That was so good," Divine says as she wipes her mouth.

I look up from the quick text I just sent to my office assistant. I need to get to the hospital soon, but I love spending time like this with Divine. Dr. Jennings was able to cover for me to have a little more time here before I have to head to the hospital today. However, I'm on schedule soon.

"I will give your compliments to the chef."

A file on her desk catches my eye. The name of the company seems familiar. I can't put my finger on it, but it nags me.

I point to the file. "Are you working on something new?"

She follows my gaze and her face lights up. "I've been working to get a meeting with this investor for some time now. I finally locked in a lunch with them."

"Investor? You're company is doing well, isn't it? Why would you need an investor?"

"I—"

Her words are cut off as a knock sounds on the door. My phone vibrates at the same time. Divine goes to the door and I respond to the text that comes in. I'm disappointed that I have to leave.

However, that file grabs my attention again. I frown. She doesn't need to sell off pieces of her business. I don't like the idea at all. From the way she talks about her ventures she's done great on her own. If she's in trouble, I'll give her the capital she needs to get her books in order.

I turn to the door and find Divine has stepped out. Quickly I open the file and snap shots of the pages on top. I want to know more about this investor. I will find out more about Divine's financials as well.

"I'm sorry," she says as she returns to the office. "I need to get back to work. I have some buyers I need to conference call with."

I stand and walk over to her. Palming the side of her face, I kiss her lips. The sweetness from the peach tarts Navid made especially for her flavors her mouth. I groan, not wanting to end this but knowing we both need to get to work.

"I'll see you tonight. Have a great rest of the day," I say, lightly brushing my lips back and forth against hers for just a few moments longer.

"See you later," she says as I release her and head out.

"Thanks for the drinks and lunch," Dada calls as I leave.

"You're welcome." I place a hand over my heart and nod.

"Bro, those sandwiches. Thanks," Terrance says.

"Anytime." I wave and leave.

Navid made extra for Divine's friends. I would say workers but the more I drop by the more I see that they're her friends, if not family. Even the part time workers that come in a few times a week.

My mind goes back to the investor. Does she need the money? Is that why she has part-time workers? I assumed it was more because of the fact that she's not in the office all of the time. Some days she and her two main employees work from her home.

I slip into my car and place a call. I want to have facts. I will not allow my woman to have financial worries.

"Hey, asshat. You bailed on us for that chick. Not that I blame you," Ryan Black says.

"What's up, Ry? I need a little favor. I'm going to text you some information. Can you put a file together on the investment company and another on Divine Favors?"

"Yeah, no problem. I'm assuming this is low key since you're asking me and not Wyatt," he says.

"Wyatt has his hands full with me. You can handle this for me. I'll send a little gift to you for your discretion."

"Say no more. I love your little gifts," he laughs and hangs up.

I send him the information in a text and look out toward Divine's place of business. I don't like this investment idea. Nothing says she's struggling but I will get to the bottom of this investor and her thought process.

Feeling a little more at ease, I start for the hospital. I can't wait until tonight. I look forward to our nights spent together.

I won't be able to fall asleep until I hear her cries of pleasure. Yet, it's the time before I crawl between her legs to feast on her. The moments where she reveals little by little who she is as a woman. Brilliant, determined, focused—I love all of this about her.

"By forty, I want to be settled into family life with a thriving business. Me, baby, and the empire," she murmured the other night while I held her in my arms.

Her, baby, me, and our empire.

That's the way it will be.

CHAPTER ELEVEN

Level Up

Divine

Omid: *Just delivered a baby boy. Need to see you.*

Me: *Can we meet later? Having that lunch I told you about.*

Omid: *Where is this lunch? I'll come to you.*

I smile at the message on my phone and shake my head. He has been text messaging me all morning while waiting on that sweet new baby boy. Last night was the first night in two weeks that he hasn't slept over. Even if he's exhausted from balancing patients at the office and delivering babies all day, he still shows up at my house to shower me with dinner and gifts.

The only reason he never showed up last night was because he delivered babies back to back until around 3:00 a.m. By 10:00 p.m., he had Navid deliver roses and dinner with a profuse apologize on his behalf. I surprised myself with how disappointed I was.

"Divine Favors?"

I look up from my phone to find the man I've been waiting for. I wipe the smile away and put on my game face. I worked hard to get this meeting.

I want to take my company to the next level and that means the right connections and a great distributor. Partnering with the right investor will open some new doors for me. This will grant me access.

I stand from the table in the posh restaurant. Reaching out my hand, I give him my business smile. He's a nice looking guy. When he smiles his light brown eyes light up.

"Nice to meet you, Mr. Alderman," I say.

"Jared, please."

"Okay, Jared." Waving over our waitress as I reclaim my seat.

Jared sits across from me and looks around at the restaurant. I picked the nicest place I could think of for this meeting. I want to make a great first impression. This meeting is huge for me.

I rub my sweaty palms in my lap. I must have spent two hours trying to decide on what to wear before choosing this cute black puff skirt, a black shell, and blue pumps. I wanted to represent my brand but still look professional.

"This is a nice place," Jared says after we place our drink orders.

I look up from my menu and smile. He's taking in my appearance. I bat my lashes so he can get the full effect of the look. My makeup line is flawless. If not for the pops of blue I used on my lips and in my shadow, I'm sure he's wondering if I even have on makeup.

"The lemon chicken and wild rice is so good here," I say and turn my blue painted lips up.

"I'm sorry for staring, but are you wearing your makeup line? I mean your skin looks flawless, and the glow. You're simply gorgeous," he says and starts to blush. "I meant that in the most professional way. I just can't believe you have on makeup."

I smile and tilt my head at him. "No worries. I get that reaction a lot. The formulas for all of the products are super light." I rub my fingers over my cheek and hold them out for him. "As you can see there's little to no transfer as well. Which for brown women is a big concern. I can't tell you the amount of tops I've ruined with other products."

"The lipsticks are what you started with, right?"

"Yes, we started with lip paints."

The waitress returns with our drinks and takes our order. Once she bounces away we get into talking about some of my competitors. Jared has done his homework. I'm impressed. I thought I'd have to come in here and school him.

"Divine, you have an amazing mind," Jared says once he finishes his lunch. "You're figures are amazing as well. I see so many places where I can help you grow the brand. You've already done such an impressive job."

"Thank you," I say and beam. "My team and I have worked hard to get everything exactly as I envisioned it."

"I know what I feel I can offer you. Tell me what you're looking for—"

"She needs nothing from you."

I whip my head toward Omid's voice. He's standing over our table glaring at Jared. My mouth drops open. I can't believe he's here.

"What are you doing here? How did you know where to find me?"

"Terrance gave me the address," he says without looking at me.

"Omid, you need to go. This is a business meeting."

He turns his head toward me slowly. His eyes are that odd color and he looks furious. I stand and place a hand on his chest. He wraps his arm possessively around my waist.

"I haven't seen you in over twenty-four hours. I will not be the one leaving."

Jared stands and reaches out his hand. "I'm Jared Alderman."

Omid looks at it like he has shit staining it. I blow out a breath and get ready to rip into him. I'm so pissed off. I'm going to kick Terrance's ass right after I hand Omid his.

Jared clears his throat. "I'll take care of the meal. Divine, it was nice to meet you. You have a great business on your hands, but I don't think this investment is one for my portfolio."

I close my eyes and nod. "Thank you for your time," I choke out.

When I open my eyes, Jared gives me a sympathetic look. "Again. Nice to meet you. Best of luck," he says and walks off.

Tears sting the backs of my eyes. I snatch out of Omid's hold. My own fury outweighing his. I can't believe what just happened. I was so close to closing the deal.

Omid

She grabs her bag and begins to storm out of the restaurant. I follow on her heels. She can be as angry as she likes. I didn't like the looks of that guy and his investment group didn't come up clean enough for my liking.

When we're out of the restaurant at the driver's side of her Jaguar, she spins on me. I cage her in, placing my hands on her waist. I go to kiss her lips and she turns away.

"I'm so fucking mad. Like, do you even understand what you just did?" she fumes. "He was going to invest in my company. That was my shoot at moving to the next level. I worked so hard to get that meeting. He has the connections I need."

"You don't need him. You have me." I wave her off.

"What's that supposed to mean?" Tears well in her eyes.

"You have done well on your own. Why sell pieces of what you've built? You don't need him or his money. You need to meet the right people, I'll make that happen for you," I say.

Her lips tremble as she shakes her head at me. Tears begin to spill over. I reach to wipe them away but she turns away once again.

"You're a doctor. What do you know about makeup? Do you even understand what Gossip means to me?"

I move closer and cup her face. "Yes, which is why I will help to place the *right* people around you and your company," I reassure her.

I want to tell her that I have more contacts and connections than that asshole ever will but she still hasn't connected the dots as to who I am. I grow more and more frustrated each day. I've tried to steer her to the questions and conversations that will reveal the truth but she shuts down every time I mention anything that can spark the connection.

If she realized who I am, she would know I'll bend the world to give it to her and I have the power to. She looks in my eyes, not trusting as easily as she once did. Twenty years ago, if I said it she believed it.

"You had no right to do that, Omid. You were wrong," she says.

"I will always do what I feel is best for you. You want the next level. I'll make that happen. Trust me," I lean in to kiss her lips and this time she allows it. Only, she doesn't kiss me back. "Divine, trust me."

"I think we need to take a break. I'm not ready to be in a relationship. I want to focus on my business," she says.

I tighten my jaw. I've been away from her long enough. Twenty years too long. I'm not about to spend another day without her if I can help it.

My phone goes off. I grind my teeth as I pull it from my pants pocket. I release a heavy sigh and answer.

"Dr. V-Shah," I say.

"Mr. Levi called. He's on his way with Mrs. Levi to the hospital, her water broke."

"Thank you. I'll be right there." I hang up and watch Divine as she tries to pull away from me. Kissing her forehead, I rub a hand up and down her arm. "I have to go. We will talk more later."

"You're not listening to me, damn it!"

"Yes, I am. I hear what you're saying. You're not hearing me," I say more harshly than I mean to. I reel in my temper. "I will have a better offer for you before the month is over. Trust me."

She looks at me through tear-filled eyes. Searching for something before she nods. I release some of the tension that has coiled within.

"I will call you later," I say and kiss her soft lips.

She nods and turns to climb in her car. I long to follow her, but I head to my vehicle to meet the Levi's at the hospital.

CHAPTER TWELVE

Pressure

Omid

I look out over my balcony as I listen to the voice on the other end of the phone. "No, that's all I need to know. Thanks, Felix."

"No problem. Wyatt said if you need anything else let us know," Felix Black replies.

"I will. Thanks again."

I hang up and stare at the phone. I've been waiting for a call from my cousin, Remi. I meant it when I told Divine I'd get her the right connections. I'm just waiting for the call to set it all up for her.

My phone rings but it's not my cousin. It's my mother. I groan and consider ignoring the call. However, my gut tells me to pick up.

"Hello, Anne."

"Omid," she sings excitedly. "Baba wants to come visit with you. I know, I know. You are busy with your study but we'll stay out of your hair."

I grind my teeth. I knew this was coming. Never mind me telling her that I would be busy. I squash my anger and change courses.

"I'm actually on my way to Italy," I say and grin. This is actually a fact. Well, I leave in a few days. "I will be there for several weeks. I was thinking of coming to visit during one of my free weekends."

"That sounds wonderful. I will cancel our flight. Maybe I can join you in Italy," she says hopefully.

I roll my eyes. "There won't be much time for that. I have one free weekend. I'll visit with you then. Tell Baba I look forward to seeing him."

She takes a moment to reply. "Of course. I'll tell him."

"Talk later, Anne."

"I love you, Omid."

I hang up without a reply. I've spewed enough bullshit for one day.

Looking up at the sky, my mind goes to Divine. It's been a week since our fight. I've been too busy to spend my nights with her. I'm getting annoyed with each day I spend without her.

My phone rings again, this time bringing a smile to my face. I answer on the second ring and lift it to my ear. "I was just thinking about you," I croon into the phone.

"You have to stop sending me all of these gifts." She sighs into the phone.

"Why would I do that, *Prensesim*?"

"I'm not your princess." She pauses to blow out a breath. I grin at the flustered sound in her voice. She will need to get used to me spoiling her. "Can you please stop sending me things? These aren't even small gifts you would get for a girlfriend."

"Ah, so you finally admit you're my girlfriend."

"Oh my God. Why are you intent on driving me crazy? Wait, how on earth did you know I'm in Vegas and my location for that matter."

"You are my Prenses, I will always know where you are. I miss you. I miss eating your pussy."

She grows silent. The sound of her moving fills the phone. A door opens and shuts on her end.

"Do you think you can buy sex from me?" She growls into the phone.

I'm taken aback. So much so, I take a step back as if she's before me. I'm stunned for more than a moment.

"I would shower you with gifts until my last breath even if you never let me in your body again. I've spent hours eating your pussy and never once asked for anything in return. I'm always seeking your pleasure," I say tightly.

There's another pause before she speaks softly. "I'm sorry. I'm just a little stressed out. Diamond earrings, Omid. That's a lot of pressure. We've only been seeing each other a few weeks. I don't know what to think of all of this."

"I'm your man. What is there to think of. I want to show you that you deserve the world. That's what a man does. I will give you whatever is in my power to give you. Period."

"The earrings are beautiful. Thank you for the laptop and all the other things," she says with less agitation.

"You're welcome. Are you still returning on Saturday?"

"I'm going to kick Terrance and Dada's asses. They're the ones feeding you my schedule, aren't they?"

I chuckle. "I will not confirm or deny this."

"Unbelievable."

"I will miss you. I have to leave for Italy Saturday morning. I will be gone by the time you return," I say.

"Oh. You're leaving?"

I turn to walk back into the house to finish my packing. I always have to prepare ahead of time. I never know when I'll get called to the hospital and then I'll have to pack at the last minute and forget things on top of being exhausted.

I smile as I think of Divine as my wife and her helping me with all of this. We will be good for each other. I will show her how a real princess is supposed to be treated and she will be the partner I've always wanted.

"I will return in five weeks or so."

"That long?"

My chest swells at the sound of her voice displaying disappointment and longing. She has been so angry with me for the last week. Her replies to my texts have been short and our phone conversations have been tense and abrupt.

"Yes, I have been offered the opportunity to share my research and take part in a case study. It was last minute. I accepted the offer yesterday," I reply.

It was a last minute offer because as usual my identity became an issue. It always does when Nobi and I do the bait and switch. We introduce my work with him as the lead and when these opportunities come up we reveal my involvement and my desire to remain anonymous.

It has slowed my advancement in the field and we've lost out on opportunities because of it. Many times due to biases. Dr. Nobi and I represent two different ideals of what American doctors should look and sound like. The overseas opportunities are usually easier to finesse.

Of course, I could throw money at every situation to turn it in my favor, but I'm great at what I do. I want to earn my place. This offer is a high honor. I will miss Divine but I can't turn this one down without damaging all I've worked for.

"Okay. I guess I'll see you when you get back."

"You will. Aşkım?"

She hesitates to answer. "Yes."

"Trust me. You will have all you want for your business. This changes nothing."

She gives a curt laugh. "Omid, if you don't fix that shit you pulled, I'm going to burn your home and everything else you own to the ground."

With that she hangs up. I'm left roaring with laughter. I have no doubts that she would.

Divine

I hang up and stare at the phone chewing on my lip. I'm still pissed as fuck at Omid. It took everything in me not to act a fool in that restaurant or parking lot.

I think our business schedules have been the Universe's way of giving me the space I need to cool off before I kill that man. I sag my shoulders. I'm going to miss him. As mad as I am at him, the thought of him being across the world for five weeks stings.

"Baby girl, you better get in here before your mother steals all of your chips," my father says as he peeks his head out of the front door of the villa.

This trip is my gift to my parents for their upcoming wedding anniversary. It was the only time I could get everyone together to do this even though their anniversary isn't for another three months. My father loves Vegas and my mother loves anytime she can get all her babies and grandbabies under one roof.

"I'm coming," I say taking one last glance at my phone, that unwanted longing playing with my heart.

I roll my eyes at myself and head back inside. I'm just overreacting because other than Marica, I'm the only single person in this house. Both of my older brothers brought along their girlfriends, my baby brother and my sister have their family with them.

It was a true task to find a villa big enough for all of us. Most places booked up so fast if they were as nice as this one. I got lucky with a cancellation. Seeing the joy in the room, I'm glad I did this.

Lance, my youngest brother has a huge smirk on his face as I reclaim my seat at the blackjack table in the living room. I'd excused myself when the delivery arrived. After opening the box, I called Omid immediately.

"Finally. Don't remember the world revolving around you," Patience grumbles next to me.

I glare at her. She wrinkles her nose at me and sticks her tongue out, causing me to roll my eyes. It's like we're little kids again.

"Who's the dude?" Lance says as he deals out the cards.

The energy in the room shifts as my entire family turns their attention on me. I look past Lance to the outdoor pool where the kids are playing along with his wife, Brandy. I debate going out in that heat just to get away from this conversation.

"Well?" Nashawn says.

"Am I not entitled to my privacy?"

"No," everyone in the room says in unison.

My mouth pops open. Patience laughs and tosses a pretzel at me. I bat it away and pout.

"Does this mean you've changed your mind about getting knocked up by a tube?" my second oldest brother Neil asks.

"Not that it's any of your business but I'm still having the baby," I say, folding my arms over my chest.

"Why?"

I look at Lance and narrow my eyes at him.

"Why not?" I shoot back at him. "Nothing has changed. I want a baby."

"So you are seeing someone?" my mother chimes in.

I shrug my shoulders and take a peek at my cards. I toss in a few chips and look around the table expectantly. My family returns my glance with pointed ones of their own.

"Don't nobody care about these cards," Patience says. "Who is he? How long you been hiding him?"

"Nah, what I want to know is, is dude paid? You built everything you have with your own hands. I'm not about to let some fool come up in your life and think he's about to get a free ride. I watched you make something out of nothing," Nashawn says.

"Word," Neil grunts.

"I was thinking the same thing," Lance says.

I throw my hands up. "I know how to take care of myself, thank you."

My father grunts, drawing my attention. I look to him and he's studying me closely. I want to fidget but when it comes to my father you hold your ground or he will pick right at the weakness you show.

"I agree with your brothers."

"Daddy, I never said I was seeing anyone to begin with." I huff.

"Problem number one. If you're ashamed to introduce him to us, something's not right."

"I'm not ashamed. Wait, I'm not seeing anyone," I say.

"Ow, this girl is a bullshitter," my mother cackles. "Like we haven't been cleaning her out because her poker face ain't shit."

Everyone bursts into laughter as she continues. "Girl, who you talking to. Your father and I worked our way off the streets of Compton. We know a thing or two. You kids have only known the better things in life because of the sacrifices and hustling we did to go to good schools."

"Tell her, baby," my father snorts. "I went nights without eating to make sure your mother ate and we paid our tuition. I busted my ass to keep moving you guys to the next best neighborhood. Greater opportunities. But I'm still from the same hood. I know bullshit when I hear it."

"Thank you," my mother says.

I drop my head to the table and groan. Patience giggles beside me. I want the table to just open up and swallow me.

"In her defense, she's thinks she's not in a relationship. He, on the other hand, is not having her BS." Marica snickers.

I lift my head and glare at my cousin. "You traitor."

"What?"

I roll my eyes at her. She just covers her mouth and tries to look innocent. I'm going to kick her ass later.

"We want to meet him," Nashawn says.

"Damn right. He better be at the next barbeque," my father grunts.

"He's going out of town. He won't be here for the next barbeque." I pout.

"Got her," Lance croons.

I palm my forehead and huff. They all laugh at me, high fiving each other. I don't know why I bother.

CHAPTER THIRTEEN

Advice

Divine

"I'm sorry I blew you up," Marica sings as she wraps her arms around my waist.

"You're not sorry about a damn thing," I grumble pushing her away with an elbow.

"Don't be like that," she laughs, kissing my cheek. "I haven't seen you like this in years. You like him."

I set down the new diamond bracelet on the kitchen island. I'd come down to make the family breakfast and do a live with my followers. The doorbell rang with a delivery the moment my toes hit the bottom stair in the foyer.

Here I am now with this beast of a diamond bracelet. I can't believe my eyes. It's like he heard nothing I said yesterday or chose to ignore it by sending something more extravagant to prove his point. I'm going with the latter. It would totally say Omid.

"He infuriates me," I bite out, sagging my shoulders, I run a hand through my hair. "But I feel this pull to him at the same time. I don't know what it is about him."

"Well, I want to meet him. I can see he has you all up in knots. He must be something," she says.

"He's my type to a T. No, let me get that right. The man broke the mold on all the things that I love in a man."

"Oh...wow," Marica blows out. "Like, make you forget about Arman type break the mold?"

"Who?" I say pointedly.

"Damn," she says releasing me to round the island and take a seat. "That's huge."

I bite my lip and look at her pleadingly. "I don't know what to do. We've been fighting and now he's leaving for five weeks. That shouldn't bother me. I should be okay with that."

"But you're not."

"No, I'm not. If I weren't here for Mommy and Daddy, I'd run back just to see him before he leaves."

Marica gives a low whistle. "So I'll be doing this baby thing alone then, huh?"

"No, I never said that. That's just one more thing I'm so confused about. I know I want to do this. I'm just not sure how he will fit into that. I've told him my plans, but we never had a real decision about it."

"Maybe it's time you do. All strong relationships are based on communication. This is one of those conversations that are a must. Sending gifts like that he's serious about you."

"That's what scares me," I whisper. "But I also know gifts mean nothing."

Marica sighs and reaches over the countertop for my hands. "Cuz, you were sixteen in an online relationship with a boy that was from across the globe. His world was so different from yours. We don't know what could have happened to him."

"I know he told me he loved me and promised we'd be together. I'm so afraid to let myself feel again. I mean, Omid is so much like him. How do I know I'm falling for him and not something from my past?"

"Wait, is this guy Persian?"

I nod. "They're from the same city. Like how crazy is that?"

Marica snorts. "Sort of insane. Do you think they might be related?"

I freeze. I never thought of that. I push a hand into my hair, my thoughts running over each other.

"I don't know. I don't even understand him all the time. He...he works with Dr. Nobi. In the same practice." I pause to let my words sink in.

"The dark haired doctor with the crazy sick eyes?" she gasps. "You've seen him?"

She fans her face. "Girl, when I saw him I thought of you immediately. Yeah, I get why your brain would be scrambled. He is...shit. I don't have words. Look, got me cursing in here."

"It's more than his looks. It's the way he treats me. Yes, I want to punch him when he gets all possessive and highhanded, but the way he cares for me and does simple things for me it's...he makes me feel cherished. I've never had that as an adult. Arman was the last male to make me feel that way," I confess.

"So what's the problem?"

"There are still so many things that feel like unknowns. Besides, have you met my father?"

She pulls as face. "Oh, yeah. You have a point. Uncle Clive isn't going to like this one bit. I mean, is Omid Muslim?"

"Yes," I groan.

"Oh, girl, good luck. I will never understand your father when it comes to all that. He's not even active in the church like that anymore, but he still has no tolerance at all," Marica says sympathetically.

I stretch my upper body over the island top. "Why me? I can't put those two in the same room."

"I think you should focus on talking to your man first. See how he feels about you going through with having the baby. If you guys can't see eye to eye on that, you're not going to have to worry about uncle Clive."

"Why is everything so much harder for me?"

Marica laughs sadly. "I'm the one having the baby of a dead man implanted in my womb. I get but so many shots to make this happen. Once the sperm is gone it's gone. I think that's what I'm most afraid of."

I look at my cousin, feeling like a total bitch. Here I am groaning about what could be my shot at a happily ever after and she has watched her own slip through her fingers. Lifting up, I round the counter to sit next to her and tug her into my embrace.

"No matter what, I'm going to be here with you every step of the way. You're going to have this baby. Keith will live on. We'll all be here for you," I promise.

"If you think he's the one, Div, don't fight it. Let him love you. Life is so short and full of surprises that are not always the best but some that are freaking awesome. I don't know if I'll ever find love like what I had again. God is blessing you with that twice."

I close my eyes as her words hit me in the chest. I have to stop throwing up a wall against Omid to shield me from Arman. It's not fair to either of us.

I don't say it out loud, but who knows if Arman was even real. I know for a fact that Omid is real. He deserves for me to give him a chance.

"I hear you. I'm still pissed at him. He better fix the mess he made." I huff.

Marica lifts her head from my shoulder. "What mess? Why have you two been fighting?"

"If you got time—"

"Girl, if you don't start talking before the rest of our nosey behind family wakes up."

I laugh. She has a great point.

"I could just strangle him," I start off as I launch into the story of how Omid ruined my business lunch and cost me my deal.

Omid

Sitting in the corner of the hospital cafeteria, I open the lid on my salad and start to stab at it. I'm exhausted and cranky. Not to mention horny as fuck.

It's time for me to figure out how I'm going to tell Divine who I am. She still hasn't figured it out on her own. I think I'm treading a thin line at this point. She will be livid if I don't tell her soon.

"What did that salad do to you?" Dr. Nobi asks as he takes the seat across from me.

"It's not the salad. It's my life," I mutter.

"Want to talk about it?"

I toss my fork down. I have no real appetite. Running a hand through my hair, I try to sort through my thoughts.

"I'm grateful for this trip but it comes at an awkward time in my life," I say.

"How so?" he asks around a bite of his burrito.

"When I was eighteen, I met a girl that I knew was the one. I fell in love with her at first sight. You know of the complications in my life. They first affected that relationship.

"I've found her. She's everything I remember and more. I'm in love with her all over again. Her laugh, her smile, the way her nose wrinkles when she's pissed at me. I love her mind. If ever I believed Allah made a woman just for me, it would be her. She is the blessing I was born to receive."

"Wow," John says as he wipes his mouth. "Sounds like you have what every man dreams of. What's the problem?"

"She's Divine Favors," I say and watch his face.

It doesn't register at first. I wait for him to catch on. When it does, his brows shoot up into his hairline.

"Now that I didn't see coming."

"Neither did I. I never thought she'd walk into our practice looking to have a baby by another man. I've thought of a million crazy things to do to keep it from happening.

"Rejecting her specimen when it arrived on her IUI day. Switching it for mine. Fuck, I could lose my license for some of the things I've had planned in my mind."

"Have you just talked to her?"

I rub my forehead. Talking to her would be the rational thing to do. I probably would've talked to her had I told her from the start who I am.

"My pride got in the way. She doesn't remember me," I mumble.

He gives a long low whistle. "This is starting to sound like a problem."

"It won't be. Not for the practice. I'll keep my personal life out of our business."

He taps the table for a few moments. I sit staring at my hands. This has become unnecessarily complicated.

"I'm curious. Why doesn't she remember you?"

I scratch the back of my head, feeling my cheeks warm. "I didn't mean for it to happen, but I sort of catfished her," I say feeling my blush deepen.

"What?" Nobi laughs.

"You have to understand. In Iran social media is forbidden. I came to America to visit and I was able to do what boys my age here took for granted. She was this beautiful girl and I wanted to know her but if my father knew I was on those sites…Remi helped me to make it look like it was his profile."

I make a sour face. I never meant to deceive her. Everything just got out of hand. I fell in love and spent most of my time trying to figure out how we could be together. I would do so many things differently if I could turn back time.

I continue as I think of that time so long ago. "I wasn't hiding my identity from her. Everything I told her about me was real. Everything I did was to keep her safe. I just never corrected her when she made reference to my pictures on the profile.

"There is also the fact that I'm older now, I have a beard I didn't have then. My voice is different. I have less of an accent, though it's still there. There are so many things that have changed over the last twenty years." I huff and run my hand through my hair.

"I can see that. It makes sense," Nobi says. "What's stopping you from revealing the truth now?"

"She wants an excuse to pull away from me. I…I think I left a lot of damage behind." I frown at my own words. "No, I know I left a lot of damage behind. She doesn't want a relationship. I tell her this I may lose her forever. I can't do that, John," I choke out.

I ball my fists in front of me. "I can't lose her again. This isn't the crush of an eighteen-year old boy. I love her. I love her more than I ever did then."

"Then you should talk to her. Tell her the truth, then go from there."

"I leave for Italy. This isn't something I want to handle with that amount of distance between us. I will return just before she's scheduled to start the treatments. I…I can't…I just don't know what to do."

"You will figure it out. You are a brilliant man, Omid. I'm glad to call you a friend and colleague. As a friend I will tell you this. When you love someone, hold onto them. You could wake at any moment and find them lost to you forever.

"Don't find yourself wishing you told her you loved her more, wishing you shared more moments with her, wishing you could have one more day to hear her laughter. Only having memories and reminders but not her to love," he says hauntedly and gets up, leaving his lunch unfinished.

I stare after him. *Always there but not.*

Knowing his story makes me more determined to hold onto Divine. I would take my last breath if I knew she was no longer on this earth.

CHAPTER FOURTEEN

Let's Talk

Divine

It's been a long day. I had samples come in for the clothing line, I spent a large chunk of the day live to get my fans excited about the new launches coming, and the list goes on and on. I want nothing more than to face plant in my pillow and sleep for a solid ten hours.

However, I'm blinking every five seconds to keep my eyes open. It's eleven thirty. I just have to hold on a little longer. Omid always calls after his morning prayer time. If I can hang in there for fifteen more minutes I won't miss his call.

This is the best time for our days to link up. His research project has been keeping him so busy. He sounds so happy about his work and the progress he's making. It's been three weeks so far and I miss seeing him. I miss him dropping by my office and I miss talking to him in person before I fall asleep at night.

Do I miss his tongue game? I'm not even going to entertain how much I miss that. His dirty talk has provided me a muse to get myself off, but it's just not the same.

My phone rings on the pillow beside me. I open my eyes, not even realizing I'd fallen asleep. I sit up and answer before I miss the call.

"Hello."

"Hello, aşkım. I've missed your voice," he croons silkily through the line.

I'm still getting used to him calling me his love. I try not to read too much into it. It's a simple term of endearment, nothing to lose my head over.

"How did things go yesterday?"

He laughs quietly on the other end. "Things went well. The women are so grateful for the treatment. They're gaining instant relief. We've had a pregnancy already."

He sounds so happy and excited to help. I never knew listening to a man be so nurturing could be so sexy. Omid has a passion for life and the preservation and procreation of it.

"That's so great. So many women suffer from fibroids, this will be ground breaking for you," I say excitedly.

"I'm thrilled with the progress. We're at a hundred percent shrinkage in ninety percent of the tumors."

"That's awesome. I'm so happy for you."

I love hearing him like this. It's a side of him that has melted my heart. His love for what he does comes through in a big way. I'm falling in love with the idea of a man who's so thoughtful and caring of others.

"It's more than I could've asked for."

"Did you get to work with that woman again? Did she have her baby?"

"Yes, she had the baby," he says.

"That's a good thing, right?"

He releases a breath. "Something still isn't sitting well with me. My instincts are telling me something is off," he says thoughtfully.

He brought up the woman the second week of his arrival in Italy. She was having complications but wouldn't seek the proper care. One of the women in his study heard him speak fluent Italian and implored him to come to the village and help.

He went after hours to find the scared woman in need of his help. Her husband had disappeared some months before. He'd expressed before that he didn't like the situation but refused not to help her.

"Do you still think her husband's disappearance was foul play?"

"I do. Her fear to seek treatment goes beyond the fear of doctors and medicine. I overheard a few of the village women talking. I've called in some favors. She will be taken care of and I'll find out what happened to her husband," he says.

I sit up straighter. I'm wide awake now. "Omid, you can't just go to foreign countries and start digging around in things that look fishy to begin with. You don't know what her husband was into."

"I have the resources. I'm going to help. I would want someone to take care of my wife and child if something were to happen to me," he says.

"Please be careful."

"It sounds like you're worried about me. Does this mean your feelings are growing for me?"

I squirm in my bed. I'm not about to tell him that I'm completely confused about my feelings for him. I'd much rather ignore the elephant in the room. It's been working just fine for me.

"Have you found me a new investor?"

He barks out a laugh, causing my belly to drop. The sound vibrates through the phone right into my ear and travels through my entire body. Every cell in me stands up and waves to him.

"I told you I have everything under control. As soon as I return home I will introduce you to your contact," he replies.

"Um."

"You will learn that I'm a man of my word. Even when it takes me longer than I'd like, I still make good on what I say."

"We shall see. All I've seen so far is a smooth talker."

He laughs again, warming my belly with the sound. I wish I could hear his laugh all night. His voice, the accent, and that laugh. All of it pulls me in every time.

"Are you ready for me to talk you to sleep. You sound tired. I'll make you come quickly and you can rest," he offers.

I bite my lip and lie back in the bed. I'm not ashamed of the fact that I let him get me off with phone sex almost every night. The man is a pro.

"I'm ready," I purr.

Omid

I'm hard just from hearing her voice. I wish I could be there to watch her fall apart for me. The sound of her breathing increasing as she gets closer is driving me to my own climax.

"Is that pussy wet for me?" I breathe into the phone. "I want it nice and wet, Divine. Just like it is when I'm sucking and licking those pretty lips. You have such a pretty pussy. You know that, right?"

"Omid," she whimpers.

"Answer me. Is it wet?" I demand.

"Yes," she cries out. "So wet. I need more."

My hand stills on my cock. Hearing her plead for more, my mind goes to me inside of her. I want to feel her wrapped around me again. I think we've come to know each other enough for things to move forward intimately.

It's one of the things on my list to discuss with her. If she doesn't kill me for holding back who I am, I want to make love to my woman. I will provide her with a more recent bill of health if needed.

She's the only one I have ever or will ever enter without protection. She's my wife. The sooner I can make it so on paper the better.

"Omid," she gasps, breaking through my thoughts. "Please don't stop. I'm so close."

"Circle that pretty clit for me. Can you do that?"

"Yes."

"That's it, Aşkım," I croon. "Now stick two fingers inside. Don't be gentle. I'm not going to be gentle when I get my hands on you."

"Oh my god. Yes, that's what I need. I'm so close."

"I can't wait to get my hands in your hair. I'm going to tug the shit out of it while I fuck you hard from behind. Are you ready to feel my cock inside you?"

"Yes, yes, yes, I'm coming," she cries out.

I speed up my own stroking. I don't always masturbate with her, but this morning I woke with a hard-on and her on my mind. Two more weeks to go and everything between us will change.

"I bet you are glowing. You always have this glow after you come. I can't wait to watch you come apart for me. Sleep, Aşkım."

"Goodnight," she says drowsily, then giggles tiredly. "I mean have a good day."

"Goodnight, Divine. Sleep well."

I hang up the phone and stare at it for a few moments. Divine has made her place in my heart deeper and deeper. I love having someone to talk to about my day. Even if it's the day after.

She has opened up to me more and more. I have hope for my return. The bond we have made in the past weeks, offers potential for her to give me a chance to make things up to her. When I tell her everything...I just pray she understands.

With a heavy sigh, I get up and head into the bathroom to clean myself and start my day. I have a few things that need to be done before tomorrow when I take off for Shiraz. My mother has been driving me crazy. Anne Sassa has called a time or two as well with her own excitement to see me.

When I finish my shower, I wrap my towel around my waist and step back into the bedroom. I find Navid waiting for me. This can't be good. I roll my shoulders back, readying myself for his words.

"Your father has called me," he says.

I tighten my jaw. Yes, this has the potential to piss me off. "What's the issue?"

"He's becoming curious about your work. It seems someone may be in his ear. I believe it's your brother, Paiman. He has been to the States recently."

"Fuck."

"Indeed. The Blacks can do but so much. This all has the potential to unravel very quickly. I don't want to see you or Divine hurt."

"That's not an option. Whatever you are thinking is not an option," I bark.

"Please calm down," Navid says in his calm and gentle manor. "Have you considered bringing this to your uncle and the twin's attention."

I run a hand through my hair. My uncle and the twins will have a solution but not one I'm ready to deal with. I know my family can be ruthless. I just prefer not to be a part of that ruthlessness.

"Uncle Jahan has no patience for my father. If I go to him this will not end well. The twins are twice as bad."

"What do you think your father will plan to do to Divine if he finds out about her? You have been in America for too long. As your advisor, let me remind you of *our* world and the rules.

"You, Omid Arman Vahid, are a prince. You're your father's eldest son. His father and his father's father would have killed you for leaving the family the way you did.

"You disgraced him with your actions and have continued to do so behind his back. You're a Gynecologist. You look between the legs of women every day. You're not the brain surgeon or heart specialist he believes you are."

He stands and looks me right in the eyes as he continues. "Now, you will refuse another arranged marriage because of the same girl he forbade you to see. Omid, her life will be in danger, as will yours. If you love her the way you say, and you absolutely can't live without her, playing nice went out the window years ago.

"He will not turn another blind eye. He will erase you both from the earth before he loses face like this again. Everything about you is against your baba and anne's beliefs. He will not have this," Navid says fiercely.

"Then what do you suggest I do?"

He scoffs. "You use this Alliance your cousins are a part of. You protect Divine from the wrath that threatens her once and for all. There are no accidents in this life. She has come back to you when your family in America has come into its greatest power. Your father sees that your Uncle nor your cousins need the title he covets.

"They have created their own. Follow in their footsteps if you want to keep your life. You know Remi and Ramses will deny you nothing. Go to them before it's too late. Your father isn't an imbecile. He will not sit on his hands for long."

I stumble to the bed and flop down. I have been angry with my parents for years. I've wished them so many things but death isn't one.

I've never seen myself becoming that person. It's what I've run from. However, I know Navid is right. My life will mean nothing when they find out what I've hidden from them. Divine's will mean even less.

"I need time to think."

Navid moves closer to pat me on the shoulder. "Take it but remember the clock is ticking. Be the prince they will fear, şehzade Omid. Not the one they will conquer."

CHAPTER FIFTEEN

Rounds

Divine

"That was so amazing. I wasn't expecting that kind of crowd," I say excitedly as Terrance and I get out of my car.

"I don't know why, you're killing it. I'm proud of you, kid. I remember when I used to come over and hang with your brothers. They would give you such a hard time, but you were a tough one.

"I knew then you'd do big things just to prove they were wrong about you being the little brat. Now look at you," he says holding up the duffle bag of cash.

We sold out of everything. It was supposed to be a two-day event. A pop up sale. I decided to do it as a soft launch for the new products. We did so well, Dada is back at the office trying to get products shipped over from the warehouse by morning.

I can't stop smiling. Over seven hundred thousand in cash, not including the cards that were swiped. My mind is blown.

"It's all paying off. All the sleepless nights, the traveling, grinding none stop. Everything is different now. I don't have to sweat the small stuff," I muse.

Making your first million is one thing. Keeping that million and growing it is another. It's like I've had to work harder.

Terrance opens the door to the bank and the cool air hits me in the face. It's the same feeling I have from life right now. It's like it's all sinking in and blasting me in the face.

"You worked hard for it. It's well deserved," Terrance says as I walk in ahead of him.

I see my bank rep as soon as I walk in. I called ahead to let her know I'd be coming in with a large deposit. I wanted to sit around with this large amount of cash for as little as possible.

She waves and I head right for her. I giggle to myself as my walk has a little more sway. I'm feeling myself. My hustle is speaking for itself.

"Divine?"

I turn at the sound of my name. A tall white guy stands staring at me. He has cobalt blue eyes, dark long shoulder length hair and a nice build. The jeans, white T-shirt, and blazer suit him.

"Gable?" I say and furrow my brows once it clicks.

The long hair threw me off for a minute. I can see why I was a fool for this dude back in college. Time has been good to him.

"Oh my God," he says with a blinding smile. "I can't believe it's you."

"I have to go," I turn to continue with my task.

"Hey, wait," he says grasping my wrist. I turn and look at his hand wrapping mine. If looks could set a fire he'd burst into flames. He drops it quickly and shoves the offending hand into his hair. "Hold on a second. I've always wondered what happened between us."

"Excuse me?"

"You good, Div?" Terrance comes closer to ask.

With my sour face still in place I nod. I turn to see the banker still waiting on me. "Go ahead. She's waiting for us. I'll be right there."

"You sure?"

"Yeah, this won't take long."

Terrance looks Gable up and down for a few seconds and scoffs before walking off mumbling. "He ain't no Omid. Better not fuck up my sandwiches and ice coffees."

I bite my lip to keep from laughing. Gable starts to talk again, ruining my brief moment of humor. "Is that your boyfriend?" he nods at Terrance.

"Why would that matter to you?"

He looks down at my bare fingers. "You look great. What happened, Divine? I was crazy about you? You stopped taking my calls. You never said anything—"

"Please stop. I heard you. I came to your dorm and I overheard you and your friend. I was nothing more to you than a score, points you were trying to earn." I move closer and lower my voice. "I gave you my virginity the week before only to find out you were an unworthy asshole."

He closes his eyes and groans. "Fuck."

"Yeah, exactly. You were busted."

I turn to walk away, but again he grabs me by the arm. "Wait, you have it all wrong. I was in love with you." I turn to glare at him. "You couldn't have been outside the room for long.

If you were, you would know I beat the shit out of him for the things he said about you. I was expelled.

"At first, I thought you weren't answering my calls because I got kicked out of school. You were so smart. I was always trying to impress you. I thought I fucked up by being a hothead. Then I found out you'd left too. I was so confused. Shit, Div, I loved you. I've thought about you for years."

I stare at him wondering if I should believe a word he says. He reaches to brush a lock of hair from my face. It's odd but it doesn't feel anything like it does when Omid performs the same gesture. It actually makes me feel hollow with a longing to have Omid here.

"That doesn't change a thing," I say. "You started dating me with disgusting intentions. I'm not that woman. I'm not forgiving of shit that's hurtful and mean just to warm my bed."

He jerks his head back and drops my arm. "Yeah, I made some really bad decisions back then just to fit in," he says to his shoes.

He continues as if talking through his thoughts. "You were so gorgeous. I...I had forgotten about the stupid game when I approached you to ask you out. I didn't think you'd say yes.

"After you did...I was too worried about what the guys would think if I bailed from the game. I never told them we slept together. I'm proud of you," he says in a whisper.

"What?" I compress my face in confusion.

"I...I follow you. My best friend's wife loves you and she talks about you all the time. One day she made us watch one of your videos. You took my breath away.

"I'm so sorry I lost you. I just want you to know how incredible I've always thought you were. That night we spent at my parents' cabin has always meant something special to me.

"Take care of yourself, Div. You're an amazing woman," he says, leaning in to kiss my cheek.

I stare after him as he walks away with slumped shoulders. I'm speechless. Could I have gotten him all wrong?

I hate what he did but maybe he did care for me. Not that I'd consider dating him again. No, it's just the opposite.

I think of Omid. I've been holding him at a distance because of Gable, a boy I've never met in person, and the married dick head. While having an entire wife and three kids is inexcusable. What if I was too hard on Gable before I found out the truth? What if the boy I loved at sixteen had a truth to tell?

For Gable, I don't think it would've mattered. The damage of his behavior was a hard pass for me. He broke my trust. However, I don't know why Arman did what he did and it shouldn't matter to me anymore.

My phone buzzes with a text. It's Omid. My smile returns.

I'm coming to you soon, Aşkım.

I think I need to allow myself this. A man that I might be able to fall in love with. Yup, still in denial about that.

Hey, work in progress.

Omid

I'm back in California. It's time I face my past and my present so that I can live my future in peace. I can't ask Divine to give up her plans if I'm not ready to secure her safety and our love.

"Thank you for coming in to see me," I say to Remi and Ramses.

Remi leans forward in his seat in the twins' office at Club Desire, L.A. I made the call to set up this meeting before leaving

Italy, giving them time to come to meet me. They have families of their own. I'm grateful for this time.

"You're like a little brother to us. You call we're there. Anything we can do we will," Remi says, his amber eyes lock on me.

"I've told you over the phone the problem. I've found Divine—"

"Yes, I told you over a year ago you could look for her, if that's what you wanted," Ramses says.

I pull a hand down my face. "I've been willing to risk my life, my career. If Baba were to find out what I've been up to...I don't fear him."

"Yet, you weren't willing to risk her life," Remi nods. "I understand. You've been a part of our world from a distance. You know of our power but not how long it reaches."

Lifting a brow, he tilts his head to study me. Ramses does the same in the odd twin way they do things. I lift my hands.

"No disrespect."

"None taken. I would use the same caution with my wife. I have in fact." Remi nods.

"Your father has an odd way of doing things," Ramses says.

"But we have respect for him," Remi adds. "However, we've never liked what he forced you to do."

I grind my teeth as the memories come back to me. I was so broken back then. I didn't know what to do. I found my way back to America and Remi and Ramses were waiting with open arms. The only family I trusted.

"I don't like that it was done in the name of Allah. She's everything I've always wanted. A mirror to my soul. How can she not be who I'm meant to be with? I will not give her up again. I will not accept her life being threatened as my wife," I say to them as I struggle with the decisions I made as a boy.

Remi stands and walks to the bar to pour four tumblers of brandy. He hands them out before reclaiming his seat. I toss back the dark liquor and relish in the burn.

"You don't see either of our wives living in fear of anything. Neither will yours," Remi says.

"Maybe the best way to deal with a prince is to send in a king," LaSalle says.

I look at him my brows creased as Ramses and Remi grunt their agreement. "It may be all our uncle will understand. Prince to prince hasn't been getting through," Remi says with a smile. "I want to be there. I'd love to see his face."

"You think my father will listen to an American. No offense, LaSalle," I say and shake my head. "You are Christian too, are you not?"

LaSalle sets his tumbler on the table and levels his gray eyes on me. "I'm no mere American. My reach is global. Your father can't shit without my say so. There isn't a man that doesn't owe me grace. If he wants you or your woman dead, he has to go through me and the Alliance to make that happen. You're one of mine. My power is your power."

"In other words, little cousin," Remi starts.

"Go claim your wife," Ramses finishes.

I sit back and breathe, daring to believe that I'm finally free to live my life fully. I think I've known it all this time but I've feared it would be a lie. As I sit here, I think I start to understand what I've known.

Ramses releases a laugh. "You've been in love with her this long. It's surreal, huh?"

"If we can't do this for you, none of it was worth it," Remi chimes in.

"My wife is calling. Since she's the only one I fear, I'm going to need to answer this," LaSalle laughs and stands.

I watch him leave to take the call. When he's gone I turn to my cousins and sit forward in my seat. I'm going to ask. I have to know.

"He will just talk to Baba, right?"

The twins laugh heartily. Ramses is the first to speak. "This is why we sent you to medical school. You were a good boy then and now you are a good man."

"He will have a talk with Uncle. We will have a talk with that fat fuck brother of yours. If they don't want to listen, we will make things uncomfortable," Remi finishes.

"Uncomfortable?"

"We are next in line," Remi says. "I have no problem returning home to remind everyone."

"I'm for that. My sons can spend some time in the homeland," Ramses muses.

"You are your father's first son as well. Never forget that. Paiman wants what you've given up. He'll never be you," Remi tosses out.

"Let me ask you something." I turn to the door LaSalle just walked back through as he speaks the words. "What's really keeping you here? You know who we are. You've not been that naïve.

"I've been around you enough to know you're a brilliant man. I've seen your temper as well. So none of this should surprise you or rattle you. What's the real problem?"

"I think I need another drink." I sigh and tug off my jacket.

CHAPTER SIXTEEN

Return

Divine

I've been walking around the house with the biggest smile on my face. My two-day pop up was a huge success and Omid should be home tomorrow. Not even the storm outside could dampen my mood.

I have 50 Cent's "I Get Money" blaring as I wiggle my hips. Another trip to the bank with Terrance today had me feeling like a boss. My merchant account even called me to make sure all the money coming in wasn't unusual activity. They were about to freeze the account.

The icing on the cake, my doctor's appointment is tomorrow. I smile when I look to my phone on the kitchen countertop. Dada has been sending me pictures of little baby outfits.

"Aw, this one is so sweet," I coo to myself.

I shoot her back a text and grab a glass of water to chug down. I've been so thirsty today. I blame all the excitement.

I found myself a little dizzy once or twice at the pop up location. I even took a nap when I got home. So unlike me.

My doorbell rings, causing me to jump. I scratch my messy ponytailed head. I'm not expecting anyone.

Marica said she wanted to spend the night alone. I think she's nervous about tomorrow. I didn't push after the second time she mentioned wanting time to herself.

My brothers usually call first and Patience's husband doesn't let her out after ten. I look at the clock. Oh, wow. I hadn't noticed that it's after midnight.

Grabbing the throw from my couch, I tuck it around me. I've been in my panties and bra since I got home. I creep to the door to peek out first. When I see the figure outside my house, I gasp and tear it open.

"Omid," I squeal.

He's standing out in the rain, drenched but looks like a god. I'm frozen at the sight of him. He's simply breathtaking.

His hair is plastered to his forehead. Raindrops are sliding down his nose and hanging from his dark lashes. His dress shirt and slacks are clinging to his tightly sculpted body.

Even his stance is drawing me in. His feet are set wide apart. His fists are clenched tight at his sides.

I dart my tongue out to wet my lips as my nipples tighten in my bra. I don't know if it's just the sight of him or the time we've spent apart that has me reacting like this. Whatever it is, I lose all sense as I stand staring at him.

"I've missed you so fucking much," he says as he takes me in.

I take off the throw tucked around me to hand to him to step inside and get dry. A sound rumbles in his chest as he moves forward into the house swiftly and kicks the door closed behind him. Ignoring the offered throw, he lifts me onto his waist and shoves his hand in my ponytail.

"I've missed you too," I barely get the words out before he covers my lips with his.

His mouth is hot and demanding. I moan into his kiss, melting into his strong arms. Something has changed. His kiss is still possessive. However, something else lies beneath the possession.

I can't put my finger on it right way. Alcohol flavors his breath. Maybe that's what's different. This new aura about him could just be from having a few drinks. After all I'm sober, unlike the last time he was intoxicated around me.

"Don't think," he says against my lips. "I want you to just be here with me. Turn everything else off for tonight."

"Okay." I nod as he looks me in the eyes for my submission.

His lips turn up. I reach to run my thumb over his full lips, while he walks us to my bedroom. He drops me on the bed with a bounce and starts to peel his soaked clothing off. I move onto my knees to help, reaching for his belt.

When his erection comes into view, I bite my lip and stare. I want him. I don't just want him to get me off. It's been selfish of me and I plan to fix that immediately. I lower and wrap my hands around him as he stumbles to kick off his shoes and slacks.

"Divine," he hisses when I wrap my lips around him.

I smile and go to work. I lock eyes with him and the storm in his sends my heart pounding. I whimper when he grabs my ponytail and starts to thrust into my mouth.

I make a gagging sound and he pulls out to give me room to breathe. The look he gives me dares me to give up as he thrusts back in. Again I gag and he pulls back, he's still daring me with his gaze.

I narrow my eyes at him, taking the challenge. I've never been a quitter. I tighten my grip and relax my throat, breathing out of my nose.

"Fuck," he growls before he starts to give me praise in a mix of Farsi and Turkish.

His head falls back when I pull back and spit on the tip. I grin as I stroke him and he lowers his head to look back at me while I cover him with my mouth again. I said I don't suck dick. Not that I don't know how.

My big sister used to give me and Marica lessons. Patience didn't have three babies by sitting and looking pretty. My sister is a huge freak and she has no problem sharing her skills.

I reach to massage his balls while he thrusts and guides my head. I go for the magic spot behind the balls right as I flick my tongue under the tip. His hand tightens in my hair.

"Enough," he says huskily. "I want to be inside you."

I wipe the spit from my mouth with the back of my hand. Omid grabs my face and seals his mouth to mine. I reach behind me to release my bra. My breasts feel extra heavy and sensitive as they bounce free.

Still consuming my lips, he backs me onto the bed. I have no choice but to follow, he pulls one of my legs from beneath me as I wiggle the other free. He stops to kiss down my body, still keeping a firm grasp on my jaw.

The sound of fabric tearing greets my ears as he rips my panties from my body. He licks at my folds but it's much too fast, just a single lick. As if he changes his mind on the course he plans to take, he licks and kisses his way back up my body.

"Oh my God," I cry out when he sinks into me.

He bares his teeth and a growl vibrates within him. I'm wet with the excitement and anticipation from sucking him. It's making his strokes smooth and easy.

"I need you," he gasps like a man drowning.

The look in his eyes is almost one of desperation. He still has a tight hold on my face as he pounds into me. I cup the back of his head trying to understand.

I know he said not to think, but this is so intense. There's so much at play. He takes my lips in a kiss that's mixed with pleading, need, and something else.

"I'm here," I whisper when he frees my mouth and looks down at me—needing to say something, anything.

He stares into my eyes for what seems like forever. He's searching. For what? I don't know. When he seems to find it, he nods and lifts my right leg, pinning it into my chest. He slows his thrusts and finds a pace that stirs something deep within.

Not within my body. Within my soul. I cling to his back. Tears prick the backs of my eyes as I realize this is what making love feels like.

The intensity in his eyes, the feel of him moving in and out of my body. Once again, he's giving me something no one else ever has. I'm having an out of body experience as I watch us come together with such passion it threatens to ignite the room.

"*Sen her zaman benim oldun.*"

I bite my lip and nod. The tears start to slip. I want this. I want him.

I'm still scared, but I can't deny the words. Just maybe I have always been his. From the time he walked up to me in that bar and claimed me without question, I've been his.

Omid

I should've gone to my own home after drinking with LaSalle and the twins. However, the more I sat there and revealed my true fears the more I knew the answer was here. She's all I need.

I need her to know how much I need her. No matter what the truth brings between us, I'm not going anywhere. I'll do better this time around. I'm older, wiser, I have what's necessary to keep her safe.

I groan as I push into her. Her tears are cutting through the cloud of emotions I've been driven by on the way to her. Emotions that run a wide range and had me twisted in knots. Anger, fear, love, frustration—the list goes on.

I meant to come here and talk. When she opened the door and took off that blanket, talking went out the window. I release my hold on her leg and face and reach for her waist.

Turning onto my back, I command, "Ride me."

She nods as the tears continue to spill from her pretty eyes. I claw up her back as she keeps the steady pace I've set. I lift and capture her lips, deepening the kiss as she starts to grind her hips into me.

"That's it. Give it all to me," I whisper.

She throws her head back. I kiss my way down her neck, collarbone, to the center of her full breasts. I make love to her soft skin with my lips.

"Yes," she moans. "You feel so good."

"Take all you want."

Dragging my hands up her back again, I glide my palms over her arms until I reach hers and lace our fingers together. I lift my eyes to watch her enjoy herself on my cock.

"Omid," she gasps when I start to thrust up into her.

"Have all of me. I'm yours," I say huskily.

She shivers. I smile against her breast that I'm nuzzling. I kiss my way to her nipple and suck it into my mouth. The sound of her cries filling the room takes me to another place.

The day I thought I'd lost her forever. The day I thought I'd never find her again. Something primal rises within.

Here she is in my arms. I've suffered from not knowing if I'd ever get to have her like this. No matter what I'll never be without her again. We'll work through everything. I demand it.

I flip her onto her back again, sliding a leg beneath her ass as I drive into her. Her cries get louder and she tightens her hold on my hands as I pin hers to the mattress above her head. I close my eyes and savor the feel of her gushing all over me, soaking the sheets beneath us.

"Oh shit, baby," she screams.

Her words bring a smile to my face. I look down at her breasts bouncing and lick my lips. The shine of sweat that glistens from her brown skin is gorgeous.

I lean into her ear. "Who's pussy is this?"

"Omid," she pants. "Yours. Oh my God, it's yours."

I lick from the base of her throat back to her ear. "It will always be mine. I and I alone possess the knowledge of how to make you come like this. Not even you will so much as touch yourself unless you have my permission. No one touches my pussy but me."

She's going to come again. I dip my head to take her sweat covered, hardened peak in my mouth as I rock into her at just the right angle to give us both what we need. I bite down on her nipple as she releases. I'm roaring my own climax through my teeth as I come seconds later.

My heart is pounding. As I draw in a breath reality sets in. We've made love. Divine is sober. This was a conscious decision, not made under the influence. I'm finally getting through.

I kiss her temple. Her eyes are closed and her body lax. My woman has been satisfied.

Spent, I slide my arms beneath her and roll onto my back. The alcohol beckons me to give my body rest. When her cute little snores reach my ears, I grin up at the ceiling.

"I love you," I murmur before I join her in sleep.

CHAPTER SEVENTEEN

Can't Continue

Divine

I'm so nervous. I almost chickened out. Last night was so amazing. I get goose bumps every time I think of Omid's touch. There was something different going on between us.

It was there this morning as he made me breakfast and proceeded to feed it to me. I didn't know he could cook until I woke to the smell of cinnamon and coffee wafting through my house. As soon as I entered the kitchen he wrapped around me and kissed me passionately.

"I've missed this," he murmured against my lips.

It was the perfect morning. I didn't want to leave the comfort of his arms but I had my appointment and to my surprise he planned to return to work today. I thought he'd take a few days to rest.

I love his dedication to his work. It's just one of the things I'm falling in love with. I've allowed myself to admit that—barely.

"I'm glad you're back," I said against his lips as he stood at the door to leave.

"We'll have dinner tonight," he replied.

I was on the verge of telling him then that I'd changed my mind. I want to talk about our relationship and maybe put this all off for now. I was just that close.

However, I want this baby. Once he was gone my home felt so lonely again. More lonely than usual.

I don't know what the future holds for me with Omid. Our five weeks apart changed a lot. As I got ready this morning, once he had left, I thought about my priorities and where I want to be in five years.

While I could see Omid in the picture. I could also see my time running out. I don't want to lose out on having this opportunity.

"You don't have to do this," Marica says beside me, pulling me from my thoughts.

"I want this baby," I say to her pleading with my eyes for her to understand.

"What did Omid say about it?"

My cheeks heat. We didn't do much talking last night. This morning he seemed a bit distracted even as he showered me with affection. Honestly, I figured it might be because of my appointment today. I didn't want to pour salt in the wound.

"Ms. Favors. Dr. Nobi would like to see you," I look at the nurse holding the door open, then back at Marica.

I thought he'd call us in together to give us the pills or needles or whatever. I'm not sticking myself for the next eight to twelve days. I'm going with the pills. Marica opted for the injections.

In any case, I thought we'd go in together. My nerves go through the roof. I swear I can hear every breath I take, every footstep I make. I gulp down, licking my suddenly dry lips.

The walk to Dr. Nobi's office takes two hours, when in reality it's only a minute or so. I'm sweating everywhere. Yet chills start to run through me as well.

"Hello, Divine," Dr. Nobi says when I step into his office.

I look between him and Omid. Omid's eyes are fastened on me with an intensity I've never seen before. Not able to find my voice, I wave like a jerk and go to take a seat.

I fall into the seat clumsily. My cheeks heat with embarrassment. I settle properly in the chair and drop my eyes into my lap.

Omid moves to take the seat next to me. I wish I could say the gesture comforts me. Instead, my heart starts to pound more. The atmosphere in the room feels like it's about to choke me.

"Normally, Dr. V-Shah wouldn't be here unless I needed to consult him. However, he overheard my medical assistant discussing the test you took this morning," Dr. Nobi starts.

My mind races to the blood work. I've never been reckless sexually. Omid is the first partner I've ever had unprotected sex with. Oh God, if I have some STD. I feel the tears coming. I've ruined my life.

Oh my God. Does Omid have some shit he gave me?

I can't even look at him. I tighten my fists. If I have some shit and he knew he had some shit, I'm going to fuck this place up.

"We're not going to be able to start the treatments," Dr. Nobi continues with a smile.

Do they always give bad news with a smile? A single tear makes it through and I quickly swipe at it. Omid reaches for my hand but I snatch mine away.

"Why not?" I choke out.

"Because you're already pregnant," Omid says, pulling my eyes to him finally.

"What?" The word comes out like a tiny puff of air.

"You're pregnant, Aşkım."

"How? It doesn't work that fast. We had sex last night," I blurt out before clamping my mouth shut.

Omid roars with laughter, reaching to pluck me from my seat. My purse falls to the floor as he pulls me into his lap. He strokes my face as I sit on him.

"You've been pregnant for quite a few weeks. I knew Allah made you for me." He pecks my lips placing his hand on my belly. "Just once, our first night together is all it took. You carry my heir and my future, Prenses."

My head is spinning. None of my thoughts make sense. I can't wrap my head around the fact that I've been pregnant for at least two months.

I palm my face. Yes, my dumb ass can see it now. My sore breasts, all the trips the bathroom—oh crap, the dizziness.

"But…I was spotting."

"Not uncommon the first month of pregnancy," Dr. Nobi says.

Omid tucks my hair behind my ear to whisper into it. "I told you, you would get your baby," he croons with a smile in his voice.

I turn to glare at him. "Did you do this on purpose?"

The smile falls from his face. "You would take the sperm of a stranger but you're upset that I've fathered our child?"

I snap my head back. When he says it like that I do feel like a jerk. I press my forehead to his.

"I'm sorry. I'm in shock," I whisper.

"Maybe I should give you two some time alone," Dr. Nobi says reminding me that he's in the room.

"No, we're going," Omid says, bringing us both to our feet. "I'll be out the rest of the day."

"Congratulations, I'm here for anything you need," he replies.

I grab my purse from where it fell to on the floor, clenching it to my chest. I'm still in shock. Omid takes my hand in a death grip and pulls me from the office. Once in the hall, he looks up and down to ensure it's clear before he takes my mouth.

I cling to his white coat as he sucks my soul out through my lips. "You're pregnant with my baby," he growls. "I need to get you home to fuck you."

"Our baby," I say breathlessly. "Did that really just happen?"

He bites his lip and nods. His eyes are that odd color and they're so filled with light and happiness. I move my hands to his chest and stare at them. I wanted a baby, now I'm getting one.

"How do I know you're not just telling me this so I don't go through with the treatment?"

"You are taking all the joy out of this, Divine. We can go into an exam room. I can do a simple Vaginal Probe if you like. It's early but it will prove the point," he says.

I shake my head. "I'm pregnant. This is happening...oh, God. I have to tell Marica."

"And then we go home."

I snort and laugh. "Fine, then we can go home."

Omid

"Wow, I'm so freaking happy for you," Marica sings as she pulls Divine in for a hug.

"You're not mad?" Divine says in a small voice.

"Mad. Are you kidding? You're getting your baby the way I always wanted you to. I'll be fine. This is the way I'm supposed to do things, not you," she replies.

Divine pulls her cousin in for another embrace. The two whisper back and forth for a bit before they back apart and Marica nods tearfully. I place a hand on Divine's back as her own tears start to fall.

"We'll stay with you for support," I offer.

Marica shakes her head. "No, Keith is with me." Her lips tremble. "I'll be fine. You guys go celebrate."

"Are you sure?"

"Yes, Divine. I'm fine. You guys go. Let it sink in, *talk*," she says pointedly. "You two look great together. I can't wait to spoil my little cousin."

They both squeal and hug again. They're too cute. Although I can't wait to get Divine alone, I'm enjoying watching this moment.

"I'll be returning the favor so don't get too carried away," Divine teases.

Marica gives her a small smile. I have total confidence in Dr. Nobi. He's going to help her fulfill her husband's wishes. The rest is Allah's will.

"You're in the best hands," I reassure her.

She nods just as the nurse comes out to call her name. Divine reaches to squeeze her hands. They give each other a smile. It comes to me who Marica is to Divine. I remember how close they were as teenagers.

"Oh wait, I drove," Divine says.

"You will ride with me in your car. Navid will take her home."

Divine turns to me. "He's not busy?"

"It's taken care of." I kiss her temple.

"Thanks," Marica says and waves.

Divine watches her disappear behind the door leading to the exam rooms. Her shoulders sag. I wrap my arms around her from behind.

"She'll be fine," I say into her hair.

"I feel bad," she says.

Turning her to face me, I look into her eyes. "Everything is happening as it should. You will see. Now. Let me get you home to celebrate. You have some people to meet this evening."

"Your family? Oh, Omid. It's too soon. I haven't let all of this sink in. I'd be a mess. I need to get my hair done. I'd have to tell my family first or they'd kill me. I'm not ready for any of that," she whispers and glances around the waiting room.

"No, sweetheart. I'm making good on my promise. You want to take your business to the next level. I have your solution."

She stares at me in confusion for a moment before it clicks. The smile that takes over her face makes my entire life. She throws her arms around me and squeezes.

"You got me an investor?" she squawks.

I kiss the top of her head. "I did something better than that." She pulls away and looks at me skeptically. "Haven't I told you to trust me?"

"Yeah, but your record isn't working in your odds." I stiffen. She blinks at me and gives a questioning look. She leans in to whisper. "You knocked me up. Your pull out game sucks."

I relax and scoff. "As if," I mutter.

Taking her hand, I kiss the back and tilt my head toward the door. "We can talk about this some more at my place. It's closer."

"I get an invite to his place now. I've moved up in the world," she teases.

Slapping ass, I lean into her ear. "You could've moved in from that first night. You've just been trying to deny me."

"Omid?"

"Yes, Aşkım?"

"We're having a baby, we're still not dating," she says with a mischievous smile.

I roll my eyes. "You're right, we're not dating," I say and give a crooked smile.

Her smile falls as she turns to me. I reach to open the passenger side door of her car. She's searching my face.

"What's that supposed to mean?"

I chuckle against her lips. "Always be careful what you ask for."

I kiss her like my wife should be kissed. When I break away she stands stunned with a dreamy look in her eyes. Her full lips swollen.

"Omid," she says breathlessly, her eyes glowing. "Why do I feel like you're not saying something I should know?"

"I…." I get ready to reveal everything, but it just doesn't feel like the right moment. "I want to give you and our baby everything. You will never want for anything."

With that, I kiss her again. I will tell her the truth. Just not now. I want to bask in this happy occasion.

CHAPTER EIGHTEEN

This is the Plan

Omid

I've never been happier in my life. I have Divine and my growing seed under my roof, in my bed. I close my eyes and take it all in.

She glides her hand over my thigh, causing me to turn my lips up. I open my eyes and look down at her. She's so beautiful. I'm wrapped around her, keeping her close in my cocoon.

"How are you feeling? Are you hungry?"

She laughs. "Omid, you've asked me that a hundred times since you fed me lunch."

"I want to make sure you two are eating well," I say, splaying my hand against her belly. "I now know what it's like to be one of my patients. The anticipation and impatience for the months to fly by."

Covering my hand with hers she looks down at the two together over her flat tummy. The smile that comes to her lips is priceless. I can't resist kissing her.

She moans, dragging a deep groan from me. I want to make love to her again, but I hold back. We've spent the day in bed. I want to give her a break. When I break the kiss she caresses my beard.

"I still don't…I think I'm dreaming," she says. "I have so much to do. It's not just a thought, you know, a plan that I hoped would take root. I was afraid to buy things and set up a nursery prematurely. Now I have to baby proof the house. Set up the baby's room. I've always wanted to put a little swing set in the backyard," she says happily.

"Navid will begin to get the house ready for you both. Whatever you want you will have," I tell her as I stroke her glowing cheek.

"Huh?" she says.

"We'll place a swing in the backyard. I'll have the room next to this one turned into a nursery. Maybe we can convert the sitting area into an adjacent nursery for the first few months to have the baby close," I start to plan out loud.

Swiping the room with my eyes, I make a mental checklist of things I need to tell Navid. I'll have my things moved from the second closet. Divine has tons of shoes. I'll have someone come in to redesign the closet for her.

"Omid, I was talking about getting my house ready."

I narrow my eyes. My wife and child will be under my roof. While her house is in a nice neighborhood and it's big enough, my home is more secure. Navid has his wing in the house and my security system is state of the art. No, there is no question, she'll be moving in here.

"My home is the better option for our family. You will move here."

She looks at me with her mouth hanging open. I shrug. This isn't up for negotiation.

"Oh my God, don't. I'm an adult. I won't be told what to do without having input."

"Divine," I say firmly. "You're now pregnant with our child. We're going to get married, you're going to move in with me, and we're going to have a happy family. Sounds good, right. There we've had a talk."

She reaches to place a palm over my forehead. "Oh, good. You're not running a fever. Maybe you bumped your head during sex. You were a little aggressive."

"You weren't complaining when you soaked the sheets I had to change," I say pointedly.

"Whatever. We've been dating all of two months. I'm not rushing into marrying you. We can discuss co-parenting. I plan to keep my house."

"You can keep your house. I never said you had to sell it. All of this other"—I wave a hand in the air—"mess you're speaking. No. You carry my child, you live under my roof. This is the way it has to be."

She purses her lips. "I'm not going to have this fight with you. Don't we have someplace we need to be?"

"Hayidah will be coming to us." I kiss her lips. "This isn't a fight. My wife, my baby, my roof."

I unwrap my body from hers and climb from the bed. Without another word, I start for the bathroom. When I finish relieving myself I turn to find her standing in the doorway with her arms folded over her bare chest.

I walk to the sink to wash my hands. Connecting eyes with her through the mirror, I lift a questioning brow. She rolls her eyes at me.

"The world does not bow to you, Omid."

I bite my tongue before I say something I shouldn't. Again, this isn't the time to reveal who I am. I frown. I've never told her of my title. When we were teens, I told her that I come from a wealthy family but never that I'm from a royal family.

"I'm not asking you to bow." I rub my forehead and turn to face her. "I've told you before. I will always do what's best for you and now that includes our child."

She points a finger at me. "You're going to learn that I'm not going to roll over every time you bark."

"I'm no dog. I don't bark."

"Grr." She stomps her feet.

I open my arms for her. "Come here." She pokes her lip out and shifts her weight to one hip. "Come here, Aşkım."

She starts for me slowly, eyeing me warily. I wrap my arms around her when she reaches me. Sliding my hands up and down her smooth skin, I nuzzle her neck.

"For now, we will agree to disagree. I don't want to stress you."

She scoffs. "That's Omid for you're going to do what you want. We're just not going to talk about it anymore."

"You've admitted that we've been dating for two months. I have won enough battles for one night," I say and laugh.

She goes to swat me, but I jump out of the way before she can. I chuckle as I wrap her head with my arms and tug her into me once again. I kiss the top of her head.

"Bully," she mutters into my chest.

"Let's get ready."

Divine

Okay, my baby daddy has damn good taste. Or maybe the credit should go to Navid. This red silk wrap dress and the silver strappy sandals are gorgeous and so me.

I don't miss that Omid has dressed in a black suit and red shirt with silver accents. His black and silver, suede loafers are on point too. I don't think there is anything he could wear that wouldn't look good on him.

"It's good to see you," the pretty woman says. She has dark hair and eyes with something dark and mysterious hidden in them. She's a gorgeous woman.

She looks like the type of woman that should be at his side. However, Omid holds me close as if I'm the only woman in the room that matters. He covers his chest with his free hand and bows his head.

"Welcome, Hadiyah. It's good to see you as well. Thank you for coming. This is Divine," he looks at me as he says my name proudly.

"It's my pleasure to meet you," she turns to me and says.

"Come, we will talk while Navid finishes preparing dinner," Omid says.

He leads us both to his living room, where Hadiyah takes a seat in one of the accent chairs and Omid guides me to sit next to him on the sofa. I look at the woman and she gives me a small smile. Navid enters the room and places drinks on the coffee table before he returns to the kitchen.

"Hadiyah will be sort of a liaison for you. Anything you need, she will make the connections," he says.

"The ladies are excited to help you in any way they can," she adds.

"Ladies?" I look at Omid.

He nods, but it's Hayidah that responds. "Should I explain?"

"Please do."

"No, I will." Omid holds up his hand. "It's not necessary for you to give away pieces of your business. You're not in financial straits. Your business is thriving. You shouldn't be paying for something as simple as access to the right people."

"Okay." I nod.

"Hayidah's job is to listen to what you need and then she will place you in contact with the right wife. You're being granted access to my family's network. My cousins are opening the right doors for you."

"Paige Mairettie has already set aside time to come and sit with you to look over your distribution contracts and to provide you with support in the legal department. The rest of the ladies are willing to help in any way you need. Product placement, shelf space, support, you name it, it's yours," Hayidah offers.

"I'm sorry who are these women?"

"The wives of some very powerful men. You have made some very valuable friends. There will be no door closed to you," she replies, reaching into her bag she pulls out a set of papers and hands them over. "I was told to give this to you."

I take the papers and look them over. A crease forms in my forehead. I read over them three times before it sets in.

"This is the deed to the warehouse I have my products in," I say as I look between her and Omid. "It has my name on it. How?"

"A gift," she says. "From four Queens to a—"

"Thank you, Hayidah," Omid says. "This is greatly appreciated. Can you extend my thanks? I'll be sending the ladies a token of my appreciation. Did you receive my gift?"

"Yes," she says displaying her first full smile. "You're too kind. I drove it here."

I jerk my head back and look at Omid. I know he didn't give this woman a car. I'm so tempted to go out and see what she drove.

"It was nothing. I'm grateful you're doing this for Divine."

"Many things have changed but my loyalty hasn't," she says.

Omid stands. "I think dinner is almost ready. Why don't we head into the dining room?"

I look up at him. A light sheen of sweat has dewed across his lip. My curiosity is bouncing off the charts. I start to raise the wall I've been allowing to fall.

Omid is hiding something. I noticed the first time he cut her off. When he goes to Hayidah's side to murmur to her, I know something is up. Her eyes grow wide and she begins to apologize profusely in Farsi until he gives her a curt shake of his head.

What don't you want me to know?

He moves back to me as I stand. Placing his lips to my forehead, then the top of my head. I hold my tongue. I don't want our personal life mixed with my business. If this woman can bring the connections I need, I'll keep my cool for now, but I have questions. Questions Omid will answer.

CHAPTER NINETEEN

Warning

Divine

I step out of my car and inhale a deep breath, my lips turning up as I look up at the sun. It's been a great day. I was finally able to have a sit down with Pam Briggs, Paige Mairettie, Valentina Donati, and Tasha Locatelli. I feel like I just came from an empowerment session.

I don't know their husbands personally but those women have power in their own right. I'm so excited about all the things that are happening for my business. It's only been a month since I met Hayidah but she has connected so many dots for me. Never in my wildest dreams did I think things would take off like this and so soon.

"That's an awfully pretty smile," Melvin's voice pulls me from my moment of peace and gratitude.

I look at him quizzically as his words come off a little harsh and bitter. I push my bag up my arm, but keep ahold of the handle in case I have to swing it. He's making me feel uneasy.

I place my other hand over my stomach. My little bump has just started to pop. Not enough for many to notice but Omid and I have.

"Hey, Melvin. How are you?"

"Like you care," he snaps.

I tilt my head at him and lift a brow while I scrunch my face. He's out here tripping today. "Is something wrong I should know about?"

"You said you weren't interested in dating. You were keeping your focus on business. You said you'd tell me if you changed your mind," his voice rises. "I've been watching. He's been coming over here for months."

"Oh hell, nah," I say pulling my bag from my shoulder.

I'm going to have to beat his ass with this bag and then my brothers will be here to whip his ass too. I won't even be mad if they come and see my tiny bump. This dude needs his ass whipped right about now.

He pushes his glasses up his nose. "I know I'm not the coolest guy or built with muscles and stuff but I'm a nice guy. You could've given me a chance."

"Melvin, I told you repeatedly that I wasn't interested. I was very clear. You were the one that insisted on asking me out over and over again. How many ways can one person say no?" I bite out.

"But you drop your draws for that sand nig—"

"Don't you finish that shit," I hiss. "I think you better get your ass off my property. We have nothing else to say to each other...*ever.*"

"I'm not good enough but he is? You're just like all the rest. You were sweet to me at first. Now…Sure, just toss me aside."

"She won't have to," Omid booms. "If you don't step away from her and get the fuck off her property, I'm going to toss you through the fucking window of your front door."

Melvin spins around to find Omid glaring down at him. He just came out of nowhere. Shit, I'm scared. Even Navid looks menacing as his stands behind Omid. Navid never looks like he'd hurt so much as a fly.

"I'll call Homeland Security on you," Melvin threats. "You're probably already on a watch list."

Omid grins and snorts. "You have fun with that."

"I'll be filing a complaint with the police. It's clear you've been stalking me," I snap. "We'll see who's complaint has more teeth."

That seems to do the trick. All of the blood drains from Melvin's face and he scurries his punk ass back to his house. Omid doesn't give him a second thought.

Instead, his tugs me into his chest. "I left the office early today to do some shopping. Navid and I were coming to surprise you with dinner and your gifts. I would've fucking torn his head off if he touched you."

"I'm fine. Annoyed but fine."

"Navid, please go to purchase two trunks and a few boxes. We will start to pack tonight," Omid commands.

"What? Pack for what?"

He gives a bitter laugh. "I've been patient. I was allowing you to warm to the idea. Now he has proven this place is no longer safe. You'll be in our home tonight."

"I'm not paying him mind. He's not going to run me out of my house," I say pulling away to fold my arms over my chest.

The rage that enters his eyes nearly makes me piss myself. I've never seen him like this. He moves closer and I take a step back.

"You're with child," He seethes. "Do you know what kind of trigger that can be for a man like that when he figures it out? I've seen the way he watches you.

"I noticed a few weeks ago. He's been becoming more bold. You weren't even aware of it. Why do you think I've been coming to your office to drive you home? Why do you think Navid comes when I can't?"

I shiver and look at him with worry covering my face. I hadn't noticed anything off with Melvin before today. I place both hands on my bump.

"I didn't know," I whisper.

He runs a hand through his hair and takes a calming breath. Pulling me back into his arms he presses his lips to the top of my head. I'm shaking as it all hits me.

"It has taken everything in me not to force you to move once I noticed. I mean, everything. If I hadn't thought it would be a big fight I would've had your things packed up and moved weeks ago. I can't allow you to stay here," he says tightly.

"Okay, you're right."

"We will take the things you need tonight. Anything else the movers can take care of. You're not to come here without me any longer."

I nod my head as I start to sob. I can't believe I didn't notice. I placed me and the baby in danger. On top of that, I have to leave my house. I love my house.

"Shh. I will take care of it. I will always take care of you," he croons.

Omid

Now that Divine is in my bed fast asleep, I let my temper show. I'm livid. I'm so close to calling the twins and asking for one more favor.

"He will pay for this."

My muscles are coiled so tight and I can barely see straight. We arrived just as that piece of shit moved closer to Divine to shout in her face. I didn't need to hear his words. Both of their body language told me enough. She felt threatened and he was threatening her.

"She is safe now," Navid says calmly.

"He will still pay."

It took me an hour to calm her tears. I had to bring her home while Navid collected a few of her things. I didn't mean to lose my temper with her, but I knew she hadn't noticed that creep's escalating behavior.

He started with pulling the curtains back whenever we'd arrive together or when I'd come over for the night. At first, I noted it as a nosey neighbor. Then he started to open his door and stand on the porch watching. Not like a concerned neighbor. No, I could see his growing agitation.

"You have to calm down, şehzade."

"Do not call me that while she's here," I snarl.

Navid sighs. "You still haven't told her. You have had several close calls. I expected you to tell her about the heir she carries by now."

I wave him off. "I'm not ready to tell her. The time hasn't been right. There's always something in the way. I'll tell her before the baby is born."

"I won't lecture you. You already know this isn't wise."

I glare at him. I hate when he does that. I pace back and forth in my study. I have too much anger coursing through me to sit.

"I have bigger things to worry about." I grind out. "I won't leave some obsessed man out there after he approached my woman."

"I can make a call. It would be more than fair to at least look into his past and have him watched for a while. From there you can make a decision on whether or not you want to make further calls," he offers.

I pause. This is my child and wife. I don't feel at ease sweeping it under the rug and thinking it's all over.

"Make the call. I want to know everything. Every move he makes. If he so much as breathes anywhere near her, you know the call to make."

I start back for the bedroom to hold my woman and child in my arms. I've heard stories about Uri Donati and his wife. LaSalle was right about me knowing who those around me are. I've never called on their services, but I never had to.

Everything has changed.

CHAPTER TWENTY

Meet the Favors

Divine

Time has run out. This little bump isn't going to allow me to hide it for one more get-together at my parents' house. Besides that, my father has been asking to meet my boyfriend. I was able to put it off in the beginning.

Omid has been called to the hospital literally right as we walked out the front door to go to my parents' house every time. On each occasion he has sent a bouquet of flowers to my mom and a bottle of expensive liquor to my dad as an apology for his absence. That has only piqued everyone's interest.

Omid does nothing small. While everyone no longer wonders if I'm dating someone who plans to freeload off of me, they do have other questions. All questions I've been trying to avoid.

"Here she is," Patience sings as I walk into my parents' kitchen. "And again, she's alone. I'm starting to think she made this dude up."

"He's real," Marica says around the pineapple chunk she just shoved in her mouth.

I roll my eyes at them both and place my bag down on the countertop. I'm so tired. I just want to take a nap. I tried to wait up for Omid last night. He's been at the hospital all night.

"He just delivered the twins he was waiting on. He'll be here after he showers and gets in a nap," I say and take a seat at the island.

My mother stops and narrows her eyes at me. She's been watching me closely the last few times I've been here. I don't know why I haven't told them about the baby yet. I think I just feel the pressure of them wanting to meet Omid.

"I've had five babies. I know technology has changed all kinds of things, but one thing that has remained the same is the gestation period. Now, this baby over here." She points to Marica.

"She's in her first few weeks. Right where she should be for the timeframe you gave me on when you two planned to be inseminated, together, around the same damn time.

"Which means that depending on your bodies reactions to your procedures you two would be around the same weeks. I was quiet at first. Waiting, but if you were pregnant from the procedure you'd be just as happy as Marica. Babbling all over the place." She pauses to fold her arms over her chest.

It's like steam is coming out of her ears as she continues. "Your ass been pregnant, Divine. I could see it in your ass two months ago. You're just like me and your sister. I can tell when she's knocked up within weeks. It shows right in her hips. That gym hasn't hid a thing."

Patience reaches under my chin to close my mouth. "She's right. I knew you were pregnant months ago."

I burst into tears. I don't even know why I'm crying. I tear off the hot ass cape blouse I have on to hide my bump.

"Oh my God. You're so cute," Patience sings as she reaches for my belly.

"She's gorgeous," my mother smiles rounding the counter to pull me into a hug, rocking me from side to side. "You've been glowing, baby. Not just from the baby but this man has you lit up."

"Divine," Nashawn storms into the kitchen. We all turn to look at him. "Some dude is here asking for you. His Arab ass got crazy ass looking eyes and shit. You want me to fuck him up and get him out of here?"

"No," I rush and stand to go to the door.

Nashawn stumbles back. "Where'd that come from. I thought Marica was the only one that got knocked up through the tube. Wait, you're too big...who's dude at the door, Div?"

"You're not my daddy. Move out of my way," I grumble pushing past him.

I get to the front of the house to find my father and brothers surrounding Omid. The game is still blaring in the living room but no one's watching it. I roll my eyes at them and move to Omid's side.

"You look exhausted. How long did you sleep?"

He places his hand on my bump instinctively as he's grown into the habit of doing and pecks me on the lips. "I slept in the car on the way to the house and then again on the way here."

"I told you to take your time."

"*Endişelenecek bir şey yok.*" He shrugs.

"It is something to worry about. You need rest. You've been going nonstop and when you're not working you're catering to me. You need to take care of you too."

"Now wait a damn minute," my father interrupts our exchange. "You mean to tell me, you've been pregnant all this damn time. Who is this?"

I turn to my family and Omid wraps his arm around my waist. "Everyone, this is Dr. Omid. My boyfriend."

His fingers flex on my side when I say boyfriend. I ignore that as I focus on the shocked looks staring back at me. My father's eyes bounce between us.

"This girl done lost her mind," he utters. "As if being a black woman isn't hard enough…we were too easy on you."

"What's that supposed to mean?" I say crossing my arms over my chest.

"You went and got pregnant by some Arab and ain't say nothing to nobody," Nashawn says.

"Shut up," I snap at him. "First of all, not everyone from the Middle East are Arabs, you jerk. Omid is Persian. I just made it out of my first trimester a couple of weeks ago. Women are welcome to keep a pregnancy under wraps until they're in the safe zone."

"Girl, please. That's not why you kept this from us," my father says. "Son, let me ask you a simple question. What religion do you practice and what religion will you expect your child to practice?"

"I am Muslim. I will want our children to know the teachings of Allah—"

"Exactly," my father bursts out. "You done lost your mind, Divine. Are you even aware of what you've signed up for? Do you know who this man is? You're dealing with a whole other culture. They're different, baby girl. They treat their women different."

"Daddy, you need to stop. You don't know Omid and you're making assumptions."

"Omid, is it? How many wives does your father have?" Daddy seethes.

"He has three but—"

I look up at Omid. This is news to me. He looks into my eyes searching as my father continues his rant.

"But nothing. The apple doesn't fall far from the tree. Three wives. You didn't know that did you?" he says to me. "I taught you to respect yourself and to find someone that would respect you and treat you like a queen. You go find the first man that's going to treat you as a possession that he can replace nightly.

"You know nothing of his culture, nothing of his world. You probably can't even show your face in his country and I'm not talking about a head wrap. You're chocolate brown ass ain't welcome, Div. Dammit."

With that, my father storms off into the backyard. I'm left stunned with tears rolling down my cheeks. I knew my father would be pissed but this has gone beyond what I expected.

"Baby, you have to understand some things about your father to understand what just happened. He'll cool down," my mother says as she brings over tissue for me. "Hello, Omid."

"Hello," he chokes out beside me. I turn into his chest and sob as he wraps his arms around me. "Sh, aşkım. *Sorun olmayacak.*"

"It's not going to be okay. He's never talked to me like that," I cry.

"Since when she speak Arabic?" Nashawn says.

I spin on him. "It's not Arabic you asshole. I told you he's not Arab. He's speaking Turkish. I know several languages for your information."

"Chill, Div. The baby," Lance says. "I don't know you, bro but that's my baby sister. I'll put in work for her. Twenty-four hours, seven days a week she got me on speed dial to come whop that ass if you hurt her. You treat her right, I ain't got shit to say."

Nashawn shoves Lance and Neil grunts. My mom shakes her head while Patience hasn't stopped staring at Omid since she stepped into the foyer. Marica has a worried look on her face as she watches me.

"I'm going home," I whisper. "You've embarrassed me. I'd like to think I wasn't raised in a prejudiced home but today has shown me different. My best friend has always been welcomed here. Why is it different for the father of my child? Y'all have a good night."

Marica rushes to hand me my things she ran to collect from the kitchen. I lace my fingers with Omid's and start out of the door. I hate the silence coming from him. I hate that his energy has shifted from the confident man I know.

"I'm embarrassed for her," Patience says as we walk out the door. "Daddy and Nashawn didn't even give him a chance. That's not how we do things. Y'all are wrong for that."

Omid

"Are you okay?"

I turn to look at Divine as we ride in the back of the car. I should be asking her that. Her father had no trouble expressing his dislikes.

I wrap an arm around her and tug her into my side. "I'm fine. Are you okay?"

I'm not fine but I don't want her to know that. The shock on her face when I replied about my father's wives twisted something inside of me. There's so much about me she still doesn't know.

Her father never gave me a chance to answer either. It was like talking to my own father. They're both set in their way of thinking. Their opinion of the world engrained and unyielding.

"I never thought I'd hear him talk to me like that. I've always known he wasn't in favor of Islam. I had to hide my first Qur'an. I was curious and wanted to learn more. He would have lost it," she snorts. "Okay. I shouldn't be so surprised after all. It still hurts, you know?"

I kiss the top of her head. "I've learned that the best way to see change in people is to show them rather than tell them. We'll show everyone our happiness. Then they will come around."

She snuggles into my side. "I'm sorry about all of that back there."

"You have nothing to apologize for. My people have been demonized in the eyes of America. I've been stopped in airports for my accent and brown skin. People make assumptions, not knowing the difference between one group of people or culture. Once you're labeled as such you're that label.

"I won't make my family out to be saints but we're not plotting heinous acts in the name of Allah. Unfortunately, as an Iranian man this is what I face. My religion is just one more knock against me. I'm not naïve enough to think my children won't have their own set of challenges. This is the world we live in."

"But my own father? My family is so close. I can't imagine my child not growing up around their grandparents or their aunt and uncles and cousins," she sniffles.

"Who says they have to?" I place my fingers under her chin and lift her face. "I am here to take care of everything you need. If you need your family to understand the man I am, I will show them. It may take time but I'm not going anywhere."

I wipe away her tears before capturing her lips. I don't deepen it because I know we're both too exhausted to do more than climb into our bed once we arrive at the house.

"You've made me a lot of promises, Omid," she says as she settles her head on my chest.

I run my fingers through the front of her hair. "I will keep every last one."

CHAPTER TWENTY-ONE

Erase It Now

Divine

I'm so sleepy and cranky. I just want this photo shoot to be over. I'm showing and everyone has an opinion on whether I should hide it or not.

We've done several outfit changes to please everyone, which is aggravating as hell and driving me insane. At the moment, I'm ready to claw someone's eyes out and burst into tears at the same time—something I do a lot of. I'm hungry, craving a strawberry smoothie, and I want out of these clothes.

I'm only five months, why on earth am I so big?

I adjust the sheer top I'm wearing and roll my eyes. My boobs are ready to burst from the blue bra beneath. I swat at the puffy skirts surrounding me. They just billow back at me in a black cloud.

"Come on, Divine. We're almost done, honey. You look great. Give me that pretty smile," the photographer coaxes.

I give a cheeky smile then stick out my tongue. We have more than enough photos as it is. I'm over this. I blow a kiss at the camera as a signal that I'm done.

"What is this?" Omid barks.

I turn for the entrance where he's standing with a basket in one hand and a tray of drinks in the other. My mouth waters. Finally someone plans to feed me.

"Food," I sing and clap my hands.

"Everyone get out."

"What? Omid, what the heck?"

"Your breasts are out. What are you wearing?" he fumes.

I brush the big curls from my face and step out of my heels. Lifting the skirts, I walk over to him. His eyes are hard and his jaw is set tight.

"I told you we were doing a shoot today."

He puts down the basket and drinks on one of the tables in the photo studio. Shrugging out of his suit jacket his drapes it around me. I slap at his hands and take the jacket off. I'm hot as it is.

"Put it on," he bites out. Turning to the photographer he commands. "Delete everything. Don't keep a single photo of her like this."

"Eric, don't you delete a motherloveing thing. Everyone out. Do lunch or something."

Everyone starts to shuffle from the room. "Y'all not going to keep telling me to get out," Terrance grumbles.

"Shut your mouth," Dada hisses at him.

Omid stands before me, still glaring at my sheer top. I fold my arms under my breasts. His eyes roll over me.

"Why do you think this is okay?" he says. He makes a gesture with his hands at his temples. "My mind is blown that you thought this would be a good idea."

"Everything that needs to be covered is covered. It's a glamour shoot. It will focus more on the hair and makeup." I huff.

"If it's focusing on hair and makeup why is everything out," he says waves his hands at me.

"Babe, you're tripping." I scoff.

He tugs at his hair. "You drive me nuts. I'm going to break that fucking camera, Divine. You have the pictures deleted or I swear I'm going to set that camera and the photographer on fire."

"Oh my God, you're crazy."

I place my hands on my hips and glare up at him. He looks at me like I'm the one that has lost it. He grinds his teeth.

"I walk into a room full of men drooling at my woman and I'm crazy? You fail to realize the effect you have on men."

"Three men. That's not a room full of men."

"That's more than enough," he growls.

"Come on, I'm huge. Nobody's checking for me, Omid. Give me a break. You haven't even touched me in almost two weeks," I grumble.

The crazed look in his eyes heightens. He storms to the door to close and lock the only way in or out of the studio. When he stalks toward me, I start to back into the table behind me.

He grabs the top of my shirt and tears it right down the middle. I gasp but don't get to react much further. He turns me to face the table and lifts my skirts. The sound of him ripping through my undergarments fills the room.

Tugging my head back by my curls, he puts his lips to my ear. "You have been so exhausted by the time I arrive home that I feel like a selfish bastard when I get hard at the sight of you and want to fuck you all night. The last two nights you've fallen asleep on the couch waiting for me. I've carried you to bed to tuck you in."

With each word his fingers are working between my legs. I whimper when he pulls his hand away. The sound of his zipper opening fills the room. In one swift thrust, he enters my slick folds that he has primed for entry.

"Omid."

"Shut up, Divine. Shut up and take this dick. No one is checking for you? I always want you. I always crave you. You're the most beautiful woman in the world to me," he rasps harshly.

I plant my hands on the table as he rocks into me from behind. The grip he has on my hips only heightens how good he feels inside me. His short, blunt nails are digging into my skin. My teeth are chattering.

"Omid, oh shit, baby," I cry.

I suck my lower lip into my mouth. My eyes cross as he changes angles and starts to really tear it up. Omid should be certified as lethal.

"You think men don't look at you and want what's mine? You're a fucking goddess. Every inch of you is gorgeous," he palms my belly. "And this, this makes you so fucking sexy."

"Babe, I'm going to come," I yell out.

"You better. *Bana dokunmak istemediğimi söyle.* You must be crazy. I always want to touch you. If I put my hands on you as much as I want, you'd think I'm the insane one."

I come but he doesn't stop. He releases my belly and hip to cover my breasts with his big hands. He groans as I start to convulse and squeeze around him. My orgasm seems to last forever.

I cry out and he slaps my ass. "What's wrong, baby? You wanted my cock? You said it's been two weeks. *Alamaz mısın?*"

"I can take it. Damn, I can take it."

He chuckles darkly and buries his face in my neck. His tongue flicks out against my skin. I open my mouth but no sound comes out.

"Don't worry. You'll never go that long without me touching you again," he whispers, pulling a shiver from me.

I might want to learn to keep my mouth shut.

Omid

"Do we have an agreement?"

She rolls her eyes while she sits on her desk with a hand on her belly, swinging her feet happily and drinking the strawberry shake I brought her. She looks stunning. The yellow sundress complements her skin.

It took everything for me to let her up for air after fucking her in the photo studio. I was pissed when I arrived to see her in that sheer shirt and bra. I nearly lost my mind.

She burps and gives me a cute little smile. "Excuse me."

"Well, do we?"

"I will not erase them. I'll let you see the final proofs that I plan to use. Then I'll give you the files for your personal use," she says and wiggles her brows.

I growl, standing from my seat in front her to kiss her lips. I pluck one of the homemade fries from her plate and hold it to her mouth. She takes a bite and I finish the other half.

"That's not what I said."

"Take it or leave it." She shrugs.

I release a heavy breath and peck her lips. "Don't forget the fundraiser tomorrow evening."

"Wait a minute. You're conceding?"

"You sound too happy. Don't make me change my mind."

She scoffs. "You gave in too easy. I need to go lock that room to make sure you don't go back in there to set it on fire."

I laugh. "Did cross my mind. The fundraiser, you'll be ready by five?"

She puts her drink down and pouts. "I don't want to go."

I cross my arms over my chest. I knew she was avoiding it. I tilt my head and study her. She looks back at me pleadingly.

"You're gorgeous. You'll be beautiful by my side. Stop giving me those puppy eyes. Besides, you'll have friends there," I say.

"Fine."

I kiss her forehead. It has been harder in the last few weeks to get her to go out. She's even reluctant to do her live recordings for social media.

She doesn't see how beautiful she is. She almost didn't come to work today, trying to avoid her photo shoot. I shake my head at her.

"Finish your lunch, grumpy pants."

She waves a hand at me. "I think you're trying to make me fat. Why am I so big?" she groans.

I smile and cover her stomach with my palms. I've been holding back on telling her what I think. She's due for a sonogram at the end of the week.

"Have you considered that you're carry two of my babies, not just one. Did I ever tell you my baba is the youngest twin?"

Her eyes round. "Seriously?"

"My uncle's sons are twins so it's very likely you're carrying twins as well."

Something in the air shifts. The wonder in her eyes falls away. She searches my eyes.

Slowly she lifts her hand to cover them and then pulls it back and cradles it to her chest just as slowly. Her brows knit. My heart starts to pound as I watch the gears turn.

The air is sucked out of the room as she pulls a face. She reaches to brush at my beard as if she can wipe it away. Her eyes squint.

"It's crazy...I don't know why I never asked. How old are you?"

Just then my phone goes off. I suck in a deep breath and answer. I listen to my medical assistant as Divine watches me.

"She says she's been spotting since this morning," Brenda says in my ear.

"No, no, she has reached week fourteen. Tell her to head to the hospital. We can move forward with the cerclage," I reply to Brenda.

"You're the best Doc. I don't know how you remember these details about each patient the way you do."

"Thanks, Brenda."

"No problem, Dr. O." She hangs up.

I look into the brown eyes staring back at me. I need to head to the hospital. This isn't the time to drop this bomb on her.

"I need to go. I'll see you at home."

CHAPTER TWENTY-TWO

My Fiancée

Divine

"Hey, you," Sephora Lincoln coos as she comes up and kisses me on each cheek. "You look amazing. I love this dress on you. Just stunning."

I met Sephora through Hayidah. She's been rebuilding my website and plans to make it more secure to keep it from being hacked. She has some great ideas to optimize my site overall. I love talking to her.

"You look amazing," I reply.

She's a curvy dark skinned woman like myself. Like Omid, she has eyes that change color. When I first met her they were honey colored. Tonight they're a gray color with hints of honey brown. She looks like a doll baby. I wish I could get her to model some of my makeup for me.

She's both super smart and beautiful. The silver dress she has on hugs her curves and plays with her eyes—a nice choice for her. The theme of the party is silver and gold.

I opted for a gold V-neck maxi dress. The other two dresses that I bought for this event wouldn't close. I was so happy I purchased all three. I swear I'm growing by the day.

"Good to see you, Sophi," Omid says with a broad smile.

"Hey, Omid." They embrace and she kisses his cheek. "Where's Dr. Nobi? I was hoping I'd get to say hello."

He looks around. Concern covers his handsome features. He shakes his head.

"I don't know. He should've been here by now."

"Oh, well I'll be on the lookout. Nick, I have someone I want you to meet," she says to a guy that walks up next to her. He has sharp green eyes and golden brown hair. His suit fits him nicely.

He and Omid shake hands. "Dr. Omid, how are you? Who's this lovely creature?" He gives me a welcoming smile as he tucks Sephora under his arm possessively.

He's very handsome. He and Sephora make a stunning couple. They seem to move together. Like two magnets that gravitate to one another.

"Nicholas Lincoln, meet my fiancée, Divine Favors."

I stiffen and look up at him. He hasn't proposed to me. I'm not his fiancée. I've had this nagging feeling inside that he's hiding something from me. I don't think we're anywhere near getting married.

Hell, I still didn't get an answer to my question. I keep getting side tracked when I go to investigate. Pregnancy brain is no joke and my insane life isn't helping.

"It's nice to meet you, Divine. I've heard so much about you from my wife. You have a line of makeup and a few other ventures, is that right?"

"Yes. Your wife has been such a great help with growing my online business. I can't wait until she finishes with the website."

"I had some great ideas we should talk about. Give me a call next week," Sephora says.

A spark of excitement hits. Her ideas have been amazing so far. Everything from interactive capabilities for trying on lashes and makeup to a membership for fitness to match the products. The beta tests she's provided are mind blowing.

"Well look what the tide brought in. The East Coast is missing some royalty," Nick says in a teasing tone.

I turn to see Valentina and Tasha walking toward us with two handsome men. Handsome sexy men. They both have swag and walk as if they own the place. The blond walking with Valentina looks dangerous, which reminds me of how I always get that vibe from her.

I get the feeling that if we ever went out clubbing or something, Valentina and Tasha would have my back. I can always use a few ride or die chicks in my corner. I've taken a liking to them both and look forward to their visits.

"If it isn't my favorite makeup designer," Valentina says as she pulls me into her embrace. "You look so adorable."

"Hey, Valentina."

If I look adorable, she's straight killing it. From the gold lace dress and sparkly gold heels to the deep waves in her burgundy colored hair. Valentina is another gorgeous woman. Her blue eyes stand out against her deep brown skin color.

"I told you to call me Val. Do we know if this is a little nephew or niece yet?"

She gives my bump a little rub. I don't mind it. She used to ask but I told her to stop. I love her energy.

"We're going to wait," Omid says.

"The good doctor," Val sings and pulls Omid into a hug. She kisses each of his cheeks. "*Grazie per l'auto.*"

"*Prego. È stato un piacere,*" he replies.

I look between the two. It's not the first time I've heard Omid speak Italian. He seems to be quite fluent.

The blond steps up and wraps an arm around Val's waist. She snuggles into his side like it's the only place she belongs. Definitely a power couple.

"I didn't know how to feel about that until LaSalle told me that you sent one to his wife as well. I thought I was going to have to make you disappear," he says with a hint of a smile.

His blue eyes sparkle with dark mischief. He has an odd accent. It's sort of like a British, Italian mix or something.

"Oh please," Val says and rolls her eyes. "Divine, this is my husband, Uri."

"Nice to meet you."

"It's a pleasure to meet you. Dr. Omid, you have great taste. Beautiful women and great choices in gifts."

The dark haired man with the gray eyes, standing next to Tasha snorts. "I still don't know how I feel about the car. However, his gift to me kept me from paying him a visit."

His words are taunting as a smile remains on his lips. Again as I look at these couples, they complement each other so well. Not just in looks but in the auras they give off.

"The cars were tokens of my thanks." Omid says beside me.

"I'm pulling your leg," he replies. "I'm used to your family giving extravagant gifts to my wife."

My mind goes to the gift Omid gave Hadiyah. Does he give everyone that helps me a car? I seriously need to dig into who the father of my child is.

I'm starting to get uneasy with all that I don't know. We've been living together long enough for me to know more about him. However, our schedules sometimes don't give us the time to sit and chat as much as I'd like. It's like his phone knows when we're getting ready to have a deep conversation and goes off as soon as we start.

"Girl, you're killing this pregnancy," Tasha says stilling my train of thought.

She's dressed to impress just like the other ladies. The roman style silver dress shows off her toned curvy body and the small baby bump. She's making pregnancy look like her day job where she's the CEO.

"Are you kidding me? You look amazing," I say.

She winks at me. "LaSalle, this is Divine. This is my husband Lasalle."

"Oh my God. You're the one gifting me the wrapped Sprinters." I go to tug him into a tight hug. "Thank you so much."

He winks at me. "My wife loves you and I couldn't let your boyfriend outdo me."

"Fiancée," Omid corrects.

Again I turn to him and give a look. His face remains expressionless, but his body gives off that—I said what I said vibe. I turn back to the others. I'll deal with him later.

"Oh, Uri," Val says. "We'll have to fly them out for a baby shower. It's only right she have one in New York and one here."

He kisses her temple and looks at her adoringly. "Done."

"You guys don't have to do that."

"You heard my husband. It's already done. Besides, that will give you a chance to hang out with us."

"I may not leave." I laugh. "I love New York."

"You're welcome anytime you want," Tasha says.

My heart swells. These women have taken me in like a little sister. I appreciate them. Especially when my family still hasn't come to grips with my choices.

"Maybe I'll get a place with the money from my house, since I have to sell," I say and poke my lip out.

"You're selling your place," Val says. "Why?"

I get angry every time I think of Melvin. I don't want to sell but it's probably best. I don't realize I've balled my fists up against my stomach until I see Val and Tasha as well as their husbands watching the gesture.

"I had trouble with my neighbor. We think he was stalking me. It's just better that I sell."

"Not think. We know," Omid bites out.

"Oh, wait, didn't we handle this?" Val says her demeanor changing.

Her husband nods. Omid grunts and looks away. I look at them all confused. I haven't been back to the house.

"I—"

Val waves me off. "If you ever feel like you're in danger you call me. As a matter of fact give me your phone. You should have me and Uri in your favorites."

She holds her hand out waiting for my phone. I look between her and Uri. She shoots me a pointed look.

"I'm not joking. Hand me your phone," she says when I don't pull out the device. "You're family. No one fucks with my family."

"Give her the phone, Divine," Tasha says with an air of authority I feel compelled to obey.

I reach in my clutch and hand the phone over. "You guys are all the way in New York."

"Means nothing," Uri says. "Val is right. If you ever need me and I mean for anything, don't hesitate to call. I'll take care of it."

Sephora laughs. "You'll get used to it after a while."

I think I'm stunned for the rest of the night. My instincts were right about these women. There's so much more to them and they're nothing to play with.

CHAPTER TWENTY-THREE

Bare It All

Omid

I've been holding this in all night. I know I have no right to be angry. I know my woman. She's figured it out. She just doesn't want to admit it or at least she's in denial.

I, on the other hand, haven't been able to bring myself to utter the words. I know the damage they will do. I'm paralyzed by the outcome of my confession.

Yet we can't continue like this. Divine questioning my every word has led to the reason she can't submit her trust to me fully. I can physically feel the gap growing between us.

"Why does it bother you so much that I introduced you as my fiancée?"

I want to kick myself the moment the words are out of my mouth. I've chosen the wrong way to start this and I know it. Still, I stay the course once it's in motion.

She whirls on me making the skirts of her dress flare out around her. She looks like something out of a dream. Navid closes the front door behind us.

He sighs heavily. "Have a good night."

Ignoring him, I keep my eyes fixed on the woman standing before me in the foyer of the home we share together. She glares back at me. The way she's studying me speaks a million words.

"Why would you introduce me as your fiancée? You haven't proposed, there's no ring on my finger."

"We can fix that in the morning."

She frowns. "I would say no."

I pull a hand down my face. "Why would you say no?"

She balls her fists and storms toward me. "Because I don't know you," she says between clenched teeth. "I asked you a simple question yesterday and you still haven't answered.

"You have a thriving practice but I sure as shit don't think delivering babies would give you the kind of money to purchase Bentleys.

"Bentleys! I thought I was hearing things when I asked the ladies what kind of cars you gifted them. I sat there like an idiot bobbing my head while they gushed about the gifts you and your cousins send as small tokens. Omid." She pauses and sucks in a breath.

Tears fill her eyes, she shakes her head as if to clear it. I swallow hard. The truth hanging over my head like a taunting villain.

"I know I'm not going crazy," she continues in a whisper. "I don't want to believe what my brain is telling me. I don't know how to process what my brain is trying to tell me. I...I can't."

She turns and walks toward the kitchen. I hang my head in defeat. All of these months I've wanted her to figure it out on her own. I know that's what's truly been holding me back.

"Our pride leads us down stormy roads," LaSalle said that night at Club Desire.

Standing here now sober, his words connect. My pride has led me to be a fool. Allowing her to figure it out on her own has been the worst thing I could've done. It may cost me everything. I can already see the tear in our relationship.

I shrug from my tux jacket and head for the bedroom. Tossing the jacket on an accent chair, I walk into the bathroom and stand before the mirror. I stare into my own eyes. Anne Sassa has always told me to be the man I want to be. This isn't the man I want to be.

I'm not a liar. I'm not a coward. What I am is a man in love. A man that would do anything for the woman he loves and our children. Including risk losing them to heal the gaping hole left from the past and my omissions.

I tug my tie free and blow out a breath. Here is my chance to be a man and do what I should've done from the start. I can't allow the fears of an eighteen-year old boy control my life. This isn't about my father, this is about me and facing the truth. I fucked up.

"Here goes nothing," I mutter.

Divine

I grumble to myself as I rummage through the refrigerator. I'm not hungry, I'm annoyed which is why I'm pushing things around but not settling on anything. I grab a bottle of water and the Swiss Rolls I had chilling and tear the pack open.

"He's not crazy. It wouldn't even make sense. All coincidence. He wouldn't. Nope, and God wouldn't do me like this," I mumble between angry bites.

I wiggle my way onto one of the island bar stools. I'm not going to open the can of worms sitting in my subconscious. I'll be a wise woman tonight. The way my hormones are taking over, I might stab Omid and torch this place.

"He hasn't seen my crazy. I swear. Why not answer my damn question?"

I place a hand on my belly and try to relax. I smile when I feel the tiny flutter inside. I'm still getting used to that. I just started to connect the feeling to being the baby's movements about a week ago.

"You'll be a fatherless child if I'm right," I fuss.

The hairs rising all over my body are my first clue to his presence, followed by his cologne filling the room and his heat against my back. He buries his face in my neck, but that familiar tickle doesn't come. I go to turn to face him but he wraps his arms around me, holding me in place.

"I've loved you since the first moment I saw you," he says, causing my pulse to race. I should be thrilled he has said the words for the first time. However, I hear the but in them. "I knew you were my wife when I stared into those brown eyes.

"I am thirty-eight. I was born in Shiraz, Iran. My first visit to the U.S. was when I was eighteen. I came to visit my uncle and twin cousins for the summer."

"You motherfucker," I seethe. "Get your hands off me."

"You have to hear me out. Listen to me, Divine."

"Get off me," I sob.

He releases me and I turn in my seat. I nearly fall off of the bar stool. He reaches to steady me but I lower to my feet on my own swatting his hands away. He backs away to give me space.

It's like a slap in the face. Looking at him shaven, it's all been there right before my eyes. I fall to my knees in the middle of the kitchen and clench my belly.

"I don't understand?"

He drops to the floor and crawls closer. I'm frozen. The amount of hurt and deception I feel threatens to choke me.

He cups my face in his strong hands but it's more like I'm being burned instead of comforted. I can't breathe. It's the same face just older and without the amber eyes. Or should I say without the sunglasses.

"You…I'm so confused."

"I reached out to you because you took my breath away." He swallows. "My name is Prince Omid Arman Vahid. I couldn't use my own name or picture for the profile. My cousins thought it would be better if I posted a picture of Remi and I together. Remi and I share the same middle name. We could say it was his profile which is why there were always more pictures of him than those of the two of us or me alone."

"You catfished me?"

"No, no, that's not what I intended. Everything I shared with you was me. I never lied to you. I just wouldn't address things you said about the pictures. Divine, I swear, I was going to tell you everything as soon as we met."

"But we didn't meet," I scream. "I sat in that park for hours. I waited for you. I…I waited."

My heart breaks all over again as that day comes rushing back. He told me he loved me. I believed him so I waited. I waited and waited. Feeling like a fool.

"I'm so sorry," he says as tears spill from his eyes. "I'm so sorry. I was coming. I promise you I was coming."

"Why?" I gasp. "Why are you so intent on making me feel like a fool? Once wasn't enough? What is it about me? Why do you feel you have to crush my soul?"

"Divine," he breathes as pain covers his handsome features.

"I loved you twice. I've allow myself to fall for you twice and you've...is this what dying feels like? I think you've killed me."

He crushes his lips to mine but I'm lifeless in his hold. "Please," he whispers as he kisses me harder. "I love you. I love you so fucking much. I would never hurt you intentionally."

He shoves his hands into my hair and grips it tightly. Moving his lips to my neck, he repeats his words of love as I remain unmoved. Tears leak from my eyes but I'm hollow. I can't form the words to my hurt and anger.

"I gave up my entire life for you. I kept my promise. I came back for you. I told you no matter what I'd find my way back to America if I had to return home. I did.

"You blocked my profiles. I couldn't find you. Your number was out of service. I tried," he pleas.

I sob so hard. He's right, after I sat in that park with my overnight bag waiting for him for hours, I was so mad and scared. Marica and I had made up a sleepover at Dada's.

"Dada's house was all the way across town from the park we planned to meet in. I was scared and alone. Do you know the things I thought as a sixteen-year old girl in a park all by myself? I felt so stupid, terrified, humiliated."

"I plan to spend the rest of my life making up for that," he says looking into my eyes.

I turn away from him. "I can't. I can't trust you. I had to sneak into my best friend's home that night after I allowed myself to admit you weren't coming. I used her computer to erase you from my life."

"I was on a plane back to Iran. My father found out about the profiles. He was livid. My brother came to the States to stay for the end of my trip. He ratted on me. My father was on the next plane to collect us both.

"Baby, I didn't leave you there on purpose. Remi and Ramses were on a plane to follow me to make sure my father wasn't too harsh with me. I had no way to send someone for you. Divine, if you only knew what happened. How I've always made the choice to protect you first."

He shifts his weight to sit on his behind, pulling me into his lap. "I love you. I can't lose you again. I made a mistake—"

His phone rings. He closes his eyes and curses. I go to move from his lap, but he tightens his hold. "Please stay," he whispers as he retrieves the phone and answers. "Hello."

I curl into myself as he listens. "John slow down...No, she's right here with me...What hospital?" He starts to get up and helps me to my feet. "We're on our way."

"What's going on?"

"It's Marica. She's been in a car accident."

"Oh my God, the baby."

"The baby is fine. Nobi is with her. They've been trying to call you. Where's your phone? We have to go."

I rush for my clutch. When I walk toward the door, he tries to place a hand on my back but I pull away quickly. I don't need his comfort.

I check my phone to find several missed calls and messages. I just want to get to my cousin. I'll deal with this mess later.

CHAPTER TWENTY-FOUR

Living Life

Divine

I have so many emotions running through me. If I wasn't shaking so badly I would've driven myself. I can't even look at Omid.

"Come, we'll use my credentials," he says.

I follow him into the hospital in silence. My heart is racing. Dr. Nobi appears, looking a bit disheveled dressed in a white coat, dress shirt, bow tie, and shiny dress shoes. His pants look a little worse for the wear.

"What happened?" Omid asks.

"Where is she? Is she okay? The baby?" I say shakily.

Dr. Nobi looks at me sympathetically. "The ultrasound shows the baby is safe and sound. However, I'll be observing them both overnight. Marica has a slight concussion, broken leg and fractured wrist. She'll be needing a lot of help for the next two months or so."

"I'll be there. She can stay with me at my house."

"You're in no condition to help," Omid says.

I ignore him. Lifting my chin, I look at Dr. Nobi expectantly. He glances between us before he speaks.

"He's right. She'll need a lot of help getting around and doing basic things but for now we want to focus on making sure the baby remains stable and that she gets some rest," he says.

"Can I see her?"

"She's been asking for you. I'll show you to her room." He nods.

Omid starts to walk with us. I turn to glare at him. "Don't," I say the single word and turn to follow Dr. Nobi.

My lips tremble and I have to fight to keep from sobbing out loud. She looks so banged up. She's connected to all types of monitors.

Dr. Nobi places a hand on my shoulder. "I should've warned you. It looks worse than it is. I want to keep an eye on the baby so she's hooked up to the monitor for the little one."

"Yeah, and my face just looks like a hamburger. I'm okay," she says with a tired smile. She then turns to Dr. Nobi. "Thanks to this guy. I'm so sorry I ruined your night."

"I told you to stop apologizing."

"What happened?"

"Reckless driver. It was a hit and run," Dr. Nobi says through his teeth. "I'm so glad fate had us on the same road. We were going in opposite directions but I saw when he ran her off the road. God, when I think of you being in that ditch with no one to know you were there."

His cheeks turn red with anger. I can almost taste it filling the room. He moves to look at the charts and monitor.

"Wow, that's crazy," I say as I move closer and sit on the side of her bed, taking her uninjured hand.

"It all happened so fast," she says. She's searching my face and her own crumbles. "I'm sorry. I shouldn't have bothered you. I probably upset you and the baby."

"Are you kidding me? You better have called me. Besides, I was a mess before the call came in."

"What's wrong?"

I shake my head and glance at Dr. Nobi. He looks up at us, his blue-gray eyes bounce between us. I take him in for a moment.

He seriously is a handsome man. He's leaner than Omid and stands about an inch or two higher. He has a pair of the fullest pink lips. The thick wavy salt and pepper hair that tumbles into his face is something I wouldn't think I'd find attractive but it works for him.

He gives a small smile and it lights his entire face. I wonder how old he is. I believe him to be older than Omid but he doesn't look to be in his forties despite the hair.

Almost reluctantly, he places down the chart in his hand and starts to leave. "I'll give you some privacy. I won't be far, Mrs. Thompson. If you need me, ring the call bell."

When he's gone, I turn to Marica and give her a look. "Mrs. Thompson?"

"Yeah." She shrugs. "He started calling me that after we got here and they fixed me up. He saved my life. He can call me Annabelle for all I care. Now what's going on with you?"

I look down into my lap. "He's not related to Arman," I murmur. "He is Arman. Prince Omid Arman Vahid."

"Okay, my head is hurting a little. Did you just say what I think you said?"

"Sure did. He shaved his face and…I feel like such an idiot."

She squeezes my hand with the one I'm holding. "I never would've made that connection. You shouldn't feel that way."

"Oh, you wouldn't have made the connection because the boy—quite sure man—we thought was Arman was his cousin. Also named Arman. The cutie in the glasses. *That* was Omid. The boy that I was talking to," I scoff.

"Holy crap," she blows out. "So what happened to him?"

I shrug as the tears start again. "I'm not quite sure. I mean, he tried to tell me but I'm so fucking hurt."

"Oh, Div. I'm sorry." I swipe at my tears. The last thing I want is to upset her. I try to push it all back. "Don't do that. You don't have to be strong for me. Come here, lay next to me. You cry all you need."

Careful of her casted leg, I wiggle my body and big stomach into bed beside her. It's like being sixteen all over again. I cry for a while as all my thoughts settle.

"You know what hurts the most?" I say after I'm all cried out and the room falls silent save for the machines. Marica strokes the hairs at my temple with her good hand.

"What's that?"

"I love him. I love how much his loves his job. I love how he treats his friends. I love how he cares for me but he hurt me so bad. Not once but twice."

"Div, I've seen the way he looks at you. I'm sure there's a reason for everything. Maybe you should hear him out. You two have more at stake this time."

"He's been making a fool of me for months. I don't think I'll ever get over that."

She sighs, her hand in my hair pausing. "Keith told me that he wanted me to live a full life if anything ever happened to him. I've been trying. I…I figured having the baby would get me back into the world. Play dates, pre-school…at some point I'd start living again, you know?

"But when my car ran off into that ditch, I came to grips with the fact that I haven't been living at all and had no real intentions to start. I've been rolling through the motions. It wasn't until I found myself trapped in my car that I realized I want to live.

"Really live. When Dr. Nobi appeared to rescue me out of there I saw that as the boat God was sending. I'm not going to let this life move forward without being present. Keith is gone, but I'm still here and this baby…it needs me to be here.

"What I'm saying is, you have loved a man with everything you are twice. You were sixteen, Div. He was eighteen. You see the drama going on with your daddy and Nashawn. Could you imagine that at sixteen?"

"No." I huff. "They would have ran him off."

"Exactly," she laughs. "Omid stood there by your side as your father pretty much said he wasn't worth spit and wouldn't treat you the way you deserve. Other than withholding this from you, has he ever done anything to hurt you?"

I sit and think. I come up short each time. He has pissed me off on so many occasions but in the end he has always had my best interest at heart.

"Maybe not," I say, not wanting to admit she's right.

"Girl, please. Him ruining that meeting was one of the best things he could've done for you. Look at your business now."

I fall into silence. Placing a hand on her little barely there bump, I look up at her. This is why I love her.

"I'm here for you, Marica. You're amazing," I say.

"You have your own baby and man to think about. I'll be just fine. God has always looked out for us. This will be no different. I'm supposed to live my life and have this baby and you're supposed to be with that fine ass doctor," she giggles.

"We'll see."

"Divine, does he make you feel good?"

I close my eyes and a shiver rolls through me. Omid knows me inside out. He knows just how to touch me, what to say, how to make me smile. He gets what my business means to me. The man listens to all of my dreams and works to make them happen.

The tears start to roll down my cheeks again. I nod my head. Marica gives a tired sigh.

"Then, that's all that matters. You're carrying royalty honey. There are worse things in life."

Her words dig in. If Omid is a prince, what does that make my baby? Holy cow. He's been dropping hints all along.

His heir.

Omid

I don't want to move her but she can't stay like this and they need to take Marica for an MRI. She lost consciousness a few times after the accident. Dr. Nobi has been in everyone's ass to make sure Marica gets the best care.

I'm grateful to him. If anything were to happen to Marica or the baby that would devastate Divine. I release the breath I've been holding and scoop Divine in my arms.

Her eyes flutter open. I stare into those brown eyes and plead with her for forgiveness. She blinks a few times.

"You can put me down. I'll walk," she says.

I nod but hesitantly placing her on her feet. She starts to amble out of the room, turning to me when I don't follow right away. Her smile is weak but it's there.

"Come on. You can explain. If I don't like what I hear, I'll pack my things and we can arrange how you'll see your child," she pauses and looks down at her stomach. "If that's what you want. You can't take my baby from me. I'm warning you now."

I move to her side swiftly, placing my hands on her hips. "I will always be in our child's life. A strong mother is the most important thing a boy can have. I would never take him from you."

She gives a crooked grin. "Who says it's a boy?"

Palming her stomach I smile. "Vahids always have first born sons. I'd be the first in at least ten generations to break traditions."

She looks up at me sadly. "So he would be a prince?"

"Yes, princess. He is a prince. Heir to the throne. A throne I walked away from for his mother."

"Yeah, you have a lot of explaining to do."

"I will tell it all."

CHAPTER TWENTY-FIVE

With Love

Omid

"I was standing in the mirror getting ready. I'd just come back from getting a haircut. Remi and Ramses were sitting on the bed teasing me. I remember turning to toss back a joke of my own. I still remember being the happiest I'd been in my life," I say as we sit on our bed and it all comes back.

"Look at him. Never seen anyone so happy to be going to get some pussy," Ramses teased.

Remi roared with laughter beside him. Ignoring them, I sprayed on more cologne. I smoothed down my T-shirt and turned to make sure my cargo shorts didn't have any wrinkles in them.

"She's going to take one look at his scrawny ass and go home. I should go with you. I'm the one she really wants," Remi teased.

I turned ready to tell him where he could shove it. I'd grown more confident in the time I'd spent in America. My jokes were funnier to keep up with the twins' taunting.

"She would—"

"Omid," Baba burst into the room.

My heart raced as I stared at him in the doorway. I knew I wouldn't make it. All of our waiting and planning had been ruined in the blink of an eye. If I had left only moments before, things would've been different. I would've made it to the park to meet my girl.

We would've spent the night together. I would've asked her to marry me and run away somewhere that we could be together. But I didn't and Baba started to scream for me to pack my things.

"But you came back to America?" she says.

I blink away the memory and focus on her sitting in the middle of our bed with her legs crossed. She has on one of my satin pajama shirts. I take a mental picture of one of the most beautiful sights I've ever seen.

I nod. "Yes. I returned a year later."

"A year," she whispers looking down at her hand resting over her belly.

"I lied about you. Told Baba there was no girl. He was furious that I'd been on the internet. It was sinful to him.

"My cousins told him he was overreacting. He felt threatened when they involved themselves and my uncle called them home. I spent a year planning my way back. On my nineteenth birthday, I was introduced to my intended wife."

"You were married," she asks with so much pain in her voice.

"No." I shake my head. "I left. My Anne Sassa contacted the twins and they sent a plane for me. I left and never looked back.

I became O.V-Shah. Navid arrived a few weeks after I did. I was unsure at first, but he proved he was still an ally.

"By then, you were gone. I couldn't find you or your profile. I had planned to ask for help to find you but my father sent me a message. To punish me he would hurt you. Uncle Jahan was livid. The twins promised me that one day they'd make it safe. I just had to be patient."

"Is it safe? Is that why you came for me in the bar?"

I swallow hard and shake my head. "You are safe. I could have come for you about a year ago. I...I just kept telling myself I couldn't risk it. I wasn't ready to risk your life. What if they were wrong? What if my father found a way? I knew all of that was bullshit. The real what-ifs were the ones that stopped me."

"Like what? I don't understand. You promised we'd be together."

"What if you married? What if you were in love with someone else? What if you didn't want me? It's been twenty years. So much could've happened in that time. It would've killed me to see you with another man. Better yet, I would've wanted to kill him. You're mine."

She laughs and shakes her head. When I open my arms for her to come to me and she climbs into my lap, my heart nearly bursts from my chest. I press my forehead to the side of her face and inhale.

"Why didn't you tell me who you were? How did you find me in the bar?"

"Allah has brought you back to me. I just missed you the morning you came in to see Dr. Nobi. That night in the bar, I didn't know it was you until I started walking toward you. I saw you looking uncomfortable. I was coming to see if I could help. Then you turned to me.

"That's when I knew it was you. I've dreamed for twenty years of our reunion and every time you knew it was me right away. When I realized you didn't know, I wanted to make you remember. I wanted you to come to the conclusion yourself. I wanted our love to awaken in you again," I breathe.

"Or you could've said...Divine, I've waited twenty years for this moment. I still love you, I'm sorry my life got in the way. I'm here now," she says with tons of sass.

I cup her face. "Divine, I love you. I'm sorry. I'm sorry I hurt you. I'm sorry I didn't tell you right away. I'm sorry I let my father keep us apart for as long as I have. I'm sorry that I lied to myself about second guessing my power to keep you safe and caused us to wait longer than we had to, to be together."

"Are you sorry we're having a baby?"

Those brown eyes look at me with such hope. I kiss her. Her submission ignites the flame inside me. Gently laying her onto her back. I look down into her eyes.

"You will be pregnant again as soon as Nobi clears you at your postpartum checkup," I say as I work to unfasten the buttons of her shirt.

"Omid."

"Yes?"

"I love you. If you ever lie to me again, I'm leaving you. Don't come for me, don't think of me. I'll be gone to you forever."

"My mission for the rest of my life is to bring you pleasure." I lower my head to kiss her right breast. "Starting right now."

Divine

I'm soaked in sweat and my own juices but I couldn't feel more loved if I tried. Omid's hands have been everywhere on my body. Massaging my feet, kneading my back, rubbing my clit.

I've come so many times my head is spinning. That's not the best part though. The best part is hearing him tell me over and over that he loves me.

He glides a hand over my sweaty, swollen belly as he pushes into me from behind. We're lying on our sides, my back to his front. He lips next to my ear.

"*Seni seviyorum.*"

"I love you too," I cry and arch my back.

It's weird not having his beard brush against my skin. I miss it but it doesn't take away from his voice alone raising goosebumps against my skin. He nuzzles my ear with his nose, as if reading my sense of loss.

He gives a short breathless laugh. "Would you like me to grow it back?"

"Maybe, you're sexy either way."

"Am I now?" I can hear the smile in his voice.

He glides his hand up to rest over my heart and kisses the side of my head. I exhale contentedly. His slow pace allows us to stay in the moment. It's lazy makeup sex. Perfect.

"You've grown into such a beautiful woman. The same kind heart that drew me in twenty years ago, but your passion for life and love is intoxicating. I love you more than I ever have. Allow me to make you a princess, Divine," he says.

"Are you proposing? Like this," I laugh.

Reaching for my face, he turns it to face him. His eyes lock on mine. He has that serious look.

"I'm not proposing. I'm asking if you're ready for me to? You've pushed back on every step we've made. I'm telling you now this isn't something I'm going to tread lightly with. When I know you're ready, you will be my wife," he says.

I cup his jaw that already has growing stubble that scratches my fingertips. I nod my submission. "Yes. I'm ready. I've been waiting forever for you." A thought comes to me. "Hold on."

I pull away and crawl from the bed. Padding into the walk-in closet he had redone for me, I go to my jewelry box to find what I'm looking for. I smile as I place the piece of jewelry around my neck. A blue silk scarf catches my eye. It was a gift from Omid.

I snatch it up and wrap it around my neck and return to the room. He's sitting up with his back to the headboard, still hard. I saunter over and straddle his lap. He guides me to sink down on him as we keep our eyes on each other.

"Oh?" He chuckles eyeing the scarf around my neck.

Grasping the back of my neck he kisses me deeply. Groaning when I circle my hips. I break the kiss and keep my eyes on him as I peel the fabric away.

The look on his face is priceless as I reveal the heart pendant he gave me all those years ago. "I've always been yours. I'm ready when you are."

Face full of emotions, he nods and pulls me into his chest. He holds me as close and as tightly as my belly will allow. He's still inside of me, but neither of us moves. We just feel.

CHAPTER TWENTY-SIX

Come Away

Omid

"That's two babies," she gasps in awe.

Dr. Nobi and I both laugh. John pats me on the shoulder wearing a broad smile. I rub my hands together trying to contain my joy. Today is one of the greatest days in my life. This is just the beginning.

"Congratulations. They both look nice and healthy."

"I…two…like at the same time."

The confused look on her face is priceless. I told her this was a possibility and I didn't remember at the time that her oldest brothers are twins. I've been positive about it for weeks now. The sonogram just confirms what I knew.

I peck her lips. "Yes, twins at the same time."

I nuzzle my nose against hers while Dr. Nobi cleans the gel from her stomach. It's surreal to be on this side but I couldn't be happier.

"Any questions for me?"

"Can we save one for later?" Divine says.

Nobi and I burst into laughter. She just blinks at the two of us. Giving his congrats once more, John leaves the room.

"We'll just buy two of everything. Navid is ready to put the nursery together."

"Simple for you to say. You're not going to be pushing two babies out. Like, wow, two babies," she repeats.

I shake my head at her. "Come on, you. We have someplace to be."

"Where are we going? I wanted to go back to the hospital to see Marica."

"She will be taken care of. We're seeing to everything she needs. Just humor me today."

She gives me a side glance. "Humor you. Not sure I like the sound of that."

"There's cake involved," I croon.

She sits up, fixes her shirt, and starts to get off the table. I laugh at her some more, but help her to stand. She's been talking about strawberry shortcake for days.

"You should've mentioned the cake first," she says as we leave out of the exam room.

We step out of the door and run into one of my medical assistants. She stops and looks at us. I have Divine tucked under my arm, holding her closely to my side.

Gretta is one of the older assistants here. She has been with us the longest. She treats me and Dr. Nobi like her sons. She's been on leave to take care of her husband who was ill with cancer.

Her brown eyes fill with tears, her lips tremble. The smile on her brown face is one of a proud mother. She rushes forward and pulls Divine into her arms.

"I heard someone stole his heart. You're such a gorgeous woman. I'm so happy for him, for you both," Gretta says as she rocks Divine in her arms. She pulls away. "Oh, forgive me, honey. I'm Gretta. You've got yourself a great one here."

"Hello, it's nice to meet you. I'm Divine."

"Your parents named you perfectly," she snickers.

"Welcome back, Gretta. Is there anything I can do for you, anything you need? Nothing's too much."

She reaches to pat my cheek. "Charlie's lived a happy life. I'll be just fine. Your generosity and thoughtfulness were more than I could've asked for. You and Dr. Nobi made his last days very special. I don't know what to do with the fishing boat now."

"We can help you sell it or find a dock for you?"

She waves me off. "No, I think I'll keep it at the cabin for now. You boys are welcome to stay there and use the boat whenever you like."

"I'll be happy to help make sure the place stays maintained."

"Such a good man," she squeezes my cheek. "What you can do is help me find that Nobi a beautiful girl like yours. Then you get a ring on this one's finger before she gets away." She winks.

I laugh. "The Nobi request may be hard but I can take care of the second one. I'll bring her by for you to get a look at it."

"I look forward to it." She turns to Divine. "If you need anything, you call and ask for me. I'll babysit whenever you two need. I used to babysit for Nobi all the time."

"You're so sweet. Thank you," Divine says.

"You two look like you want to get out of here. Congratulations. That's a lucky little one."

"Little ones," I say puffing my chest out. "Just found out we're having twins."

She clasps her hands together and coos before waving us both into her waiting arms. Divine and I move forward into her embrace. She gives us a little squeeze.

When we pull away Gretta wipes at her tears. "You've made my day." She cups Divine's face. "Okay, I have work to do and you two need to celebrate. Enjoy the rest of your day."

"Thanks, Gretta." I cover my heart and bow.

"Such a sweet boy. You deserve all of the happiness."

She smiles widely and starts off in the direction she'd been going when we came out. Divine stares up at me with a huge smile on her face. I wrap my arms around her.

"What?"

"You. Everyone loves you. You bought her husband the boat, didn't you?"

I shrug. "John and I purchased the cabin and the boat. He loved to fish. We thought it would be a great place for them to create some final memories in his last months. It was the least we could do."

"You're amazing. The least most people would do is send flowers to the funeral, not buy them a cabin and boat. Man, I wish everything didn't make me cry. I've cried more in the last five months than I have in my entire life." She pouts.

"You have two reasons for your tears. Two very special reasons. Come on, your cake is waiting."

She throws her arms in the air and does a little wiggle. It's adorable. I think I fall in love with her right here and now, all over again.

"Yay, now you're talking."

I tug her in for a deep kiss. "I love you."

"Maybe cake can wait." She wiggles her brows.

My laughter fills the hall of the office. I'm bursting with more joy than I know what to do with. No one can stand between me and my forever.

Divine

He's up to something. Not only is he beyond well-groomed today, he hasn't stopped smiling all morning and that was before we had the sonogram. I would say it's the excitement of the babies but I know Omid well enough to know he's hiding something.

As we sit in the back of the car, I narrow my eyes at him. We're not headed to the house. I'm all out of ideas, I've stopped guessing at this point.

"What?" He smiles, leaning over to kiss me.

"Where are we going?"

His laugh lights up his eyes. He looks younger, more relaxed. "You don't like surprises, do you?"

"Nope."

He gives another hearty laugh, squeezing me into his side. His good mood is infectious, making it hard for me not to smile back at him. The last few days have been tense, making me relish in the feel of his happiness.

Our relationship hasn't been the problem. It's my family. With Marica in the hospital everyone has been back and forth to visit her.

I've run into my father a few times. If you lit a match in the room, I'm sure the place would explode. My father walked right by me and Omid.

Last time I saw Nashawn, he gave me a hug but the glare he gave Omid started a hissing match between us. My youngest brother, Lance had to get in the middle to break us up. My mother keeps her distance to keep the peace in her marriage.

"You just don't understand," she murmured in passing.

I don't. I get texts here and there from her but that has become hurtful. She knows my father's wrong but she's holding up his behavior by holding me at arm's length.

I've started to keep to myself at the hospital when Omid doesn't get me in before and after visiting hours. As much as it hurts and as hard as it is, I'm sticking to my guns. They all need to grow up.

Patience has just been a trigger for everyone because she's not picking a side but she's not keeping her opinions to herself either. She has become like a match in the room.

"Just relax," Omid says against my temple.

Reaching for the buttons of his shirt, I release a few to slide my hand inside. His heat is comforting and pulls me in. I snuggle closer and rest my head on his shoulder. Before I know it, I drift off to sleep.

Omid

This couldn't be more perfect. She fell asleep just as we pulled up to the plane. I carried her on board without her doing more than stirring just a bit.

I'm not surprised that she's slept through the eight-hour flight. She was up most of the night nervous about the appointment. In addition, she insisted on getting up early enough to see Marica before heading into the office to see Dr. Nobi.

Her eyes begin to flutter open as the wheels touch down. Navid sends me a nod to let me know everything is moving according to plan. I smile when Divine lifts her head and the side of her face has creases from lying against my chest.

There's nothing that can mar her beauty in my eyes. She lifts her arms to stretch as she smiles back at me. Suddenly, realization hits, she half lowers her arms and looks around the plane.

"You kidnapped me?" she teases.

"Maybe just a little." I wink.

"Where are we?"

I stick my chest out proudly. "St. Lucia."

"What? How long have I been sleeping? Oh my God, Omid. I have so much work to do."

"Eight hours give or take. Don't worry. Terrance gave me your schedule. Navid packed your laptop, cameras, and your ring light. He has everything you need," I reply.

She gives me a goofy smile. "You're so getting head. I can't believe you remembered that I wanted to come here."

Navid coughs and Divine blanches. She turns to look behind us then back at me. "I'm so sorry. I'm still waking up. Oh my God. This is so embarrassing." She covers her face.

"I've caught him with his pants down a time or two. The old man isn't a saint."

"Don't worry. I heard nothing," Navid says with a hint of humor.

"Yes, you did," Divine groans.

"It's my job to be seen and not heard. I hear all but nothing at all."

She turns to peek around her seat. "Thank you. You're always so kind."

"You make the prince a happy man. I'll do anything to ensure your comfort," he replies.

I unfasten my seatbelt and then hers. "Now that we have that straightened out, we can get off the plane."

She narrows her eyes at me but gets up to disembark. We climb into our waiting transportation. Once settled, I hand her some water and a baggy with a snack. Her eyes light up when she sees the sliced apples and box of raisins.

"I can't wait to stick my feet in the water," she says as she looks out the window munching on an apple slice. She turns to me with wide eyes. "I can't put on a bathing suit like this."

"Hush, Divine. I've picked several suits that you're going to look fantastic in. Besides, I'll be the only one to lay eyes on you. We'll be on private property."

She rolls her eyes over me. "I see you, Omid. I see you."

We fall into a comfortable silence as the sun starts to set. I've never been more sure of myself in my life. I'm a few short miles away from the biggest moment in my life and I'm on top of the world.

CHAPTER TWENTY-SEVEN

Under the Stars

Divine

This place is so beautiful. I feel like I'm in paradise. Walking into this beautiful bedroom, to be greeted by the sound of waves crashing and the amazing view of the infinity pool and the ocean, put the biggest smile on my face. Omid has a great view from his property back home, but this has a different feel.

Or it could just be the pampering. I've been treated like a queen from the time we arrived. Omid fed me dinner before bathing me in roses.

After, a team arrived to give me a full spa treatment. A massage, nails, hair, and makeup. Now I'm getting ready for whatever Omid has planned for the rest of the night.

"You guys see this? Makeup slayed," I say to the camera. "My man has me on an island feeling like a queen for real."

I turn my face to give them all the angles. The natural face and glow are popping. The girl that did my makeup came through and she used my products to do it with.

"Thanks, Shelly," I say as I read one of my follower's comment. "I'm trying. These babies have a girl tired."

I laugh when the comments go crazy and they start to type in they knew I was pregnant, others flip out because I said babies and not baby. I smile as I read through the comments. I figured since I'm five months and the photos from the shoot will reveal the truth soon, I might as well share.

"Yes, I'm pregnant with twins," I reply to the rush of inquiries. "We're just on vacation...He wanted to take me somewhere to relax...I don't know about that. I don't think I can get him on camera," I respond to their comments and laugh.

"Divine, *Elbise al bebeğim. Gitmeliyiz,*" Omid calls from the other room.

I cross my eyes and stick my tongue out at the camera and giggle. I read the comments as I get ready to close. They've all heard him in the background.

"Yes, that's him," I laugh. "He's speaking Turkish and yes, it's sexy. He's telling me I need to go y'all. Thanks, guys. I'll talk to y'all later. Don't forget we have that sale going for the liquid lip. Get your Gossip on. Everything's in my bio. Love ya, bye."

I end the live and smile at my reflection in the mirror. My hair is so cute. The woman braided the sides back and barrel curled the rest, pinning a white rose in one side of the faux hawk.

"Divine," Omid calls impatiently.

"I'm coming," I grumble back. He's usually the one taking forever to get ready. Good lord, the man can primp for hours.

Walking to the garment bag that was left for me, I unzip it and lose my breath. The white and gold dress is exquisite. It looks fit for royalty. It's a halter, maxi style but it's so elegant.

I take off my robe and slip the gown on. When I look in the mirror, I have this glow. It's more than the make-up, it hits me how happy I am. Omid walks up behind me and kisses my bare shoulder.

"Come, Aşkım. The stars are out."

I turn and place my hands on his chest. He looks so handsome in his white and gold linen shirt and pants. I smile at the matching outfits. He brushes his fingers across my cheek.

"Where are we going?"

"You'll see."

He takes my hand and leads me from the room. Butterflies fill my stomach. I'm excited. This has been so romantic so far. I can only imagine what's next.

We exit a side door and head out toward the beach. Music fills the air but I don't know where it's coming from. Omid pulls me into him and starts to sway with me.

I place my head against his chest and close my eyes. The sound of his heartbeat grounds me. The sound tells me I'm not dreaming.

"Thank you. This trip has been great and it's only been a few hours," I say.

"It's hasn't begun."

I lift my head and study his face. I have so many emotions rising. "It hasn't?"

"No." He looks down into my eyes. "I wanted to dance beneath the stars with you. I want you to remember we always come back to this."

"This?"

"You and I. No one comes between this. Nothing. We will always find the stars. They're a constant. We can always look to them for guidance back to this no matter where we are.

"*This* is the moment when I give myself to you. The moment when I show you that you mean the world to me," he drops to one knee.

I cover my mouth and the stupid tears start. He holds up a ring box with a ring big enough to blind me. I look from the box to the man holding it.

"Omid?"

"I've known who you were to me from the first time I saw your face. The fact that you're standing here before me only proves what I knew in my heart. I'm asking you beneath the stars that have watched our love live, even when we lost sight of it, and will continue to see it grow, will you marry me, Divine?"

"Yes," I choke out.

Removing the ring from the box, he slips it onto my finger. I cup his face and bend to kiss him. He places his hands on my stomach.

"I have one more thing to ask. I've waited long enough to have you as my wife. Our families aren't on the same page with us. I'm not going to wait for that to happen. Take this walk down the beach with me. There we will commit to each other," he says.

"You want to get married tonight?"

I search his eyes. He lifts to his feet and nods. "When I make love to you tonight it will be as your husband."

I bite my lip. I haven't dreamed of a wedding since I was sixteen. I wanted all the bells and whistles then but that was the dreams of a girl.

This reality is more beautiful than anything I could have dreamed of. I don't know if my father will ever speak to me again. I could be gray and old if I wait for him to come around to walk me down the aisle.

"Yes, I want to be your wife."

Omid

"Mrs. Divine Vahid," I murmur into her ear. "My princess."

We stand before the window that looks out over the beach and pool off the bedroom. Our reflections staring back at us through the glass. She's still in her dress, while I'm shirtless and barefoot.

I glide my fingers from her shoulder down her arm. "My wife," I whisper.

The ceremony was quick but will forever remain the most meaningful time in my life. I wish it were something we could share with the ones we love. I didn't miss her glances to where our families should've been.

Although, her eyes said she was still happy we were getting married, I saw the longing. Someday, we will have the blessing of her father. I will see to it.

"The wife of Dr. Omid, I think I like the sound of that."

"Do you?"

She reaches up to cup my face, her eyes fixed on mine in the reflection. I nuzzle her neck and watch her shiver as my whiskers tickle her skin. Slowly opening my mouth, I flick my tongue against her skin before sucking it into my mouth.

"Omid," she pants.

"I can't decide how I want you. How should I take you, wife? How do I please you tonight?"

"Undress me," she replies breathlessly.

My lips turn up. Sucking her skin into my mouth again, I release the clasp behind her neck. The top of the dress falls, revealing her gorgeous breasts. I cup them both, kneading them in my palms. I continue to kiss and suck her neck.

Releasing one of her mounds, I start to pull the zipper down at her side. I take my time, teasing her skin with my fingertips as the silky patch is revealed. She moves her hand into my hair.

The fabric billows to the floor. I don't rush to take her panties off. Instead, I run my hand over the fabric covering her swollen belly until I reach the apex of her thighs. Palming her mound, I bask in the feel of her heat.

"You're so beautiful."

I brush her hair over her shoulder and kiss a trail from her nape down her spine. Hooking my fingers into her panties, I gently pull them over her belly and down her legs. Her hands go to the glass.

"Please."

"I plan to please you. Spread your legs."

I lick at her ass, nipping one cheek before going to the other to lick circles across her flesh. Reaching between her legs, I find her soaking wet. I continue to dance my lips across her globes, tasting and pleasing.

"Mine. All mine," I say as I push two fingers inside her.

Her head falls forward and she starts to rock her hips. I grasp her cheeks and open her for a taste of her core. It's like my first ever. The flavor of her essence seems sweeter. I groan diving in for more.

"Omid, *kocam aşkım*," she whimpers.

My heart swells as she calls me her husband and her love in Turkish. The language is beautiful coming from her lips. I crave hearing it again.

"More."

"*Seni seviyorum kralım,*" she replies.

I nearly roar, lifting to my feet. Her King. It's the only title I've ever wanted to fight for. I remove my pants quickly and grab her by the waist with one hand, while I guide my cock to her entrance with the other.

"Your king? You love your king?" I hiss in her ear as I rock into her slow. I grasp her hair and hold on tight. "You're the queen of my soul. You were made for me."

She lifts on her toes as she cries out. We lock eyes in the window and I tell her all the things I'm too emotional to say. I feel like I've waited a thousand years to be with her. Knowing that she's now my wife is a high I can't describe.

Placing my hand on her shoulder, I thrust into her deeper. I drag the same hand down her back, watching it glide over her smooth flesh. Her muscles flex beneath my touch.

"Yes," she breathes.

I feel her climax coming. I'm not ready, we're coming together as man and wife this time. Pulling out, I kiss her shoulder and let my tongue move across her skin. Lifting her in my arms, I carry her to the bed. Placing her on the edge, I rest her legs on my shoulder and slide back into her slowly.

"I love you."

"You're everything to me, Divine."

She looks up at me with those brown eyes filled with so much love. I skim my palms over her thighs. She rises and falls back to the mattress moaning her pleasure. I move inside her until my spine tingles and my calves burn.

"Now, Divine. Come for me now, aşkım."

I think I leave my body when I release my seed into her as she comes around me. I place my head on her stomach and close my eyes. My entire world rests beneath me.

"Omid," she says.

"Yes?" I lift my head to see her face.

She brushes a hand through my hair. "I always knew it was you."

"What do you mean?"

She gives me a sleepy smile. "In the pictures. I was always drawn to you. I don't know how to explain it. From the first message, I was drawn to you. I was a little disappointed when I made the assumption that it was your cousin."

"I can't wait to throw that in his face." I boom with laughter. "You have to tell him this. He will never believe me."

"I never should've told you." She rolls her eyes.

I pull from her body. She moves back on the bed, settling on the pillows. I climb in beside her and wrap my arms around her. Releasing a contented sigh, I kiss her lips.

"I'm glad you did. Your heart has known mine just as mine has known yours. I was always coming to get my heart, Divine. Always."

CHAPTER TWENTY-EIGHT

Accept Our Love

Divine

My wedding and honeymoon were amazing. One week on the island of bliss. Now it's back to reality. I've been sitting outside my parents' home in tears.

I swear, I can't wait until these babies are born. I've cried enough for a lifetime. I wipe at my face as Neil comes out and walks to my passenger side door. I unlock it when he places a hand on the handle.

He climbs in and shuts the door. "Man, how many months are you?"

"Hi to you too," I grumble.

He laughs and bumps me with his shoulder. "Lance thinks you're pregnant with twins."

"Maybe because I am."

He shifts his body toward me and nods. "I figured as much too," he looks at my hands in my lap. "I knew that was coming as well."

I lift my hand to tuck my hair behind my ear. I'm still getting used to the fact that I have rings on my finger. I feel an ache in my chest knowing I got married without my family.

"We haven't stopped loving each other because of everyone else's opinion. These babies are growing each day. He's their father and I love him. Why should he not be my husband?"

"Eh, I'm not saying he shouldn't. I've been quiet. I got my own issues. I'm happy if you're happy. I just wish I wasn't missing out on so much in your life.

"I bought my girl your new makeup line and she got them lashes. Got me waking up to Bambi in the morning," he jokes while shaking his head.

"You're so silly."

"What? How the fuck she be so flawless in the morning? I swear, I'm going to stay up all night one of these days. I think she sets an alarm to get up before me to put all that shit on." He gives a snort.

"Don't worry, when you marry her you'll see the truth."

"That's why I'm not marrying her. I'm scared. I don't think I've ever seen her without makeup. I'm not with that deception. She going to have to come clean if she wants that ring," he says.

I laugh and hit him in the arm. Neil doesn't talk much but when he does, he can be a trip. He knows he's in love. I wouldn't be surprised if he proposes soon. His ex-wife was a horror. He deserves better.

I sober up my laughter and look him in the eyes. "Are you out here to tell me I'm not welcome?"

"Psst, you bugging. Daddy on some bullshit and Nashawn just doesn't know how to shut the fuck up. Mommy's hurting, Div. She shouldn't be stuck in the middle."

"I didn't place her there. She did."

"Come on, you know Daddy. He's old school. Remember the first time I brought a white girl home?"

I burst into laughter. Now that was a scene. My father's head nearly exploded.

"He got over it. He'll get over this."

"He did not get over it. If I remember correctly, you two broke up over it," I point out.

"Nah, we broke up cause Daddy was right about some other shit about her. That relationship was a wash from the start. Anyway, he didn't trip the next time I brought someone from another race home."

"Yeah, he did. Just not in front of you," I mumble. "Has he always been prejudiced?"

Neil pulls a hand down his face. He looks out at the house then back at me. He has a sour expression on his face.

"Yeah," he says and we both burst into laughter.

"It's not funny."

"It's not. And it's selective, which is insane. We've had friends that have been from all races and cultures come through the house. He just loses it when we start to date outside our race," Neil muses.

"I wonder what happened?"

"What you mean?"

"Mommy said I had to understand some things about him to understand his reaction to Omid."

"I think it has something to do with grandma. Granddaddy wasn't her first husband. Uncle Sid and Aunt Lorrain have a different father. Heard Granddaddy was super militant too. I don't know. Things were different when they came up. Who knows."

I sit quietly for a beat thinking his words through. None of them makes for good excuses. Neil reaches to hold my hand and gives it a squeeze.

"That still doesn't excuse Mommy," I mutter.

He grunts. "I used to get so mad at her when she'd sit back and let him go in on us. I learned something though. One time I wanted to go on a trip with some friends. He wasn't going to let me go. Mommy sat back and let him go on and on about priorities and focusing on my school work instead of chasing girls.

"I went to sneak out that night and I overheard her talking to him. She was sticking up for me and softening him up so I could go at the same time. You know what I learned from that?"

"What?"

"She always has our backs. She just doesn't divide their union in front of us. Trust me, Div. She's been working on him. Come inside. She deserves to see you. She has your back. It's going to work out."

"Did you get to go on the trip?"

"He said I could, but I changed my mind. Glad I did. Some local girl accused my boys of assaulting her. It turned into a fight. Two people were shot."

"Oh my God. I remember that. Your friend was there with his girlfriend. They'd been together all night. The girl just picked him at random to accuse."

"Yup, Daddy may have saved my life. Lives were ruined all because some chick wanted attention from her boyfriend. He doesn't always say things right but his concerns come from a good place. At least, he has good intentions. You're his baby, Div.

"He has always spoiled you. No man is going to be good enough for you. If he's not laying the world at your feet, he's not even close to being right," he says.

"But that's the thing. He does. I don't want for anything. Not emotionally, physically, or financially."

"Then, this too shall pass. I know that's all I want for you. Someone that loves and respects you. You think I didn't know about that fool you were dating. I beat his married ass. I don't say much but I watch everything."

"Wait, what?"

"I found out about the wife and kids and I paid homie a visit." He shrugs.

I sit stunned. I found out my ex was married because someone had beat his ass. I never knew it was my brother.

"Thanks, Neil."

"Anytime, brat."

I smile at him. I used to hate when he called me that. Heck, I couldn't stand Neil when I was younger. My brothers made my life hell. Still, at the end of the day, I love them all. I'd drag any girl that bothered them in a heartbeat.

"Come on, I have to pee."

"Was wondering how long you were going to make it without the bathroom and some food."

"Ugh, I'm starving."

Omid

Navid pulls up outside of Divine's parents' home and I stare at the front door. My wife is inside. She has been here for the day. It's a step forward. Me being here could be a step back.

"In that house is everything you love," Navid says. "You've sculpted your life for her without even realizing it. I've watched you do it. To sit here now, after all the obstacles you've crossed to make her your wife—all the obstacles still to come—it's not you.

"Go show them you're here to love and care for her. You don't have a bone in your body that's able to hurt her. You two are a force together. Go be with your wife. Allah has carried you this far," he says.

"You and Anne Sassa have been the parents I've needed in my life. If I don't tell you how much I love, respect, and cherish you, forgive me. I do more than you know," I reply and climb from the car.

I ring the doorbell and wait. The sound of boisterous voices floats out from inside. The door opens. I believe this is the oldest twin, Nashawn. He looks behind him then steps out and closes the door.

I fold my arms across my chest and pull a hand down my beard. His eyes settle on my wedding band as I make the gesture. He mirrors my posture.

"She really went and married you," he says with a mix of awe and hurt. I bristle but he continues. "Ever since she was little, if you told Div no, she'd find a way to do it anyway but that's not the case with you.

"She loves you. To go to war with my dad for you...that's not Divine's defiance for life, that's love."

"Your sister and I have loved each other for a long time," I reply.

"From the day she was born me and my brothers vowed to make her tough. We never babied her. She probably hates us for it, but it's made her who she is. I love that girl.

"My baby sister is the most amazing woman I know. Did you know when she started the makeup thing she was living on my couch? She wouldn't take a dime from our parents and she had it in her head she was going to use the internet to make money. Man, she didn't even know it would turn into makeup and shit.

"A friend of hers was getting married at the time and she had three dollars to her name. She couldn't pay for the dress to be in the wedding and she wouldn't ask for it from anyone. Her so-called friend dragged her for not making it happen.

"I swear from that day she had this look in her eyes and she's had it since. She built millions off of three dollars," he says as he glares at me.

"I am Prince Omid Vahid before I am Dr. Omid. My uncle took me in as one of his sons when my father and I severed. I've never known lack and never will. My wife and children will never want for anything. I'm proud of my wife but her money is what I wipe my ass with. I don't need to live off her."

"That's good to know but that's not my point. She has that look again. This time it's connected to you. Div is committed to you." He pauses slaps his hands together and points them at me. "If you're not committed to my sister like she is to you. Get your ass the fuck off this porch. Cause I promise you, I'll break my foot off in your ass if you ever hurt her, make her cry, or second guess who she is.

"Prince, sheik, Aladdin, none of that shit means anything to me. I'd catch a body for my sister. Ask my other brother-in-law, there's no room for error," he finishes.

I snort and grin at him. I can respect his love for Divine but he's going to respect me too. I mimic his hand gesture and point back to him.

"We can both agree on one thing. Divine will always be cherished and pampered but don't mistake me for some punk or fool you can intimidate. I will respect you as you will respect me. You don't have to like me but you will learn to accept our love because that's what makes her happy.

"Let's start with getting some things straight. I'm Persian, not Arab. Aladdin is an Arabic title. Both Middle Eastern, not the same.

"I may look up skirts for a living but I've never been a pussy. Stop talking to me like I'm going to let you beat my ass," I say calmly.

"Well, damn, Div. I like his ass more and more." I turn to to see Divine and her sister now standing in the doorway.

"You satisfied, Nashawn?" Divine asks.

"Yeah," he nods at me, holding out a hand. "He cool."

I nod and take his hand to shake. One down. At least one more to go.

"Hey," Divine says as she comes to stand in front of me.

"Hey," I say and cup her face.

"Baby steps. I think we should go home," she says and gives a weak smile.

I nod. "Whatever you need."

CHAPTER TWENTY-NINE

Time for Us

Divine

"Look at you," Gretta coos. "You're taking to this pregnancy so well."

"Thank you and thank you for doing this," I say as we slip into Omid's office.

"It's no problem at all. I remember when I'd do stuff like this for my Charlie. I'd get dressed up and surprise him at work. There's a body under these scrubs, believe it or not," she laughs.

"I hope I still look as good as you do at your age." I give her a smile.

She waves me off and helps to clear Omid's desk for me to set up our romantic lunch. He's been working a lot and I wanted to surprise him. I've been fast asleep when he's arrived home most of this week.

"You don't look your age as it is. I thought you were a lot younger than Dr. Omid. Not that he looks his age."

"I was surprise when Omid told me how old you are. Happy belated birthday by the way. I wish I could've come in for the little party they threw," I reply.

"I told them not to fuss over me."

I place my hands on my hips. "You only turn fifty once and you're killing it by the way. I would love to do a shoot with you in my makeup or maybe a live with me glamming you up. My followers would love that," I muse.

"I just might take you up on that. I've been asked out on a date. A little polish never hurt anyone."

"Oh my God. I would love to do this for you. Even without the pictures. This is such a big step for you."

She pauses and I see the tears well. Gretta is a gorgeous Black woman. I wouldn't think she was a day over forty, if that. I would love to see what she looks like under the scrubs. From what Omid tells me, she hits the gym all the time to stay fit.

"Charlie wanted me to move on. He made me promise. I'm not sure if I'll take this fella up on his offer, but I've thought about dating. My kids are all grown and off living their lives. I'd love to have someone to talk to. You know?"

"Yeah, I understand."

"Enough about me. Come, he'll be headed this way soon."

I move around the desk to embrace her. "Let me know when you're ready. I'd be honored to help showcase your beauty."

"I'll let you know." We both turn to the door as Omid's voice carries from outside. "You finish up. I'll buy you a minute or two."

"Thank you," I whisper and get the rest of the things in place.

I light the candles I brought with me and look around. Taking a deep breath, I sit on the edge of his large oak desk. I release a short laugh. I can't believe I'm so nervous.

"Okay, okay, Gretta. I promise. I'll bring Divine by as soon as I can," Omid laughs outside the door.

The knob turns and he enters. He's looking down at a chart in his hands. Suddenly, he looks up with furrowed brows. The sexy smile that comes to his lips sends my tummy fluttering.

"Hey, handsome. Thought you might want to spend a little time with your family. Hungry?"

He looks me over. At a week away from six months, I'm a lot of belly. I spent two hours picking the right outfit. I settled on a yellow baby doll dress with a shear top layer. My swollen feet wouldn't let me be great so I had to slip on a pair of gold flats.

He closes and locks the door. Placing his hands behind his back, he moves closer with that sexy walk of his. The hunger in his eyes makes me giddy.

He places the chart down beside me before cupping the side of my head and brushing my ear with his thumb. "I've been thinking about you all morning. I've been trying to get away to come have lunch with you," he says with a smile.

"Great minds think alike," I say wrapping my arms around his neck.

He dips his head and kisses me. I don't think I'll ever get tired of his dominating way of consuming my mouth. He's all tongue, teeth, and lips at the moment as if I'm lunch.

"I want you so much but I know I don't have time for all I have in mind," he groans.

"You'll just have to settle for eating with us," I say.

"Now that's not a bad idea," he replies, pushing his hands up under my dress.

I grab his wrists and laugh. "Gretta told me you don't have that kind of time. We have thirty minutes tops to eat the lunch I brought."

"What have I done so wrong to you?" He pouts.

"What are you talking about?"

"You come to my office like this and want me to keep my hands to myself. Why torture me?"

The laughter I've been trying to hold floats through the room. The babies begin to respond to the sound and vibration of my body. Excitement fills me and I reach for his hand.

"They're moving. Come, feel your children."

We wait as I look into his eyes. As soon as he feels it, his eyes light up and I know. These are the small moments I've cherished with him in the last three weeks.

I fall in love with him more and more each day. It's like discovering who we are to each other all over again. We're living out the dream we once had together so long ago.

"What are you thinking?" He asks as he searches my eyes.

"Remember we'd talk all night. Sometimes about nothing. Other times you'd listen to me rant about needing to get away from my siblings and wanting to build a business and be successful."

"Yes, I remember. It was your ambition that led me to go through with medical school. You encouraged me to do so much that summer."

I tilt my head. "Really, like what?"

He pulls a chair closer and grabs the fresh fruit salad I brought with me. Opening the lid, he starts to feed me. His eyes grow distant for a moment.

"I started looking at colleges here in the States. I entered a few gaming contests like you pushed me to. I was going to tell you that I won one. When you would tell me about your favorite places to go, I found them and checked them out for myself."

"Seriously? So why couldn't we meet at one of those places?"

"I was never alone when I'd explore. I had to have one of my uncle's men with me. Remi and Ramses were willing to cover for me when they were around, but you remember, they had to take care of business in New York."

"Yeah, I remember that."

"That limited my freedom. They were my ticket to being free that summer. Actually, I should've gone with them to New York. I was in America to spend time with them but I couldn't bring myself to leave the state, knowing you were here," he says.

He eats some of the salad before feeding me more. I sit thoughtfully. So much has come to light about all those years ago. I shrug it off. The past is the past. I love our life now.

"Oh, I forgot to tell you. Navid found two of the cribs I wanted. I had such a hard time finding two. It was like I'd find it at one place and they'd have one in stock but by the time I'd find it in another place they'd sell out at the first location. Ugh, that was driving me crazy."

"I'm glad you found what you wanted. I would've had them handcrafted if you didn't."

"For what I'm paying for them you would think they were," I snort.

I will always want the best for my babies, but the insane amount of money for some of the things I like has been interesting. Navid has encouraged me a time or two to get whatever I wanted. I'm still getting used to that.

Yeah, I've built wealth, but I've been wise with my money. Some of the things Omid and Navid choose not to bat a lash at blows my mind. Omid's wardrobe alone puts my shoe addiction to shame.

"Nothing is too much for our children. Speaking of which, why haven't you been using our accounts? I saw the baby clothes you started to purchase. Our balance hasn't changed."

"Honestly, I forget to."

I shrug and hand him the lamb and rice Navid prepared. Handing me the empty salad tray, he opens the lamb dish and starts to share it.

"How's business?"

"Everything is great. The website is fully functional. I'm thinking about a new palate and some new lip colors. My followers are up as well." He gives a little laugh. "What's so funny?"

He shakes his head. "I always love when I think of your social handle. I searched for you as Divine Favors every so often."

"Ah. Yeah, I actually started out as Nika Favors. I changed to D Beauty Favors once things started to take off."

He drops his eyes to my feet. He frowns and places the food on the desk. Unfastening my shoe, he starts to rub my foot. I moan and lean back on my palms.

"God, I love you."

Omid

I laugh at her words. I love her more with each second. This visit has made my entire week. With Dr. Nobi on leave, I've been taking on twice the load.

I'm not complaining. John hasn't taken a vacation in years. It's just been busy and harder for me to sneak away as often as I would like to.

"I know you've been busy but have you been resting enough?"

"I do nothing but nap," she groans. "Dada has been at the house more to help me get things done. Otherwise, I'd be so behind."

I kiss the sole of her foot. "We'll make time for a staycation soon," I say.

She closes her eyes and visibly relaxes. "Sounds good. How has work been? What's new with you?"

I think of the news I received this morning. I was going to call her to share but I got side tracked with a run to the hospital, by the time I returned I needed to attend to the patients waiting for me. This has honestly been my first moment to breathe.

"I'm being honored with an award for some of my research."

She opens her eyes and they sparkle as she looks back at me with excitement. "That's wonderful news. Congratulations, babe. We have to celebrate."

"They're going to present it at a ceremony next month."

"I'll be huge, but I'll be ready. I'll find something to wear," she says. I can see her mind creating her plan.

"I'm not going."

"What?"

"I can't risk the photos circulating. It's just better if my family doesn't know what I do here in the States," I tell her.

She pouts. "But you work so hard. You deserve this. By the way, when I come here and they call me Mrs. V-Shah it totally throws me off."

I chuckle. I was adamant that she take my true last name. It's not the first time she's mentioned having to remember the two names.

"You will get used to it," I tell her. As for the award, I've gotten used to things being this way. "Receiving the acknowledgement is what's most important. I will send my regrets and thank them for the honor."

"If you're okay with that." She frowns. "I hate that you're not going to have the experience of the accomplishment."

"It's a little thing," I kiss her toes.

I start to make patterns on the bottom of her foot with my tongue. She lowers her lids as I look up at her through my lashes. She sucks her lip into her mouth.

"You're not leaving here without me making you come," I breathe.

"I didn't come here for that."

I release her foot and shrug my coat off. Releasing my cufflinks, I roll my sleeves up. Moving my chair forward, I place my hands on her thighs. This time she doesn't stop me when I begin to push her dress up.

Her breasts heave with anticipation, my slow touch raising goosebumps along her skin. My cock starts to twitch in my pants.

"Then you're in for a treat, Aşkım," I murmur, kissing her belly.

She leans back, spreading her legs for me. I hook one over my shoulder and I begin to kiss my way up her thigh. I get to the apex where her fruit awaits me and my office phone rings.

"You have to be fucking kidding," I groan against her hot pussy.

"It's okay, I'll see you at home. You have permission to wake me if I'm sleeping when you get in."

I inhale her pussy once more before reaching for the phone on my desk. Reaching down, I squeeze my cock. It's going to be a long day.

CHAPTER THIRTY

Interruptions

Divine

"Go sit down," Omid barks at me.

I look up like a baby caught misbehaving. I'm supposed to be lying down and resting, but I've found my way back into the nursery. I only planned to fold a few things and organize.

"I just want to get these things put away," I say.

"You're seven months pregnant and you've been running all week. I want you to rest," he demands.

"Fine. And I'm not seven months yet." I put down the little onesies in my arms and poke my lip out.

He narrows his eyes at me and folds his arms over his chest. He's been more bossy than ever. Dr. Nobi has returned to the practice, allowing Omid this time to be home to help me.

The man is driving me crazy. Okay, yes, I've had insomnia and I haven't cut back my workload but doubled it. I'm also two days from being seven months. I'm definitely trying it. However, he acts as if I shouldn't do something with these hours that I can't seem to use for sleep.

"Come here, you." He holds his arms open for me to walk into.

I go willingly into his comforting embrace. Leaning my face against his chest, I savor the sound of his heartbeat.

"I thought you were going for a run."

"I am. I wanted to kiss my wife before I took off. I entered the bedroom and you were gone."

"Oops." I giggle.

He slaps my ass lightly. I go to fuss at him but he kisses me, silencing my protest. He slips his warm hand into my panties beneath his T-shirt I'm stretching out. I groan into his mouth.

His phone rings and he growls. "I have to take this call. Go lie down for a bit. I'll be right there before I head out."

I nod as he lifts the phone to his ear. I'm a little disappointed but suck it up and head to our bedroom. The doorbell rings and I change directions. Navid has been out running errands all day.

I blow out a breath as it seems to take me forever to get to the door. I can't see my feet anymore but I have to wonder if they're even moving down there. I finally get to the door and open it.

When I do I'm hit with a wave of shock. There are a ton of people on our doorstep. The ones that stand out are the little woman glaring daggers at me and the older looking version of Omid. Only this man has amber colored eyes.

"Where is my son?" the woman says. "Who are you?"

I lift a protective hand to my belly. I don't like the way either of them are looking at it. Looking around at all of the faces there's only one that's even remotely friendly.

I'm drawn to her. However, it's the young looking, tall olive skinned woman with highlighted hair peeking out of her hijab and hazel eyes who begins to speak in Farsi. "Who is this woman? Why would she be in Prince Omid's home dressed like this?"

A heavyset guy holds up a gold ringed hand to her. His eyes roll over me. I tighten my fist in my T-shirt. That doesn't stop his hungry gaze. If anything, his eyes drop to my legs.

"My parents and my brother's fiancée would like to see him. Is he here?"

"Fiancée? Oh, hell no. *Omid*," I start to yell through the house. "Omid. Omid, you better get your ass to this door."

"She's with child. There is no need to stress her," I turn to see it's the one person that had a smile for me speaking.

She's a pretty tall woman with kind eyes. There's something about the way she's looking at my bump. It's almost a look of longing.

"Omid," I scream again.

I don't know these people and I don't trust them. My husband comes flying around the corner with concern and confusion on his face. He scans me with his eyes as he gets closer.

"What is it? Are you having pain—"

His words cut off and he becomes rigid. In a few short strides he closes the distance between us and places his body between me and the people still standing outside of our home. The tension coming off of him is palpable.

"What are you all doing here?" he says.

"Is that any way to greet your family?" The woman who called herself his mother says.

"Who is this?" the man I'm assuming is his father asks.

Omid seems to grow ten feet taller. He scoops an arm around me to bring me into his side protectively. "This is my wife.

"Your—"

"You've heard me correctly, Baba."

"I'm so happy for you," the lady with the kind smile bursts out. Everyone seems to turn and glare at her.

Omid gives me a gentle squeeze. "Anne Sassa, come. Divine, this is my Anne Sassa. Anne Sassa this is Divine and my little ones," he says proudly as he palms my stomach.

"He has a wife and heir," the younger woman says.

"Who are you?" Omid says with no small amount of disdain.

"You introduce her before me?" The woman that called herself his mom says, ignoring the younger woman.

"You bring strangers to my home to question me," Omid snarls back.

Sassa hasn't moved forward yet and I think it has something to do with the glare his mother is leveling her with. The tension is only increasing. I start to tremble with a mix of anger, frustration, and confusion.

"Gulzar is no stranger. She's your fiancée," his mother says and lifts her chin, glaring down her nose at me.

Omid gives a bitter laugh. "You have dragged this girl here for nothing. Divine is the one and only wife I will ever have. Paiman, why don't you take this one off my hands as well? You can take her back to Iran with you since you won't be stepping foot into my house."

"We're not welcome here?" his mother gasps.

"He isn't welcome," Omid says tightly. "He understands why."

"I think I'm going to be sick," I murmur and pull away from Omid to head to the bedroom.

I don't know what the fuck is going on but this isn't what I signed up for. It's better I walk away than watch some woman that thinks she's my husband's fiancée, eye fuck him while she thinks no one is watching. I have a five star ass whipping for that ass. Remembering I'm nearly seven months pregnant, I reel it in and walk my trembling body from the scene of the potential crime.

Omid better fix this shit. I'm not about that life. Fiancée my ass.

Omid

I'm brimming with anger. Navid has been concerned with not being able to reach Sassa in the last few weeks. Navid has always kept her up to date on my life and she has always shared things we've needed to know from back home.

It doesn't hurt to have a pulse on my siblings. Bazar and I get along well, which is rare in noble families. Wars over rank and power aren't uncommon at all. Paiman is a prime example of noble half-siblings that aren't worth shit.

I've known he's been up to something. I don't have to ask to know he instigated this trip. He's probably behind the reason Sassa has been out of touch and didn't warn us about this visit. It hasn't slipped my notice that she didn't come forward to greet Divine when I introduced them.

I want to follow after my wife. I don't like the trembling in her body. This isn't the time for her to be worried or upset.

I look at my family still on my doorstep. "Paiman and this woman will not stay under my roof. The rest of you are welcome. However, I will warn you. This is my home, my life, my way. If you don't think you can accept it then it's best you find somewhere else or follow this woman back to Iran."

"You will send her away without getting to know her?"

"Why the f…why do I need to get to know her, Anne? This is what I mean. If you can't respect my marriage you should leave now."

"I came to learn who my son has become. I'm tired of the rumors and whispers of who you are. I have men coming to me on your behalf. I want to have these talks with you as a man. I'm no fool, Navid doesn't give me the full truth.

"Paiman, take Gulzar to a hotel with you. Get a suite. Your mothers and I will stay here with Omid."

"He has no respect for our family or Allah. Why do you allow him—"

"Paiman, I didn't ask you to lecture me. Do as I say," my father snaps at my whiny ass brother.

You would think he was twelve years younger than me and not one. Bazar is more mature than him and he's just coming into being a man. My brothers are like night and day.

I step back and allow my father to lead my mothers into my home. I do notice that Paiman's mother is absent. Anne Padma is a bitter woman. She has never been happy that my mother produced an heir before her. She has loathed me from the time I was born. Much like her entitled son.

Paiman glares at me as he stands on the other side of the threshold with his wife and the woman I don't intend to get to know as my fiancée. I close the door right in their faces. Just as

I do, I hear the door that leads into the house from the garage open.

It doesn't take long before Navid appears. He looks around unfazed as if he were prepared for this. "Staff will be joining us to accommodate this visit. Would you like me to provide anything else, şehzade?"

"See to their comfort for now. I have to attend to my wife."

Navid nods.

"Omid," my mother starts.

"Anne, not now. You've come here and disrupted the order in my home. I will talk to you all later."

I turn for my room with my focus on getting to Divine. I know she's angry. She has every right to be. This is her home and my family has just upended our life with their intrusion.

I already know this isn't going to be a pleasant visit. Yet I can't find it in me to care about what my baba will find or what either of my parents will think of my life. My wife is all that matters. She and my children. I need to ensure their happiness.

I climb into the bed and spoon Divine, draping my arm over her to palm her stomach. The babies move against my arm and hand. I close my eyes and inhale. When I hear her sniffle, rage consumes me.

"I don't know that woman, nor have I ever met her. I knew nothing of her until she came to the door. She's not even the same one they tried to push on me in Dubai," I say.

"What does all of this mean? Do I have something to be worried about?"

The pain in her voice is so heavy it weighs me down. I hear the words unsaid. *Was her father right about me?*

"It means nothing at all. Not to us. My brother wants to make sure he secures what's not his by revealing my life choices to my baba. I don't give a shit either way. My anne loves to meddle in my life. She has been trying to arrange the *right* marriage since I was a baby. I have ignored every attempt.

"You're my wife, this is our home, and this is our life. We will continue to live as we have and I will only be married to you. The mother of my children," I reply.

"The way they looked at me. Like garbage or shit under their shoes. Me and my children will never be accepted by them," she murmurs.

"My life is here in America. What my family does in Iran is their own business. What they accept is their problem, not mine. We will not live waiting for them to accept who we are."

"But they're your family."

I turn her to face me. The pain in her features slices through me. I can see this is about more than my family. Her father still isn't receptive of me. The rest of the family has warmed to the idea of me as her husband but her father has remained set in his way.

"And I love them for who they are. However, this is my life. I will not be forced to do things that make me unhappy, nor will I ask my wife to. Our happiness…that's my goal."

"What about my safety? You were worried about my safety before. Now that they know about me, doesn't that change things?"

"No," I say tightly. "The message was made clear that this is my life. I don't know why they're here. I'll find out. However, you're safe."

"Okay." She nods but I can still see the worry etched in her face.

"I love you, Divine. This changes nothing."

"All right. I'm tired. I'm going to take a nap."

I clench my jaw and nod. I let it go for now. There's nothing more I can say.

CHAPTER THIRTY-ONE

Not Having It

Omid

Divine has been fast asleep for hours. I don't know how I feel about that. She's had insomnia for weeks. Now she's sleeping like a baby. This stress isn't something I want for her.

I just may ask everyone to go to a hotel. Out of sight, out of mind. I rest my head in my palms as I sit on the couch with my elbow on my thighs. The same couch that Divine and I sat on just yesterday, laughing and talking about our future.

With her birthday in four months, I've already started to plan something for her. That's where my mind was as I talked on the phone with the party planner. Now, I'm planning to strangle someone if my wife is even the least bit unhappy when she wakes.

"Hey, you," her sleep heavy voice pulls my attention from my thoughts. I lift my head to find Divine in one of those sundresses I love.

She reaches to run a hand through the front of my hair. The worry from last night still in her eyes. I place my hands on her stomach and kiss her swollen belly repeatedly. She releases a smile.

"Come here," I say, gently pulling her into my lap.

"You know I'm too big for this?"

I peck her lips. "You will always be just perfect for my arms. Are you hungry?"

"Is that even a question? We're always hungry."

"Navid has brought in a chef. He's making a spread for everyone. I'll go get you a plate," I say.

She stiffens. "Everyone?"

"Yes, my parents remained."

She drops her head and starts to crack her knuckles. "Oh."

I can see her thoughts racing. Her brows furrow. I swear I can see her ready to take flight. I won't allow it. She belongs at my side.

I lift her chin with my fingertips. Searching her eyes, I place a soft kiss on her lips. "They will go before you do. I told you last night, nothing will change. You have nothing to worry about."

She releases a breath and nods her head. However, she's still not trusting in my words. I go to reassure her again, but Navid and Sassa enter the room.

They're both carrying two plates of food. Divine's stomach rumbles, causing my priorities to turn to feeding her. Navid hands me the plates in his hands as Divine moves to take a seat next to me. When she settles I hand her the one with all her favorites on it.

Sassa hands a plate to Navid and they take seats in the two accent chairs. Sassa has her eyes on Divine as a huge smile covers her face. The excitement in her eyes speaks so much of the supportive mother she has been to me all my life.

"You're having twins?" Sassa asks when she can no longer contain her excitement.

"Yes," Divine says covering her mouth as she chews.

"Oh, forgive me. Eat, eat. We can talk later."

"It's okay. You're Omid's Anne Sassa, right?"

"Yes, that's me."

Divine gives the first real smile I've seen since the arrival of my family. Sassa has a way of bringing that out in people. I remember as a boy she was always the one to stop my tears on the few occasions I would have them.

"Omid speaks very fondly of you."

Sassa beams at the comment. I've shared with Divine on more than one occasion how important this woman is to me.

"Forgive me if I am wrong, but I don't think I am. You're the young lady he met his first summer here?"

"She is," I reply, reaching to brush a hand down Divine's back.

"I knew it. He has that look again. I knew he was in love when he returned home at eighteen. No matter how much he tried to deny it. I knew he met someone special."

"Good morning," my mother says as she enters the room with a cup in her hand. The day hasn't started unless she has her tea and nabat.

Tension fills the room. While her words are cordial that glare she gives my wife and Sassa aren't. I grit my teeth and toss my plate on the coffee table. My appetite is gone.

"Good morning," Divine replies with a forced smile this time.

"Please. I don't know your name," Baba says as he appears. "I'm Javed. Omid's father."

"Ah, you're awake," my mother interrupts. "Good, we'd like to talk to you, Omid."

I snort and shake my head, her ability to roll over others is impeccable. I still can't believe they have just turned up on my doorstep. So typical of them but I'm still pissed that they've done this.

"My name is Divine," she says to my father who's still looking at her expectantly.

"This is Omid's mother, Hana."

My mother takes a seat on the loveseat beside him. It's clear she's ignoring Divine. My wife does the same. Turning back to her plate as if my father didn't introduce my mother at all. I laugh internally and lean to kiss Divine's temple. When I turn back to my parents, my father's gaze is locked on us.

"You told your anne that you were busy with a study. It looks like you've been up to more than practicing medicine," Baba says.

"I have been busy with work." I shrug. "I have also been busy with life."

I place a hand on Divine's stomach and she covers my palm. Our little ones are up and moving around. I allow the presence of the three of them to keep my calm.

"How long have you been married? Were you married when you arrived in Iran for your last visit?" My father continues his interrogation.

"No, I wasn't married then. We've been married for two months now," I reply.

My father sits forward in his seat as his gaze bounces between the two of us. "But she was pregnant then?"

"I wasn't aware at the time, but yes, she was."

He nods.

"Gulzar is a good match for you. Her family is a good match. You'll do well to marry her. If you pass on this engagement it's going to get harder to find suitable matches for you," my mother says.

My father pulls a hand down his face before opening his mouth to speak. I can't, I just can't. I'm not going to tolerate this disrespect in my home. I don't know what they thought they were coming here to do, but I'm not having it. My mother hears nothing I say to her.

I explode.

"I'm not marrying that woman or anyone else," I roar and tug at my hair. "How can you not understand that I've never wanted that life. I told you that I wanted to create my own. Fuck, I ran away from you. We didn't so much as speak for eighteen years."

"Omid—"

"No, Baba. I'm tired of this. Hear me. Divine is my one and only wife. I'm not marrying anyone else. You don't like it, you do what you must, but if that means threatening my wife and children, you can get out now. You were warned. My family is off limits."

"Omid stop this," my mother snaps.

"Let's go. We have a plane to catch," I say to Divine.

"You're leaving?" My father stands with a frustrated expression on his face.

"You arrived unannounced. We had plans."

I'll be blue in the face before I get through to my parents. I'm done here. I hope they're gone when we get back.

CHAPTER THIRTY-TWO

New York

Divine

I breathe and rub my lower back. It's been hurting more than usual today. Taking a few more cleansing breaths I try to calm my nerves. My mind has been full with so much since Omid's family dropped in on us. Not to mention, Sassa finding her way on the plane with us.

I wince at the discomfort and shift on the couch a little. After a couple more breaths some relief settles in. I just need to relax. Everything back home can wait. We're here to have a good time.

"Hey, you," Val says as she sits next to me on the couch in her living room.

We're having dinner here tonight. My baby shower is tomorrow afternoon. Val and Uri insisted that Omid and I stay with them for the few days we'll be here in New York.

"Hey."

"You want to talk about it? You've been somewhere else since you arrived, it's not like you."

I comb a hand through my hair and scratch my scalp. The frustration building again as my mind combs through all that's on my plate with the business, the babies coming, things with my dad, and now Omid's family.

"I don't know where to start."

"Sassa seems interesting," she replies with her head tilted at me.

I grunt. "She's nice. Nicer than my other in-laws. Omid seems to love her."

"That he does, but we're not talking about him. We're talking about you. What's up?"

I squirm in my seat. I'm angry and hurt every time I give this subject any real thought. I feel like a fool, if I'm honest with myself.

"My father isn't talking to me. He feels I've made a poor choice with Omid. He warned me that Omid's family wouldn't be accepting of me. He told me that I needed to know more about him before things got this far." I point to my belly. "One of his concerns is Omid taking another wife. Now I'm wondering if this is one of those times when my father is right and I'm just being a hard headed brat."

"I see." She nods. "Maybe I can help a little. We all have a reason for being a part of the Alliance. For Remi and Ramses part of their reason was Omid. The twins do as they please. They wanted that for Omid as well."

"The Alliance?" I repeat, looking at her in confusion.

Val smiles. "Let's just say while we're all dangerous in our own right. There's a lot that makes Omid's friends and family powerful as well. There are levels to who we are."

"There's also so much you have to understand about Omid himself." Val and I turn to find Sassa moving into the room slowly. "May I?"

"Yes," I say.

She comes all the way into the room to take a seat. "Omid has been special since he was a little boy. He sees the world differently from others. His curiosity for life makes him question everything.

"Before his summer here in America he spent a lot of his time glued to his father's side. However, it was clear he would begin to be his own man. When he returned to Iran, he returned different.

"A part of him had been left here. It was only a matter of time before he would return. He was passionate about you and the life he wanted to build here.

"Leaving his home and breaking his engagement put his life and future in danger. I still don't know what made my husband spare him. I've seen Javed become a harsh man in his anger.

"What I am trying to say is, you mean so much to Omid. You will always come first," she explains.

I rub at my chest and frown at the onset of heartburn. I have a lot to think about. In my heart, I know Omid has shown me nothing but his loyalty. His words have matched his actions. However, my mind keeps trying to tell me that my father was right. I rushed this.

"I'm overthinking everything and I'm hormonal."

"This might be true but you're entitled to your feelings and to express them. It took me a while to understand how much my husband cared for me in the beginning. I wish I could hold up a mirror for you to see what everyone else does when Omid looks at you," Val comments.

"But does love conquer culture and beliefs. I'm not Persian. I saw the way his mother looked at me. What if my children aren't good enough for them and they want him to have an heir that's...not mine?"

"Then they will be left wanting," Omid's voice pulls our attention. "My love conquers all. I will say this before witnesses because you don't seem to believe me when I say it only to you.

"Allah created one blessing just for me. A blessing so perfect it gives to my soul, my heart, my mind, my flesh. A blessing carved to match the depths of who I am, tethering me to a flame that mirrors my own. Divine you're that blessing. You feed all of my happiness."

He moves across the room and pulls me from my seat. Cupping my face he looks me in the eyes. I search his gaze. The love and sincerity I see there calms my racing heart.

"My belief is that you were made so divinely for me, there's no need for another. You provide all I need," he places his free hand on my stomach. "Including the perfect heirs. Outside of you, all else is irrelevant."

He takes my lips and kisses me deeply. I'm breathless and a little dazed when he breaks the kiss. He passes his thumb across my lips.

"I choose you. I will always choose you."

I nod. This time allowing it to fully sink in. My doubts melt away as his eyes repeat the words that have penetrated my heart.

"I love you."

"I love you, then something beyond."

I smile at his words. My shoulders feeling lighter. I've forgotten we're not alone until Val speaks.

"Shit, Uri. When was the last time you told me something like that?"

"It was this morning." He waves her off. "You were moaning too loud to hear me."

We all burst into laughter. Omid embraces me and kisses the top of my head. It's just what I need, when I need it.

CHAPTER THIRTY-THREE

Baby Shower Bliss

Omid

"You're...well. You," Divine stutters as she looks up at Remi.

He chuckles and tugs her in for a hug. "I'm the man of your dreams, I know. I'm sorry you got stuck with second best," he teases. "You can call me Remi."

Divine laughs as he releases her. "Actually, Omid wanted me to tell you that I was drawn to him first. I was a little disappointed when I thought you were him." She gives a cute little wince.

I roar with laughter as Remi looks between the two of us. "I'm horrified," he says.

"Don't be. You looked older and my soul knew who Omid was," she says with a smile to soften the blow.

"You were supposed to let it sting," I grumble.

"You're so mean."

"You don't know how these two torture me." I nod toward Remi and Ramses.

The baby shower has just started and all of the guests are coming over to the crystal-covered thrones Divine and I will be sitting in for the afternoon. Divine looks much happier today. For that I'm grateful.

I've been toying with the idea of a practice on the East Coast. Seeing how much Divine cherishes her friends here in New York, it may be something I toss around in the future. Who knows?

Ramses pushes at my shoulder. "We had to make you tough. Give you thick skin."

"If you say so." I snort.

"I hope you forgive me for misleading you," Remi says.

"I understand." She lifts her shoulders and raises her hands.

I wrap an arm around her, pulling her into my side and kissing the top of her head. Remi and Ramses watch the two of us, doing that twin thing. Each of their heads tilted slightly as they study us.

"This was worth it," Ramses says to no one in particular.

I look down at Divine. "Yes, it was."

I may not have been on the front line of all that my cousins did to make my life happen for me, but I appreciate it all. I owe them so much. I kiss Divine's lips, feeling humbled and honored to have her in my life.

"So you have guests?" Remi says.

Divine stiffens in my hold. I hate that the mention of my parents causes her so much tension. I'm not looking forward to returning in the morning. I don't know what awaits me.

I was happy to have Anne Sassa follow us to New York. She and Divine have been able to get to know each other. I think I even see a bond forming within the short time we've been here. Sassa is genuinely happy for us.

"I do."

"Have they found out about the practice?"

"Not that I know of," I say tightly.

Remi purses his lips before he speaks. "Rest assured you won't have any issues as far as your family is concerned."

"As for your career. We're leaving that up to you. We didn't want to expose you so it wasn't brought up. I truly think you should sit with your baba and have a conversation."

I nod. It's my only and final response on the matter. This is meant to be a happy occasion. I don't want to worry about any of this until we return home.

"Well, here are my gifts," Remi says, pulling an envelope and gift-wrapped box from his jacket pocket.

"Oh, I think the gifts are supposed to go on that table," Divine says.

I kiss her temple. "Not this."

She looks up at me then takes the offerings before retrieving similar gifts from Ramses. I smile at the look of confusion and curiosity on her face. I wink at her.

I already know they have both given her monetary gifts and jewelry. The same as I presented at their showers. Their gifts for the babies have already been placed with the others. These gifts are for her.

"*Tebrikler kuzen*," they give their congratulations at the same time and turn to allow the next guests a chance to come and greet us.

Brad and Tam are locked in an animated conversation with Nico and Reese, giving me a chance to focus on Divine for a moment. I take the gifts and set them aside before I turn back to search her face as she looks up at me. She has a mischievous smile on her lips.

"What?" I ask dipping in for a quick kiss.

"Nothing," she sings and shakes her head.

"I know that look. What's going on in your head?"

She turns in my arms and places her hands on my chest. Her eyes are sparkling giving a further indication that she's much happier today. I brush a lock of hair off her face.

"This is my life," she says shaking her head. "I look around at all these successful people and they're my friends. I break bread with these women. I'm cool with their husbands.

"You're used to wealth. I'm new to this level. It's…surreal. I started my business with next to nothing. Now look."

"We're all just people. Money changes nothing. It's just something we have an abundance of. It doesn't alter who we are at heart."

"I see that now," she muses. "We're just a few months away from meeting our little ones. Your friends have gone out of their way to make this special for me. I mean, some of them came in from all over the world. I can't find it in me to be mad that this room isn't filled with my own family."

I tighten my hold around her waist. I'm glad she's happy but I wish I could tell her that her family hasn't forgotten her. It's the reason we have to leave in the morning. They're throwing her another baby shower tomorrow evening when we return.

"Remember, our friends. You and our children are very loved and cherished."

"Yeah, I think we are. I'm sorry I didn't listen to your words and receive your actions. I was scared. I'll admit that now. The thought of losing you, having to do this on my own. Not knowing if everything would change—"

I silence her with my lips. "You don't have to worry about any of that and you don't have to apologize. It was a human reaction. Let's enjoy this."

"*Fai una bella coppia*," Nico croons drawing our attention.

"*Grazie,*" I reply. "Nico and Reese, this is my wife, Divine. Divine, this is Uri's brother Nico and his wife Reese."

"My husband is right, you two make such a beautiful couple. It's so nice to finally meet you. The girls talk about you all the time."

"Thank you. It's nice to meet you as well."

"Can I say that I love your make-up. Val hipped me to it and I'm hooked. I love that feeling of not having any on but still having that polished look and glow. You have a costumer for life," Reese says.

Divine lights up. My chest swells. I'm so proud of my wife. Every time I hear someone tell her how great her makeup is and how much they love her products, I can't help but be amazed by her.

"Oh, thank you so much. You just made my day."

"Tell me," Nico says. "How did the doc here end up with such a talented and beautiful wife?"

"You know, I keep wondering the same thing," Divine taunts, nudging me in the ribs. "I swore I wasn't dating. Now look at me."

We laugh just as Val's voice comes over the speakers. "Okay everyone it's time for a few games," she says with mischief in her voice. "Fellas, you're up first." A collective groan fills the room

as Val cackles over the mic. "Have a seat, Divine. This is about
to get good."

Divine

I haven't laughed this hard in my life. I think I've come close to
peeing my pants more than once. Watching all of these big
gorgeous men play these baby shower games has made my life.

First was the bottle sucking contest. Ryan Black won that
one. The jokes from his brothers after his victory alone had me
in tears.

"I'm not surprised he won," Wyatt said. "He spends all his
time sucking on tits."

"Best times of my life," Ryan shot back.

"Best way to shut him up," Noah grumbled.

Braxton popped Ryan in the back of the head and ducked
before Ryan could slug him. "I'm sure he found a way to cheat,"
Braxton accused. "He'd have to stop eye fucking his girl long
enough to suck anything down."

They went on for another good two minutes before their
women had to collect them. The fun times continued with the
egg race. They guys had to blow up balloons and wear them
under their shirts while racing to get the egg between their knees
into a waiting jar.

Imagine a room full of fine ass men, over six feet tall with
pregnant balloon bellies racing with eggs between their knees. I
thought that was the best part of the day. Not only was it funny,
but Omid won. However, I was wrong. The humor had just
begun.

As if watching the guys try to tie their shoes with a balloon under their shirts wasn't funny enough. I'm in tears watching them all play baby delivery. The first guy to get the balloon from under his shirt without using his hands wins.

"Go head, Noah," Tasha cheers as he leans back and starts to dance the balloon loose.

His arms are flailing at his sides as he leans back and wiggles the top of his body. I lift a brow. He looks like he would have some serious moves out on the dance floor.

I turn my attention to some of the other guys trying to figure this out. It just gets funnier by the minute. All of the women in the room are doubled over in laughter.

"Oh my God, I can't." I laugh. "Look at Brad. Is he dropping it low?"

"Girl," Val laughs beside me. "Will you look at my husband. Does he think glaring at it is going to do something?"

I look over at Uri and sure enough, he has his arms behind his back as he glares down at the balloon beneath his shirt. He rolls his eyes and starts to pace back and forth. More laughter spills free.

"He's too cool for this shit," I burst out, tears streaming down my cheeks.

I look at Nick or at least I think it's Nick. Unless you see Gavin signing, you don't know the difference between the two. He has his arms in the air as he shakes his body.

"Omid looks so perplexed." Paige snorts as she laughs. "Like, I do this for a living. Why can't I get this one out?"

"Please, make it stop. I can't breathe."

Val wraps an arm around my neck and kisses my cheek. "I'm glad you're having fun."

"Thank you. I'm never going to forget this."

Her blue eyes sparkle at me. She looks like a proud big sister. I have a pang in my chest as I think about Patience. I wish she could be here. I wish Marica were here as well. At five months pregnant, learning to walk again hasn't been the easiest. She's frustrated most of the time. Although, I think there's more to it.

Shaking those thoughts off, I focus back on the party just as both Noah and Brad get their balloons out. The room erupts in cheers. Bean runs over to Noah and jumps onto his waist. Brad wraps Tam in his arms and spins her around.

I look around the room at our friends. There's nothing but love in here and it has so many shapes, colors, and sizes. I wish my father could see this. There isn't a couple in this room that doesn't have a story, but the one thing you can be sure of, they have love.

That's what's most important, everything else is just outside noise. I look at Omid and he starts for me with the balloon still under his shirt. He stops in front of the throne I'm sitting in. Leaning over me, he hovers just inches from my lips.

"I want to see you smile like this every day of our lives."

"Is that right, handsome?"

"*Evet aşkım.*"

"In that case, I think I could smile just a little more if you kiss me," I purr.

Without another word he crushes my lips with his. I feel like I'm floating above the room as my toes curl, my scalp tingles and goosebumps race across my skin. If kisses had a language of their own, this one would be whispering of love and forever. It's the kind of kiss that says life is perfect and can only get better from here.

CHAPTER THIRTY-FOUR

Too Early

Divine

I lean into Omid's side as we walk to the front door of our home. I'm tired but I had so much fun. I wish we didn't have to rush back so soon, but I know Omid has to return to work.

"I'll draw you a bath and we can soak together," he says as he unlocks the door.

"Sounds good," I yawn.

He pushes the door open and I walk in first. I stop in my tracks at the sight before me. My tired brain starts to boil. I swear I can feel my blood pressure rising.

"Omid, you've returned," his mother sings while sitting with a full tea set in my home. Having tea with the woman she brought to my door with the intention of marrying off to my husband.

This is his family so up until now I've allowed him to handle things on his own. I left it to him to handle this mess. Now, this level of disrespect. Nah. I'm Janise and Clive Favors child. My fuse is but so short.

"How dare you?" I snap.

"Excuse me?"

I ball my fists at my sides. "Omid made it clear to you this is our home. I'm his wife and I'm the only damn wife he will have. You bringing this woman in my house, under my roof is the most disrespectful and trifling—" I double over in pain. "Omid."

I just barely gasp his name out. I feel like I'm peeing on myself as liquid begins to run down my legs to the porcelain floors. I start to panic. It's too soon. I'm only seven months. This can't be happening.

"Shh, listen to me," Omid commands in a firm voice, accent thicker than usual. "We're going to get you to the hospital. I'm here, Divine. Everything will be okay."

"It's too early," I whimper in pain.

"Twenty-eight weeks is pre-mature but the survival rate is in our favor. I'm one of the best OBs in the State. You and our children will be fine. I need you to calm down."

I nod but another wave of pain hits, knocking me breathless. I close my eyes and start to rock from side to side. Omid takes my hand and I squeeze tightly.

"Something's wrong. I feel so much pressure. Something's not right."

Before the words are out of my mouth, Omid has me lifted into his arms carrying me out to the car. He places me across the back seat as he yells in a mix of Farsi and Turkish for Navid to get us to the hospital. I lift on my elbows as he parts my legs and lifts my dress. He peels away the soaked panties.

"Shit," he bites out. Pulling his phone from his pocket.

"What's wrong?"

He places a hand on my belly and looks me in the eyes. "Baby A is crowning— Yes, this is Dr. V-Shah. I'm coming in with my wife. The membranes have ruptured. She is twenty-eight weeks. Baby A is crowning, we're going to have at least one baby in transit. Be ready with a stretcher and two incubators. Locate Dr. Nobi."

He ends the call and tosses the phone aside. I bite my lip to keep from screaming as pain sears through my abdomen. The urge to push consumes me.

"Good, baby. Just like that. Go ahead and push. I'm right here. Push for me," he says soothingly.

I'm so scared. What if they need medical attention right away? I look toward the front of the car trying to see if I can get a glimpse of where we are. That's when I realize Sassa has climbed in with us. She's looking over the passenger seat nervously.

"*Beklememen gerektiğine emin misin?*" she says to Omid.

"This baby isn't waiting for anyone. I've delivered hundreds of babies. I can handle my own," he says as he keeps his focus on me. "On the next contraction, I want you to give me one more good push, sweetheart. We're about to meet our first little one."

No sooner than the words are out of his mouth, I'm bearing down and pushing with all I have. A tiny little cry fills the car and I feel like I'm breathing for the first time. The look of awe on Omid's face is priceless.

"Praise to Allah. We have a boy," he chokes out, handing me our son to place against my chest.

He's so tiny. I'm almost scared to touch him. "We're here," Navid says as the car comes to a stop.

Everything else happens in a blur. My baby is taken and rushed into the incubator. I'm placed on a stretcher, while Omid barks orders at everyone. He and Dr. Nobi work together as the second baby takes it's time to appear.

"*Bir prenses*," Omid croons when our daughter finally makes her appearance.

"Is she okay?" I ask when she doesn't cry immediately like her brother.

When the blood drains from Omid's face I start to lose it. He rushes the baby to the corner where he works frantically. Dr. Nobi tries to step in but Omid isn't having it.

"No. I have it," he barks.

The nurses move to carry out his orders. My grip on the bedsheets is so tight my fingers hurt. Tears are rolling down my cheeks but I refuse to make a sound.

I feel like I'm looking down on all of this from above. I start to pray like I've never prayed before, berating myself for getting so angry. This is all my fault.

What tears through to my soul is the sob that leaves Omid's mouth at the same time our daughter starts to cry. His knees buckle, but he rights himself and allows Dr. Nobi to step in. Omid stumbles toward me and wraps his arms around my head. He rocks back and forth as he gives thanks in Turkish, repeatedly praising for our daughter's life.

"She's going to be fine," Dr. Nobi says. "Just a little airway obstruction. I'll be monitoring both babies through the night.

Congratulations. Dr. Omid, would you like me to finish up here or—"

"Please, John," Omid chokes out. "I just...I trust you. Thank you."

"No worries. I would've done the same," Dr. Nobi nods.

I'm still speechless. I can't believe what has just happened. I'm exhausted and grateful all at once.

Thank you, God.

Omid

I stand watching my children in their incubators. Reaching into the port, I stroke my little princess's head. She gave me a little scare.

I respect Dr. Nobi and I know he would've done his best for my little girl, but I just went into action. Hearing her cry for the first time will be something I remember for the rest of my life. Taking my hand out, I lower my gown and unbutton my shirt.

I want to hold her skin to skin. I'm ninety-nine percent certain both of my children will leave here healthy. They both weigh in just over three and a half pounds but the prognosis looks promising. I'm a proud baba of a boy and girl.

"You're just as beautiful as your anne," I whisper to her before bringing her to my chest and closing my shirt and gown around her.

I close my eyes and say a few more prayers. I don't even want to think of what triggered Divine's early labor. Navid has been instructed to move my parents to my condo. It's currently unoccupied. They can stay there as long as they like as long as they stay away from my home.

"Look who had the same idea." Dr. Nobi's voice causes me to open my eyes.

Divine is at his side looking tired but beautiful. I sit up but she raises her hand and shakes her head. She ambles over to the chair Nobi offers her. Once she's seated, he retrieves our son and brings him to her. She sits with the baby against her breasts.

"They're so small," she whispers.

"They're strong. They'll be just fine," I reassure her.

"We were still talking about baby names. We never settled on any."

"Now is better than ever."

"I'm going to step out for a bit to let you two have a moment," Nobi offers.

I nod. Turning back to Divine, I watch her with our son. It dawns on me that she has yet to hold our little girl. Getting up, I walk over and place our daughter by her brother. Divine's face glows with happiness.

"Look at them. It's real. They're real. I have two babies."

"So what should we name them?" I ask, kissing her forehead then squatting at her side.

"He was born first so he should get his name first."

"How about Firuz?"

She blinks thoughtfully. "Firuz?"

"Man of triumph. I think it fits him."

She gives me a big smile. "I like it. Firuz Arman Vahid."

"Prince Firuz Arman Vahid." I correct.

Her eyes soften. She looks down at the twins. The love in her gaze is what every precious baby deserves.

"She looks like a...

"Fairuza it's the female version of her brother's name. What do you think?"

"Princess Fairuza Araz Vahid."

"I like," I say and puff my chest out.

I brush a hand over Firuz's tiny hand. I can't express how much love I have for these two. I look up at Divine.

"You've made me the happiest man in the world. You did so good, aşkım."

"Are we going to mention the elephant in the room?"

I tighten my jaw. "When we return home, our little family will be the only ones there."

"What about Sassa? She wanted to be here when the babies were born," she says.

I release some of the tension. My tense jaw softening. The two have hit it off. "She's welcome to stay as long as she likes."

"They're going to be okay, right?" she says in such a small voice. "I'll never forgive myself if something is wrong with them. I just got so mad."

"Shh. Water under the bridge. We're going to focus on getting these two big and strong so we can take them home."

"How long will that take?"

"We'll have to see, sweetheart. It will be a few weeks most likely. Maybe two to three weeks before your due date. It all depends on them."

"These tubes," she says with trembling lips.

"They'll be gone as soon as they can eat and breathe on their own. About six weeks."

"Six weeks?" Her shoulders sag.

"It will be fine. I promise. You can pump for them to still receive your breast milk. They can have it through the OG."

She looks up at me with so much confidence in my words. "Okay."

"Let's get them some music. I've been working with playing music for my preemies. They react to different sounds and frequencies to heal and get stronger faster. It's one of the studies I've been working on," I say.

"My brilliant husband," she smiles.

"My amazing wife. Love you."

CHAPTER THIRTY-FIVE

Gifts of a Prince

Omid

I ordered these gifts for Divine the moment she reentered my life. When I found out that she was pregnant I doubled the order and paid a ridiculous amount of money to have them both ready at the same time. I had planned to give her both at the baby shower here in California.

I rub my hands together as I wait for Divine to come out of the house. We're on our way to pick our twins up to bring them home. It's been seven weeks. Dr. Nobi has cleared them both to be released from the hospital.

I'm vibrating with excitement. The babies, Divine's gifts, I'm brimming with joy and anticipation. The twins have been making improvements with each day. Firuz is seven pounds now and Fairuza is seven pounds and five ounces.

"Omid, babe, I'm ready. I'm just trying to get this email out," Divine says as she comes out of the front door looking down at the device in her hand.

My lips turn up at the sight of her. She looks amazing in a pair of black high waisted pants and a blue blouse. Her hair is piled on top of her head in a topknot showing off that gorgeous face. She's as sexy as ever.

When I don't respond she looks up at me standing in the driveway. Standing between a Bentley, Continental GT and a Bentley, Mulsanne. Both custom blue and black cars to match her Gossip logo. The iridescence of the paint causing them to shine and sparkle in the sunlight.

"Holy shit," she gasps, her mouth falling open. "His and her cars, Omid?"

"No, both belong to you. A late wedding gift and a push gift. I've been waiting for them to come in since I ordered both custom."

"For me," she whispers.

I hold my arms open for her to come to me. She moves forward into my embrace. I hold her tightly and kiss the top of her head.

I grin down at her when Navid turns on the music on queue. With two babies in the house, I don't know when we'll get to have a small moment like this again. I hold her in my arms and start to dance with her in the driveway of our home.

"Both for you. It's the least I can offer to thank you for being my wife and the mother of my beautiful children."

She looks up at me through wet lashes. "Just when I think I couldn't love you more you go and do something that makes me fall in love with you all over again."

I kiss her lips and savor her. I love this woman so much it aches to be away from her. The passion I have for her knows no bounds.

We sway to the music as we get lost in each other. This is one of those moments I want to last forever. If I could capture it and put it on display, I would in a heartbeat. Like a snow globe of our most precious moments.

"I have to give you cars more often," I say when I break the kiss and pull my tongue from her sucking mouth.

"It's not the cars. Those are amazing and beautiful gifts, but it's *this*. There may not be any stars, but the dancing. It's what you promised. Us always remembering *this*. We're bringing our little babies home. I'm terrified and overwhelmed but you just managed to take that all away."

"It's my job to be anything and everything you need."

"I have something you need to be," she gives me a sheepish grin.

"Oh, I'm giving you a few more days rest. You've been at the hospital every day for seven weeks. After you get some rest, I'm attending to business."

"That's what I'm talking about," she sings and licks her lips.

I laugh and slap her ass. I go to tell her to experience her new cars before we leave but her phone buzzes. She looks down at it and sadness covers her face.

"What's wrong?"

She lifts her shoulders then lets them fall heavily. "It's Marica. I promised her we'd do this baby thing together but it's like she's pushing me away. I don't know what to do."

"Marica has a lot on her plate. I'm sure it's nothing personal."

"I just don't want her doing this alone and the more I try to help the more she tells me she's fine."

"She has help. Actually, I think they're helping each other. Give it time. I think she's still figuring things out for herself. The accident was unexpected and changed a lot in her life. She knows you're here for her," I reassure her.

"Speaking of which. What's all that about? What's going on with them?"

"Not my business."

She purses her lips at me. I peck her nose. I learned a long time ago that you have to let adults find their own way. I'm not about to start meddling in anyone's business. I have a home of my own to run.

"You know more than you're saying."

"I know I'm going to the hospital to pick up my son and daughter. My wife can come with me if she likes," I croon and start for the car Navid placed the car seats in.

Divine grumbles to herself as she follows me. I open her door and kiss her cheek before she gets in. She rolls her eyes but I know she won't be mad for long.

Divine can never stay mad at me more than a few seconds. When I get into the driver's side, I reach for her hand and lace our fingers together. She looks at me, her face still a little pinched.

I give her a crooked smile. "Let's go get our prince and princess."

Her entire face lights up. She gives my hands a squeeze. Just as I thought, her anger has melted away.

"Let's go get our future."

Divine

They're finally home. I can't believe it. I look down at them on the changing table kicking they're little legs, smiles on their little faces. It blows my mind how big they've gotten and how far they've come in just a few weeks. From being so tiny, I was afraid to touch them, to being two healthy little babies.

"I need to check what I'm eating. You two are tearing it up. Phew. Little stinky butts," I coo.

They both blow bubbles at me. So stinking cute. Heads full of dark hair and cute little cheeks. Their eye and skin color are a mystery still. They have a dark gray eyes so far, the shell of their ears are colored a deep brown leaving me guessing that they'll take more after me.

I snicker as the thought crosses my mind. My in-laws aren't going to be happy with that. Well, with the exception of Sassa. She loves the twins to pieces.

My mother has been to the hospital as much as she can as well. Things have been a little tense but I'd never keep her from her grandchildren.

"Girl, that man bought you two cars?" I turn to find my mother standing in the nursery doorway.

"I was just thinking about you."

She gives me a side glance. "It better be good things."

I give her a smile. It's good to hear the teasing in her voice. "Just thinking of how much I wished you were here," I say to keep a light mood.

"I had a time finding this place at first. I can't believe it's the first time I'm coming here."

"About that. Is Daddy okay with it?"

She frowns. "At this point, I don't give a damn. I'm not missing out on anymore of your life or these babies' lives. Clive is going to have to work through his own demons. I'm not losing my baby because he's set on being bullheaded."

Her words are like a balm to my heart. She moves closer, placing a hand on my back. "I'm proud of you. Your husband is so happy. He speaks of you like a goddess that just granted him his greatest wish."

"I love him. He's not the man Daddy thinks he is."

She brushes a hand over my hair. "I know, honey. I have eyes. Sassa is sweet. I like her."

"She is."

"Look at you two," she coos at the babies as I finish up getting them into their new diapers. "Do you need any help? Omid just had to rush out to the hospital."

I groan. This is going to be a challenge. He can't take any more time. With the babies coming earlier and so much going on at the practice, it's just not possible. I understand, but I know it's going to be taxing. Sassa offered to help out when Omid started to talk about hiring a nanny.

I reach for my phone and sure enough he texted me that he had to get to the hospital ASAP. I think of how he took care of me and pray he gets there for the baby and mother who need him. I put the phone down and pick Firuz up as he starts to cry.

"I'm going to put them down for a nap if I can. They've been fed and changed," I say.

"No problem," she sings as she picks up her granddaughter. "I just love the smell of fresh babies."

"You should've arrived a few seconds earlier. These two can stink the place up fast." I snicker.

"Sounds like a little girl I used to know."

I stick my tongue out. We work to get both babies settled in silence. When both are in the crib and the monitor is turned on we tiptoe out of the room.

"You hungry?" I ask as we walk toward the kitchen.

"I could eat something."

Once in the kitchen, I make us both a little salad and sandwiches to go with it. I laugh to myself when my mother finds her way into my refrigerator retrieving lemons to make lemonade. Omid is going to love that. My mom makes the best lemonade in the world.

I know the moment she's going to dig into the uncomfortable topic of my dad. I shift in my seat and pick at my salad. I wish there was a way to avoid this.

"I love your father, but he's been through a lot that has jaded him on so many things in the world. Your grandmother was Muslim before she married your grandfather. Her first husband abused her and from what I've heard the religion.

"Later your grandmother married your grandfather and your dad grew up hearing how Islam was the devil. He was taught everything negative there is to think about it," she starts.

I go to interrupt, but she holds up her hand for me to let her finish. I nod. She continues, her features taking on deep sorrow.

"Despite all of that your auntie Lorrain decided to follow the practices of Islam and married a Muslim man. He already had two wives he brought over from Egypt. To me, he was a nice man. I think a mixture of your aunt's upbringing and her lack of understanding what she signed up for were the problem.

"She didn't get along with the other wives and his family wasn't that welcoming either. She was a younger black girl and they were Arabic.

"She became severely depressed. She had a mental break and spent some time in a treatment center. Her husband divorced her." She pauses and purses her lips.

"Again, to me he was doing the right thing by her. Setting her free. He truly did care for her. To your father and Uncle, well, they saw things differently. It drove a bitter conviction home.

"Your Grandfather harped on having respect for women, being a man to your wife. Your aunt never truly recovered from all of it and your father blamed the religion and her husband," she says as I pick at my food.

"But why blow up at me and act like this?"

"Divine, you're your father's baby. He's so proud of you. You could get away with anything you want and that man would turn a blind eye but to watch you suffer like his sister did…that would kill him. All he heard when you brought that man home was Islam and wives. Case closed. That's not something he could swallow."

"But that's not the case."

"I know that, honey. I pray every night that he'll wake up and see it too. I know he will. Omid is such a sweet man. Do you know he's been calling me? When your ass got all stubborn, he took it upon himself to pull me to the side to exchange numbers.

"We were throwing you a baby shower the night you returned from New York, but you went into labor." She smiles, reaching to pat my hand.

I sit with all she just said. I can see my father being upset when she puts it that way. It all starts to fall into place. His years of fussing about Islam. His reaction to Omid. I think I get it now.

It doesn't excuse the behavior but it gives me context for it. My dad loves his siblings. I can see why this would leave a sore spot. My aunt has always been a little odd to me. Now I understand.

"What should I do?"

"Give your father time. He misses you something awful. You should've seen the pout on his face when he found out the babies were coming home.

"It's killing him more not to be a part of your life. He's going to cave soon. I've walked in on him going through your baby albums a few times," she snickers. "Stubborn ass man. I'm working on him, Divine. Just give it a little more time."

I blow out a breath. My dad is a tough nut to crack when he's set in his way. It's why I haven't tried to force Omid on him. I know that for now it will only make things worse. Like throwing fuel on a flame.

I'm not trying to cause a war. I just want to get through to him. "Okay. Mommy?"

"Yes, baby."

"I'm sorry. I should've been—"

"You're your father's child. Both stubborn as hell. I've chalked this one up to that big ass head you got from your daddy."

My mouth pops open. "No, you didn't."

"I sure did," she laughs. "I love you, child."

"I love you too, Mommy."

CHAPTER THIRTY-SIX

Happy in Love

Omid

"Omid," she gasps as I lick her inner thigh.

It's 3:00 in the morning. I haven't seen my wife in hours. I know she needs these few hours of rest before the twins wake demanding food and a diaper change but I'm being selfish.

"I love you," I murmur against her skin.

I move to her core now that she's fully awake. I'll never grow tired of the scent, sight, and taste of her pussy. My mouth waters. I've wanted this for weeks. I keep my attention on her clit with my tongue. My thumb teasing her folds.

She bows her back off the bed, twisting from side to side. I grasp her thighs and pin her down. I start to feast on her pussy lips. Flattening my tongue to her clit, I apply the right amount of pressure to send her juices rushing.

I reach for her center again and find her nice and slick for me. Pushing two fingers inside her, I start to kiss my way up the center of her body. I pause at her torso to kiss and lick her smooth skin.

I already miss the twins living inside her. We'll have to do something about that. I glide my hand up her sides as I suck a patch of skin into my mouth.

She plants a foot into the mattress and lifts her hips into me. "Please."

I slap her ass. "It's coming. Don't rush me. I know exactly how I want this pussy, you wait for it."

She glares at me and I stare back at her. Dragging my tongue to her nipple, I end the evil looks she's sending me. I suck her nipple into my mouth and pull hard. Her milk squirts into my mouth, I growl.

She feeds my children with these lush breasts. Her gorgeous body housed the two most precious people in my life besides her. Not able to ignore the call of her pussy any longer, I line up with her entrance and slide into her warmth.

"Yes," she pants. "God, yes."

"Damn, I miss this," I groan.

I rock into her slowly, letting my heavy cock drag in and out of her heat nice and slow. Planting one hand by her head, I use the other to grasp her ass. It's all I can do to ground myself. My feet dig into the mattress. Her juices soak me as I drive deeper.

It's so good, I have to clench my teeth to force my climax back. She claws down my back, rocking her hips up to meet mine. When she starts to slow whine her hips, I throw my head back.

"Fuck," I bite out.

Grabbing the backs of her thighs, I push her legs back into her chest. Looking down our bodies at where we're connected, I switch angles and thrust into her. I pull out and rock through her folds, dragging across her nub.

"Omid, please," she gasps.

I turn her onto her stomach, straddling her hips. Grasping one ass cheek, I slide into her from behind. I have her pinned down to the bed as I start to pound into her.

"Shit, this pussy is so good. Quiet, Divine. You wake the babies this ends," I grunt. She continues to cry out. "I said be quiet and take this fucking dick."

She grabs the sheets and turns her head to bury the sound of her cries. She starts to punch the bed as I roll and rock into her. I flatten my chest to her back and lean into her ear.

"You miss that cock? You want this cum inside you?" I lick her ear. "Answer me."

"Yes," she gasps as she lifts her head.

"Yes. Yes, you miss this cock? Or yes, you're ready to take my cum inside this hot pussy?"

"Both. I miss you so much."

I slide a hand between the bed and her body, reaching for her button. I play her body like a master. Her walls tightening around me call for my seed. It's not going to end so fast. I'm too starved.

I pull out and go back to teasing her sweet pussy with my tongue. Lifting her ass in the air, I torture us both. Three hard slaps to her ass have her crying out into the bed. I move to thrust back into her, placing a thumb at her puckered hole.

I slide my hand over the sweat dewing on her back. Cupping her breast, I guide her body back onto my cock. Watching the bounce of her fat ass with each thrust, I salivate to have more.

I'm greedy for her hungry pussy that's already grasping me so tight my eyes roll back.

I dip to lick up the center of her back. She shivers and quakes. I love that she still responds to me every single time I'm in this tight haven.

"You feel how hard you make me? This is why you're always on my mind. Yes, throw that ass on me. Fuck your husband, baby. Soak my cock like my good girl. Shit," I hiss.

"Omid, please let me come," she whimpers knowing I'm holding her just outside the reach of her orgasm.

"No."

"Please," she pleads.

"No. I'm going to wear this pussy out. I've been without you too long. I need you. You're not coming, not yet."

She answers with making her ass clap on my dripping wet cock. I clench my teeth, lifting to my feet in a squatting position and drilling into her lush pussy. She screams into the bed. I smile with glee. Altering cheeks, I slap her ass.

She's coiled so tight but I'm avoiding the strokes to her spot. When I pull that trigger, I want us to be face to face. This is just me priming the pump. I want her dizzy with pleasure when I make her explode.

"Shit, I want to look into her eyes when you come. Come ride this dick," I command.

Divine

I've woken up to a straight savage. It seems like it's been forever since he has touched me like this. I guess he's reminding me of the beast he is in the sheets.

He pulls out and sits in the center of the bed. He folds his legs as if sitting in a yoga pose. I straddle him and he guides me onto his length. I plant my feet while he guides me up and down on him.

Our eyes lock and start a conversation only we understand the words to. I shriek when he takes my waist and shifts my weight back as he does all the work of lifting me up and down. I wrap my hands behind his neck and hold on tight. The strength in this man floors me.

"I love you," I pant.

"Without question, I love you, Divine," he says huskily.

He leans in to lick the side of my breast. Shifting our position again, he adjusts me until I'm on my knees bouncing and rocking on him. To think, I was exhausted when I passed out. Now, I feel like I could go for hours of this.

I let my gaze fall to his tight body and olive skin. Damn, my husband is sexy as hell. Looking into his eyes again, I watch him watching me. His almost colorless eyes absorbing me. I feel like he sees things no one else does.

I start to kiss all over his face. He takes my lips and makes my mouth his own feast. My essence flavors his tongue. When I suck on it, he groans and hardens inside me. I didn't think he could get any harder.

I moan and swirl my hips on him. His nails bite into my skin as he drags them down my back. He lifts his hips propelling me backward. I land on my back as he unfolds his legs. We're nose to nose as he takes over.

Locking my legs around his waist, I cradle him. He laces our fingers together, never breaking the kiss. His slick chest to my sweaty one, his heart pounds against mine.

He moves to nuzzle my neck. I'm reaching a fever pitch. I don't know if I'm going to make it through this torture.

"Omid," I beg.

He looks down into my eyes, licking my lips then pecking them gently. "Come with me."

He starts to thrust just right. The man is hands-down a master of pussy. I start to convulse, every nerve in my body feels alive. When his hot seed rushes my walls, painting them with his life force, I come so hard my sinuses burn.

"Holy shit," I cry out.

He captures my mouth in a slow tender kiss. I free one of my hands from his to run it up and down his back. When he shivers, I smile against his lips.

"I'll feed them when they wake. You earned your rest," he laughs quietly.

"Always a pleasure, Dr. Feel Good." I giggle.

"Go to sleep, you're delirious."

That I just might be. That was some damn good dick. I'm not even mad he woke me.

CHAPTER THIRTY-SEVEN

Snapped

Divine

I'm nervous. This is the first time both of our families are getting together. It's my birthday.

When Omid's father reached out to him for the hundredth time I told my husband it was time we both faced our fathers. This just seemed like the right time to do it. A dinner where everyone could be on neutral ground.

At least I thought it was a good idea. Now I'm not so sure. The tension around the room is thick. We chose Nick and Kevin's restaurant where we had our first date. The private room is large enough for both of our families to fit into—even though Kevin closed the rest of the restaurant to focus on our party anyway.

"Look at this face," Patience coos at my son.

She holds him in the air as she fusses over him, causing him to smile and drool on her. She had to nearly pry him away from Lance, after Neil held my son hostage first.

It's been a few months since the babies have been home and they get so much love and attention. My siblings plan to spoil my children. I see it already.

I look around and feel a little sad Marica couldn't join us. Her son made his appearance last week. I'm so happy for her and little Keith.

"They're both so adorable," Brandy says.

"Thank you."

I look over at my father who hasn't stopped glaring at my husband. "Would you like to hold her, Daddy?"

He looks at Fairuza and his eyes soften. The look of longing hurts my heart. This doesn't have to be so hard.

When he doesn't answer, I get up and walk my daughter over to him. "Thank you," he murmurs once she's in his arms.

I nod and return to my seat. Omid wraps an arm around me and kisses my temple. I place a hand on his thigh and squeeze.

"We'll need to find something to eat later," Omid's mother says.

"What's wrong with the food here?" he asks.

"I doubt it's Halal. Not everyone is so lax in honoring our beliefs."

Omid's jaw tightens. "Why would I invite you somewhere that you couldn't eat? The meal was prepared for everyone. My friends have gone above and beyond to accommodate us *all* this evening."

"Thank you," Omid's father says. "Divine, you're a business woman, yes?"

"Yes. She is," my husband snaps.

I squeeze his thigh to calm him. He shifts in his seat. His agitation clear.

"My daughter does very well for herself," my father speaks up. "She's built her company with her own two hands and made her *own* millions."

"Smart girl. Intelligence is a great asset." Javed nods.

"Omid is a smart man when he wants to be," his mother says. "Although, I'd like to understand his profession. I'm confused—"

"About what?" Omid bites out. "I'm an OB/GYN. I deliver babies and take care of women's health. What's there to be confused about?"

"How does that work? Isn't that against your religion?" my father chooses now to speak up.

If looks could kill, my mama just gave my father the look of death. He grumbles something to himself and turns back to the baby. Omid leaves his words unanswered.

The tension in the room goes to a thousand. I can see the uncomfortable looks on all of his family's faces. Yup, this here was a very bad idea.

He starts to bounce his leg and I'm not sure how much longer his temper will remain under wraps. The babies both start to cry bringing a much need reprieve.

"Come, come to your, *büyük baba*," Omid's father says to Firuz.

Patience hands my son over, he gives his grandfather a once over before he settles. I hand bottles to my father and Javed. Soon the twins are sucking down milk happily.

"See, büyük babas have magic," Javed croons, bringing a smile to my lips. I look around the room to see that's not the case with everyone.

I'm sorry. I just don't know any other way to put it. I don't like Paiman. Omid's brother rubs me all the wrong ways. I don't like the way he looks at me and I don't like the glare on his face as he watches his father hold my child. I start to bristle, no longer the calming force in the room.

When I see Hana with a similar glare, I start to get real pissed off. Omid's hand on my side starts to rub up and down soothingly. I roll my eyes and turn away from them.

Luckily the food arrives. Everyone occupies themselves with eating. Javed ignores his food to play with Firuz. While my father jiggles eating and my daughter like an old pro.

"This is delicious," my mother says.

"Yes, it's very good," Sassa chimes in.

"America seems to be agreeing with you," Hana tosses the snide remark at Sassa.

Omid heaves a heavy breath. His patience is nearly spent. I know it.

I snort when I look at Paiman's fat ass acting like he doesn't want to inhale the food on his plate. His wife sits beside him looking like she's thinking the same thing or reading my mind. She shakes her head and continues to eat her food.

"I tend not to take issue with life," Sassa replies. "As such, I can find happiness in many things and places."

I want to high five her and fist pump at the same time. Hana shoots daggers at her with her eyes. I cover my mouth and laugh. Omid bumps my leg with his.

"That shit is hilarious," he leans to whisper in my ear. "You see why I love her."

I nod my head as a snort slips free. I glance at my family and they're holding back their own laughter. Even my dad has mirth in his eyes.

"Omid, he reminds me of you when you were this small," Javed booms as if his wives aren't having a little catfight at the dinner table. "He will have your eyes."

Hana scoffs. "I doubt that. He was not that dark. Gulzar would have given him beautiful Iranian babies."

I'm ready to get in this bitch's ass. Before I can Omid does a damn good job for me. I mean, he takes everyone by surprise.

Omid

My glass is half to mouth when my mother makes her disgusting remark about my child. I stand so fast my chair falls back. I toss the glass in my hand across the room. It hits the wall and shatters.

"*Aklını mı kaçırdın?* You must have lost it. What the fuck is wrong with you? Is it not enough you're the reason my wife went into early labor. Are you trying to give me a fucking stroke now?"

"Omid," she gasps.

"Don't *Omid* me. You make my head want to explode. Listen to me and hear me. Don't fucking disrespect my wife and children again. Don't mention another woman in front of her, don't insinuate that I'll take another wife, don't compare her to women that will never amount to half of who she is, don't breathe a damn word that makes her feel like less than the princess she is.

"In a span of months, Divine is more of a mother than you have ever been to me. I love this woman and my children with everything I am. I'd bleed for them." I pound at my chest.

"You come here not knowing a thing about me or her. This woman built her own business off of three dollars. She's running that business, raising my children, and every night she still has a smile on her face asking how she can please me?

"Not intimately, but mentally. She listens to what I'm saying, to where I want to go in life, what I want to do. She respects my choices." I pound my fist on the table.

"Omid," my father tries.

I turn my glare on him. I'm not done. My ears are on fire.

"*No*. Why are you here, Baba? To tell me I disgraced you? Guess what? I don't give a fuck. I'm one of the best in my field.

"I've developed medications that have helped women." I lift my hands. "I use these hands to help bring life into this world. Allah is always with me. My survival rate is impeccable.

"Twenty years! I loved and waited for this woman for twenty years. She has always been and will always be the only woman for me." I turn to Mr. Favors.

"How many wives does my father have? Three. How many will I have? One. What religion do I practice? I practice Islam and will teach my children the teachings of Allah, but their mother will also teach them her beliefs because her god has answered her praises just as mine has.

"Make no mistakes. When my daughter was born and wasn't breathing, it was the prayers I prayed mixed with the ones my wife prayed that gave me the strength to focus and be my wife's motherfucking *everything* to get our little girl breathing.

"That's who I am to her, that's who she is to me. Don't judge me before you get to know me.

"I'm the man that's going to love her with every breath I have. I'm the man that's going to provide everything she needs and makes sure she wants for nothing. I'm the man that's going to walk over the corpse of any man that dares touch her or threaten her life. I know that shit with everything I am." I reach down and grab my wife's hand, pulling her from her seat.

"Everyone in this room take a look and understand this. I am and will always be Prince Omid Arman Vahid and this…this my only wife. The queen of my soul, the fire of my life. Princess Divine Nika Vahid.

"We don't need anyone else's throne, we've built our own. Respect it or don't come around my family. And don't *ever* talk of my children as if they're less or beneath you."

My chest is heaving. I need fresh air. Closing my eyes, I reel it in as much as I can. "Excuse my language." I pull Divine's hand to my lips and kiss it. "I need to step out."

"Omid," Anne Sassa says softly.

"I need a moment to myself. Please, no one follow me."

I tug at my suit jacket and turn to leave the room. I find myself outside the restaurant pacing back and forth. I promised myself I wouldn't lose it.

It's Divine's birthday. She deserves better, which is why I wasn't going to sit there and allow them to keep going with the bullshit.

It's late. The street around the restaurant is quiet. I look up at the sky and close my eyes. I grind my teeth. This could only be my life.

"Such bullshit," I mutter.

Opening my eyes, I shove one hand in my pants pocket and pull the other down my face. I'm so lost in thought, I don't take notice of the man walking toward me until he's right upon me. He thrusts a hand out at me, but I block it and throw a palm into his throat. I'm taken by surprise, still my reflexes are quick.

Someone else grabs my shoulder. I grab their hand and twist it as I turn to face the person. The squealing of tires fills the air as I continue to fight off the two men trying to attack me.

All I can think about are my wife and children inside. I will not be mugged or murdered on this street. I kick out and snap the leg of one. He cries out and crumbles to the ground.

Throwing an elbow at the face of the other, I dance away from him. It's then that the doors of a van open and four more men jump out. Realization hits. This isn't a random robbery.

If my father is behind this I'm going to flatten his entire world. With renewed strength, I keep fighting. That's until someone pricks me in the neck. I stumble to the side and my vision blurs. Someone throws something over my head as I start to fall forward.

No. I try to roar the word but nothing comes out.

CHAPTER THIRTY-EIGHT

Trusted Help

Divine

"Did that boy just talk to me like that?" my father says.

I palm my face and place my elbows on the table. My head is spinning. I don't know whether to laugh or cry.

"Man, Daddy, you deserved that. You asked him all them questions the first time you met him but you never gave him a chance to answer. Told you then you were wrong," Patience chides.

"Javed, this has gotten out of control. You need to do something about this," Hana says.

I scoff. She's still at it. I lift my head to see Javed glaring at her.

"Enough," he barks. "I've lost years with my son to make you happy. He doesn't want the life you're trying to force on him. Stop your meddling. Do you not see the beautiful grandchildren you're costing us? I won't have it. Shut your mouth. Don't say another word."

"About time," my mother mutters.

The table erupts into chatter. My mother gives my father a piece of her mind. Javed barks orders of who he's sending back to Iran without him.

Meanwhile, I get this feeling in my stomach. Something isn't right. The nagging feeling just grows with each second that passes.

I know Omid wanted to be alone, but I can't sit here any longer with this sense of dread clawing at me. Seeing that the twins are safe and watching the uproar around them like a soap opera, I push back from the table. Standing, I grab my cell phone.

When I start out of the private room, I take notice of the commotion going on outside the restaurant. I pick up the pace, going from a walk to a run. When I push out of the front doors, Kevin catches me around the waist gently pushing me back.

"Go back inside," he commands.

"What's going on? Where's Omid?"

He places his hands on my shoulders and levels his hazel-green eyes with my brown ones. "Please, Divine. We're handling it."

My heart is pounding. I try to side step him but he moves with me. Frustrated, I return my gaze to his and ball my fists at my sides.

"Handling what? Where's my husband?" I try to look around him.

"My security cams have footage of him being abducted. We're on it," he says calmly.

"What?" I gasp. "You're a chef. What do you mean you're on it? Call the police."

He shakes his head. "That's not going to help. Nothing is ever as it seems around here, Divine. I'm more than just a chef. Trust me."

His words ring in my head. I know who I trust. I know in my gut who will find my husband and return him to me safe. I pull my phone and call the one number I never thought I would have to.

I hold my breath while the phone rings. "Hello."

"Hello, Uri," I say when he picks up. "Please, I need your help. Someone has taken Omid."

CHAPTER THIRTY-NINE

Black on Black

Val

With all of our children and busy schedules we have to spend our late nights training and honing our skills. When we can turn it into sexy time too, it's a win-win. Eyes on Uri as he stares at my breasts heaving in my sheer bodysuit, I lick my lips and flip backward, tossing out a blade.

He ducks and smiles. Running at me, he throws a left then a right. I weave out of the way, grasping his wrist. He flips the hold, wrapping my wrist in his long fingers instead. Spinning me into his body, my back hits his front. His sweaty chest presses into me, his breath tickles the hairs on my neck.

"What's the matter, Bella Donna? You're getting slow in your old age?" he teases.

He slides his hand over my breast, down my stomach, between my legs. I moan and bite my lip. He pushes aside the fabric and slips his fingers inside.

"No, not slow. Tired of playing. You can't beat me, so just shut up and fuck me," I taunt.

His laugh rumbles through my back, his cock twitching against my ass through his pants. I close my eyes when he pushes his fingers into me. He latches onto my neck sucking. I spread my legs, giving him more access.

He works me like the master he is. My cries fill the workout room just as his phone rings. I stiffen, it's too late for anyone to be calling. Which means it's business and not the good kind.

Uri pulls his fingers from my body, grumbling to himself. He pops the digits in his mouth as he moves to retrieve his phone and answer. "Hello," he answers and listens to the voice on the other end.

I move to the other side of the room, my heels clicking on the floor. Rolling my shoulder, I grab two blades from my leg strap and get ready to throw them at the target.

"Slow down, Divine. Tell me what's going on," Uri says.

Chest heaving with sweat, I pause in my tracks at the mention of her name. I whip around, clenching the blades in my hands. My eyes narrow as I watch Uri listen to her.

"It will be okay. I'm on the way. I will make calls…Don't worry, *mia amica*. I will find him. It is done."

"*Che cos'è?*" I ask, moving to stand in front of him.

"Omid has been abducted outside of Kevin's restaurant," he murmurs as he shoots off texts.

"Excuse me?"

He lifts his eyes to look at me. "I will take care of it."

I slide the knives back into the holster on my thigh and reach for my phone on the table. I start to dial and walk away. I'm coiled tighter than a snake around its prey.

"Morte Nera," Uri calls.

"You know how I feel about her. None of my girls will be without their husbands, Hush. You fuck with my family you get nothing but Morte Nera," I call over my shoulder.

"People are starting to think we're crazy. Can we scale back a bit this time?" I can hear the mirth in his voice. I'm not in the mood.

"No."

He roars with laughter behind me. "We leave in ten. Put on some clothes."

I wave a hand at him and put the phone to my ear. "Hey, Val what's up?" the sleepy voice on the other end says.

"Someone has disrespected me in your city."

"Say no more. What do you need?"

"Wake your husband and his brothers. Find Omid Vahid and when you find him, you keep him safe while you wait for us. Whoever has him answers to me."

"It's the Black Brothers poker night. They're already here. We're on it. See you soon."

She ends the call and I make my next one. "Sim, we're going to L.A."

"Got it. Anything special?"

"I get the feeling I'm going to need you and Michael to do a little something for me."

"Sounds doable."

She hangs up. I see a text from Tasha letting me know she's getting dressed and will be at the plane. No doubt Uri called LaSalle.

Don't worry, sis. Your husband will be home soon. Only one meeting their maker is the motherfucker that took him.

Wyatt

"You're always cheating," Brax grunts at Ryan, tossing popcorn at him.

Poker night has become the new thing since going to the bar is less our speed these days. Occasionally, we'll go for drinks at some lounge type bar to kick back but this is where it's at.

Glancing around at my brothers, I can't help grinning. I'm proud of them all. They've all gotten their shit together and are happy.

"It's not my fault you suck," Ryan shoots back at Brax. "You're just mad Heather's going to kick your ass for losing all your money to me."

Braxton flips him the bird. Johnathan tries not to laugh too hard as his daughter lies against his chest fast sleep. My kids have probably taken over my bed trying to sleep up under their mother. I'll be lucky if I can get my cock wet tonight. Nora has found her way into our bed every night this week.

I've been gagging Nelly with her own panties to get quickies in at the office. I shake my head again. Boy has life changed.

I probably scarred my son for life after he walked in on me with his mom cuffed to the bed. Don't have to worry about John's freaky ass teaching that one anything. I still don't know how long my son was standing there.

"What's that look about?" Noah asks me.

"Man, my home is turning into a mad house. I woke up with Evan's foot in my mouth this morning."

"Ha," Noah laughs. "At least it wasn't a little shitty ass."

"Tell me about it. The twins are taking over all free time with all the shit Kamara has them signed up for. I tripped over soccer cleats and soggy swimsuits this morning."

"You don't have anyone to pick that shit up, King Toby?" Brax taunts.

"Fuck you."

Noah snorts. "I'm still asking myself why I keep making babies?"

We all laugh at that. My phone buzzes on the table next to my wrist as I look at my cards. I look down at the text Uri Donati just sent and my blood starts to boil. I toss my cards on the table and start to bark orders to my brothers.

"Just got a text from Kevin," Felix says. "He's sending me the footage from his cams. The more eyes, the faster we can find him."

"Got a text from LaSalle," Toby calls out.

"Boss, just got a call from Val. She wants us to find the Doc."

I look up in time to see Johnathan glaring at his girl. Shit never changes around here. These two will drive you crazy if you let them. I purse my lips.

"Already on it," John says. "You're staying home though."

"Yeah, okay. Sure, babe." I don't know why he thinks she'll ever listen to him. She stands with her phone to her ear, staring at her nails. "Yeah, Cass. I need to drop the kids off for a bit. Great. Thanks."

"Un-fucking-believable," John grumbles.

"No time for it tonight," I snap. "Omid is one of our friends. Let's do this. Find him. Now."

CHAPTER FORTY

The Wrong Man

Omid

I've regained consciousness and I'm livid. I can taste the salt from my blood as I drag my tongue across my busted lip. They haven't removed the sack from my head, probably out of fear. They've fucked up.

I wasn't the target. They've been arguing as they wait for whoever's calling the shots. I remain as calm as I can, hoping someone saw something and help is on the way.

"What the fuck is this?" A new voice growls. He has an Italian accent. "I wanted the wife. Why the fuck is he here?"

They start to explain in Italian what went wrong. "We've been trying to snatch her for weeks. She's never alone. She's either with the big black guy, the old Arab or this one. You said we were out of time. When he appeared alone we grabbed him. Someone is better than no one."

They have to be talking about Terrance and Navid. However, what has me burning with anger is the fact that they were trying to kidnap my wife.

My wife.

"Whoever you are, you've fucked with the wrong man. Do you know who I am?" I scoff. "No, you couldn't. There's no way you would've come for me or my wife if you knew who you were coming for."

"You're a pussy doctor. Why the fuck should we be worried about you?" The newest guy snorts.

I tilt my head and release a deep laugh. Of course. They've kidnapped Dr. O.V-Shah. No one in this room knows they've taken Prince Omid Vahid. If they heard the name Vahid alone they'd piss their pants.

"*Incontrerai la tua morte*," I snarl.

His laugh rings out. "I'll meet my death? You're the one that will pay for not minding your own fucking business. Nobody asked you to stick your nose into shit that has nothing to do with you."

"What the fuck are you talking about?"

"The little bitch in Italy. You're going to stop helping her and her little bastard. Then you're going to call off the search for her husband. He don't need to be found."

My thoughts turns a few times before the young woman in the village in Italy comes to mind. I haven't checked on her in months with everything going on here. I've made sure she gets money and I still have people trying to find her husband.

"Let me guess. You're the husband?"

"We were never married. I faked the marriage. I have a wife and kid here. I needed that little problem to go away. I thought she and the kid wouldn't make it once she started to have trouble. Then here you come, fucking shit up by saving her," he replies.

"Aren't you the world's biggest gentleman."

"Yeah, fuck you too. You can't be so great yourself. The fat Arab that found me had a whole lot to say about your ass," he seethes back.

I sit up at this. My brother comes to mind right way. I won't correct him on the fact that we're not Arab. No, I want him to keep talking about the fat Arab that sent him for my wife.

"You're after my wife for him?"

"Fifty grand to deliver her to him. After that he promised to get you out of my fucking business. Your people meddling and asking questions is bad for business. Bad enough we have to work under the table with this fucking Alliance in play. Whole world has gone to shit," he grumbles.

"Do you know the penalty for touching a member of the Alliance or one connected to them?"

"Those bastards will slaughter any unlucky son of a bitch that goes after…Wait…what do you know about the Alliance?"

"What name did the fat Arab give you? Who did he tell you I am?"

"You're a cunt doctor. Dr. O.V-Shah."

Just as I thought. Paiman sent them to their deaths. No doubt on purpose to cover his tracks. My brother wants the type of power the twins have. He knows what would happen to him and these fucks if they're found out.

"He lied. Or should I say he didn't give you the full truth. My name is Omid Vahid, cousin to Remi and Ramses Vahid. Does that ring a bell?"

Silence fills the air. You could hear a pin drop. The tension that fills the air has me licking my lips. He understands exactly what I'm telling him.

"Ah fuck. *Fuck.* Shit. Fuck, fuck, *fuck.* We need to get the fuck out of here. *Now,*" he bellows.

They start to scramble. Panic and fear takes on a scent. I tug at the ropes around my wrists.

"What about him?"

"Leave him here. We'll make an anonymous call or something when we're far the fuck away from here. Shit. We need to go. Everybody let's go."

I grin with satisfaction. I wish I could see the looks on their face. Uri sat me down in New York and revealed all the things I didn't know. I've always known my cousins were dangerous men. I just didn't know how dangerous until Uri shared the things they've chosen to shield me from. I can't say any of it surprised me.

Remi and Ramses have always been different and lead mysterious lives. They're the type to get things done. I've never asked how.

"What the fuck happened to the lights?" Someone shouts.

"Fuck!"

Arms wrap around me and I go to struggle. "Relax. It's me, Noah. It's about to be a blood bath in here. I'm going to get you out before those two psychos get to work."

I relax and nod as he pulls the sack from my head and unties me. He places night vision glasses on me. I look around me to see Wyatt, Braxton, and Noah with large guns as they surround me.

"Let's move," Wyatt says. We move quickly, heading out the door of the building they held me in.

When we're outside, Lasalle and Tasha stand waiting with their arms folded as if overseeing it all. "It's all yours, Morte Nera. You guys have fun."

Val

We stand outside the old movie studio building waiting for the signal that they have Omid safe and secure. He's been in there long enough. Snipers have been in the rafters, ready to pull the trigger if needed.

I'm glad we waited. The leader of this operation arrived just before those of us from New York arrived. Felix was able to get all the information we needed on him within minutes. He's the one I want.

Wyatt's voice hits my ear giving me the all clear. Morte Nera comes to life, thirsty for blood and revenge. They'll all pay tonight.

"Thanks, Black," I say into the earpiece. "Turn the lights back on. I want them to see their deaths coming."

"You got it," Felix replies.

I look into Uri's eyes and cock my guns one after the other. He nods and we enter the building they were keeping Omid in. I lick my lips and move forward, the taste of death in the air. I can hear their souls whimper with the knowledge that I'm near. I have no remorse. They deserve this.

Head shots, head shots. Fuck with mine I'm coming for your brains. I bob my head to the chant in my head. Uri and I move in sync. He's at my side breathing, moving, and shooting with me. Black death and the Hush that comes with it.

We've warned the world. I don't know why they refuse to listen. We won't come for them if they follow the rules.

Don't fuck with ours.

I'm even kind enough to use infrared tonight. They get a single warning before the end. I think it's courteous of me.

"Behind," Uri says. I move out of the way before he shoots at someone trying to come up behind me.

I nod my thanks. "Let's finish this."

"Done."

I see the one I'm after trying to get away. Uri nods for me to go after him. I wink at my husband and blow him a kiss.

He covers me as I run down the bastard that disrespected the family. Come to find out he's had his hands in shit we've forbidden. The Alliance is firm in its rules. I'm taking this personally. He's been in Italy committing these transgressions. My husband and I won't have it.

"Don't make me chase you," I warn. I toss a blade into his shoulder when he doesn't heed my warning. I send another into the back of his leg. "I guess you have a fucking hearing problem too."

I saunter over to where he has fallen to the ground whimpering. He hasn't begun to know pain. I squat beside him.

Reaching for the blade in his shoulder, I drag it across to the other side opening him from shoulder blade to shoulder blade. My tongue sticking out of the side of my mouth, my lips turn up in a smile.

His screams are the beginning of his penance. Reaching for the knife lodged in his leg, I drag from the crease of his leg down to his ankle. More screams pour from his filthy mouth.

"When I say no selling drugs in my Italian cities, I'm not saying it to hear myself speak. You seem to think I gave you an exception. Or wait, did you think my husband gave you a pass. Baby?" I call out. "Did this piece of shit get a pass from you?"

The gunfire has ceased. They're all dead, save for the two I ordered be held for me. The girls have them.

I plan to send a message. I don't like being disrespected. Doing what you want under my nose is pure disrespect. Touching one of my family members—blood or not—well, you're just asking for it.

"No, Love. I didn't," Uri says calmly.

This piece of shit won't stop screaming in pain. It's getting on my damn nerves. I fire a shot into his hand. That will teach him not to touch things that don't belong to him.

"Shut the fuck up," I snarl. "You were man enough to come for my family. You be man enough to face the consequences."

He clamps his mouth shut, sobbing and sniveling. "I…didn't know. He wanted…me to get…the girl. My guys fucked up…and took the doc. He didn't tell me…the right name. I had no…idea who the doc was. It was…supposed to be…the wife. I…didn't…know."

I tighten my jaw. He's not helping himself. He's sending me further into my rage. They were after Divine. I'm going to finish him and everyone else involved.

I've taken to her like a little sister. She's sweet and innocent, not that I don't think she'd fit into the Bella Mafia. It's just not for her. I'm protective of all my girls but more so of Divine.

"Shame. You should've done your own homework," I say unmoved. "Tell me, who sent you. Give me a name."

"I don't...have one. He was a fat Arab. From the pictures...he gave me...of the doctor they...they look like they could...be related." He takes pause and sobs. "His eyes...were darker. He came to me...gold rings. He wore...gold rings."

I pull the blade in his shoulder down and across his back, causing him to holler. It's the sweetest sound to my ears. Yanking both blades out, I stand and kick him over. He screams as his open wounds hit the concrete floor beneath him.

I look to my husband. "Would you like to hush him or should I?"

Uri rolls his eyes at the incessant screaming and puts a bullet in his head. "I have no patience for this shit anymore."

"I know. That wasn't as fun as it used to be." I shrug my shoulders and clean my blades with the handkerchief he hands me.

"We're getting old," he mumbles.

"Maybe," I say nonchalantly. "The fat bastard dies."

Uri nods. "I'll talk to the twins and Omid. It's their family. If they give the word...it's done."

I mumble to myself. I don't want to ask anyone shit but out of respect I will. He's going to pay for this.

That I promise.

CHAPTER FORTY-ONE

Safe at Home

Divine

I've been pacing for hours. Uri said he'd take care of it. I've been praying that my husband is returned to me without a hair on his head harmed.

Fairuza has been crying nonstop for the last hour. My nerves are so frazzled, I don't know if I should join her or ask someone to watch her so I can go find her father myself. It's not helping that my brothers are sitting in my living room watching me like three bodyguards.

They wanted to go with Kevin to find Omid, but he told them to leave it to the professionals. My head is still spinning with the fact that Kevin heads Nick's security team. He was right, none of Omid's friends are who they seem. I'm hoping that means they will do just what they promise.

"Man, it's been over eight hours. Each hour closes the window on this shit," Nashawn says.

"If you don't shut your ass up," Neil says and pulls a face at him.

"I'm just saying."

I huff. "We know what you're saying. We're saying please stop saying it."

"Whatever," he mumbles.

Lance stands and comes over to me. "Let me see if I can calm her down a bit."

I reluctantly release my daughter. Having her in my arms was one of the things keeping me glued together. I pass a hand over her little head while she wails away.

"Phew, we're going to have to do something about that," Val says drawing all of our attention.

"Well, damn," Nashawn says.

Uri steps up and wraps an arm around her waist. LaSalle holds Tasha at his side as well. However, it's the man standing next to them that has all of my attention. His lip is busted, his hair is a bit disheveled, and his suit jacket is gone but he's here.

The shock wears off and I run into his arms. Omid lifts me from my feet and I lock my legs around his waist. I place my forehead to his.

"Are you okay?"

"I'm fine."

"I called Uri. I didn't know what else to do."

He brushes my lips with his. "You did the right thing. Thank you."

Val clears her throat. "I'm taking my niece and nephew for the day. You two go be grown-ups. Auntie Val has this. You have milk stashed?"

"In the kitchen."

"Great. We'll be back tomorrow."

Val walks over to Lance and plucks Fairuza from his hold. The contrast of Val's Laura Croft getup and her mothering nature should jar me but there's something natural about it. Tasha moves to the playpen for a sleeping Firuz.

"Make it two days. I'll take them next," Tasha says. "We know what it's like. We've been there."

There's a story behind her words and the way she looks at LaSalle. I wonder what happened. These two are such a power couple. They seem so untouchable to me.

Omid nuzzles my neck, pulling my attention from the others. The look of need in his eyes tightens my belly. Something happened while he was away. Something that has shaken him to his core. I can tell.

He places me on my feet. Moving to Val and Tasha, he takes a baby at a time to hug and kiss before returning them to the arms of their protectors. That's who those women are.

I can see that now. They protect their family. I may have called Uri, but I get the feeling Val had a lot to do with my husband's return.

"We'll head out too," Lance says. "Glad you're home safe, homie."

I get a little choked up when each of my brothers hug Omid, one by one. This is a big step forward. I hope that all of my family can learn to be accepting of my husband. Mostly meaning my dad.

We see everyone out and Omid turns to me. I'm against the door before I can register he's about to move. I wrap my legs around him and lock my fingers in his hair. I try to be careful of his lip but he doesn't seem to care.

His kiss is different. It's…desperate. Almost like he's kissing me for what could be the last time. He pulls away from the door and starts to move through the house.

We end up in the master bathroom. He steps from his shoes and walks us into the shower fully clothed. He reaches to turn on the water while kissing his way down my neck.

"Baby, what happened? What's wrong?" I gasp as his feverish touch drives me crazy.

"I need you." He gives the simple reply, nothing more.

I nod and reach for the hem of my shirt, pulling it over my head. He works on the leggings I put on when I arrived home and spent an hour just trying to find things to do with myself. He drops to his knees, just barely allowing my feet to touch the tiles. I reach to unclasp my bra as he steadies me and peels my panties down my legs.

He lifts me onto his shoulders and dives into my core. I shove one hand into the front of his hair as I claw at the wall behind me with the other. My hair is soaked, hanging heavily in my face and around my shoulders. I lick my lips as I stare down at him devouring me.

"Oh yes," I pant. He tilts my hips to gain more access. "Oh shit. Yes. Yes."

Omid

I can't stop eating her pussy. I need to feel her close to me. Knowing someone wanted to harm her, to take her from me has me split in two. She will never leave my home alone again.

I start on the buttons of my soaked shirt. I need to be inside of her. Reluctantly, I release her and set her on her feet. Lifting to my full height, I tug my shirt off and toss it to the shower floor. My pants and boxers are next to drop.

"I love you," I breathe against her lips as I cup her face.

"I love you too."

I cover her lips, inhaling her like air. Dipping, I wrap her thighs with my arms and bring her to my waist. My cock rubs over her wet folds before I press her to the shower wall and slide inside her tight heat.

It's like taking my first breath. I lock eyes with her, needing the connection. I place a hand beside her head, anchoring myself to the moment.

"You always feel so good. I'd lose my mind without you."

"You'll never be without me."

Her words cause me to drive into her hard. Her back hits the wall and she cries out. I reach to brush her wet hair from her face, revealing her beauty to me. Those brown eyes stare back at me with so much love and trust.

We've come so far. Too far for me to let anyone harm her. I shake that thought away, it just makes me crazy.

She cups my jaw, a questioning expression covering her face. I take her lips in answer, pouring all of my love into her as we make love. Each stroke soothing my need and driving it at the same time.

"Whatever it is, we'll get through this together," she whispers.

I nod and press my forehead to hers. My calm in the midst of my turmoil. I couldn't ask for more.

"Come with me, aşkım."

"*Dilediğin gibi kralım.*"

Her king. She guts me every time she says that and she knows it. As she promises, upon my wish she comes just as I coat her insides.

I rub my nose against her cheek. Not ready to let her go. I envelop her in my arms and relish in her nearness.

"We will be at this for a few hours. Prepare yourself."

She laughs. "Kind of figured that."

Divine

He comes back into the bed and hands me a box. We've finally come up for air. I've been well loved and turned out.

"I never got to give you your birthday present," he says as I take the box from him.

"What it is?"

"Open it." He grabs me by the thighs and pulls me closer.

Legs draped over his, I rip the paper from the box. When I lift the lid there's a chain with a key on it. I lift the chain from the box and hold it up between us. I bounce my gaze between him and the key.

"You said you wished you had an office space closer to the house and nearer to my practice. I found you the perfect location and office space. We can go look at it in the morning," he explains.

I sit just staring at him for a moment. My expression blank. He's giving me the key to a new office space?

"Let me get this straight. I mentioned a new office space and you found one to rent for me. Just because I said it?"

"No, I purchased you the space just because you said it," he corrects.

"I'm just going to say thank you because I don't know what else to say."

"You're welcome. Happy birthday, Divine. I love you."

This is a birthday I'll never forget. That's for sure.

CHAPTER FORTY-TWO

A Father First

Omid

"You will learn to be a great man," I murmur against the top of my son's head.

I inhale his sweet scent. Divine and I just finished giving the twins a bath. Music plays through the house as we spend a lazy Sunday at home. Divine took Fairuza to the kitchen to check on dinner, leaving me and my boy here together for a moment.

"You have learned to be a great man." I turn at the sound of my father's voice to find him with Fairuza in his arms. "Not the man I would have molded you into but still a very great man."

"Hey, baba."

"Hello, my son."

He comes across the room and tugs me into his embrace. He holds me as tightly as he can with the two children between us.

I'm surprised when he holds on a little longer than I'm expecting.

"I've wanted to do that from the time I arrived in America," he says when he releases me.

I look at him in confusion. He pats my cheek. The smile on his face is open and welcoming but I'm still cautious.

"Why didn't you?"

He laughs. "You have seen me as the villain for years. I didn't realize how much so until your friend and cousins arrived in Iran. I was angry all those years ago.

"I made many mistakes. I made threats I didn't mean. Said things that weren't me. Your grandfather would've followed through on it and so much more. He was always a hard man."

"Yeah, uncle Jahan had to hear how pissed he was at me. At all of us."

My father gives a half laugh. "I wish I could've done what Jahan did. Instead, I've worked to cover him so he could be who he wanted to be. When your grandfather passes a lot of things will change. I've wanted you home to instill much of that change. Paiman is entitled. Bazar is still young.

"It's now that I see you're happy in the life Allah has chosen for you. Do you understand why I've been so lenient with you?"

"Uncle Jahan and the Alliance," I say kissing my son's forehead as he starts to whimper.

He looks down at Fairuza fast asleep in his arms. Gently, he places her into the crib. He looks at her like she created the world and offered it to him.

"You would think that," he says when he looks at me. "Of all my wives, I've had a special place in my heart for Sassa. I was devasted when I couldn't give her a child. My father encouraged me to marry Padma. He believed that Sassa was why Allah didn't want to bless me."

"Seriously?" I scowl.

"You see, I was supposed to marry Padma first but once I saw Sassa I chose her. She was beautiful in spirit as well as her face. I wanted desperately to have that light.

"You know how things are. So much discord and fighting. I wanted the peace I saw in her," he says with a distant look in his eyes.

"So Büyük baba thought she was cursed for you picking her over Padma?"

"Yes. When I married Padma she didn't produce an heir either. That's when baba introduced me to Hana. Very pretty face, but her heart has always been in the exact place I didn't want mine. When you were born, it only made her worse. Padma became pregnant the next year with your brother and you know the rest." He waves a hand.

"She became a nagging witch because she was the first to give you an heir."

"Your mother is spoiled and entitled. I will deal with her. She will not be in your hair any longer.

"Here is what I want you to understand. I thought I was the cursed one. I thought I would never have children of my own. Three wives before my first son was born. You were a miracle to me from Allah.

"You have always been special. I've allowed you things I haven't the others because you were born with a purpose. A purpose known only by you and Allah.

"If that's women's medicine, praises be to Allah. You've fallen in love with a woman named Divine, my son.

"I don't think that's a coincidence. I've been trying to tell you since I arrived that I'm proud of you. I came to America to learn the truth. What your life is truly like because the man that arrived in Iran for the first time in nineteen years was a man that I respect."

"What are you saying?"

"I'm saying, every time I've opened my mouth to get to know my son better, my crazy wife has opened her mouth to ruin it. I told her to leave Gulzar in Iran. The only reason I kept Sassa from calling to warn Navid was because I wanted to know the truth. I wanted to know you."

He places a hand on my shoulder and gives a squeeze before bringing me in for a hug. "You're the most precious thing to me, Omid. You're always welcome in my home. You're the son I prayed for.

"I'm very proud of you. Navid has shown me all of your great work. I wish you would use your real name. Let it be known to the world that the prince has saved lives and given hope to men and women that are desperate for children just as I once was."

Wow.

My mind is blown. I never would've thought any of this. I guess I didn't give him a chance when I think about it. I was always on the defense.

Which only confirms one thing. Paiman acted alone. All signs have pointed to that truth but this is what I needed to be sure of.

"I'm sorry I didn't give you a chance."

"I understand. She's special. I would protect her with everything in me as well. The way I protect Sassa from your mother." He grins.

"I'm glad you have the twins and friends willing to give their lives for you. I don't know what I would've done if I lost you forever. I love you, Omid. We will be in each other's lives moving forward."

"I love you too, Baba. I will make the time to come home more."

Divine

I wipe at the corners of my eyes. I didn't mean to eavesdrop but shit my company's name is Gossip. It's not like I was seriously going to walk away.

Hearing Omid and his father reconcile has me thinking of my own dad. We need to make all of this right. Life is too short. I almost lost my husband.

I run for the front of the house and grab my keys. Jumping into the coup, I head for my parents' house. I'm bound to find my daddy sitting in front of the TV.

I'm so focused on my mission, I forget to say I'm leaving. When my phone rings in the car, I feel like a jerk for not saying something. "Hey, babe. I wasn't thinking. I'm running to my parents'," I say when I answer the call.

"Everything okay?"

"Yeah, I need to talk to my dad. Are you okay with the twins? I'll come right back."

"How about we go together? You're not that far yet, right?"

I think on it. It's time we stop dancing around my dad. "Yeah, that sounds good. I'm turning around."

I smile as Omid and his dad stand with the carriers getting them into the bigger car. I'm so happy they have mended their relationship.

Once we're all in the car, Omid drives us to my parents'. I sit between my children watching them sleep. When they grow up, I wish them nothing but happiness with whoever makes them happy.

I want them to love with their hearts and not their eyes. I want them to know God, not a religion that limits them or places God in a box. I want them to be good humans.

When we get to Mommy and Daddy's I can see the smoke from the grill billowing out from the back of the house. We get the babies out and I point Omid and his dad toward the front door. My mother will let them in. I want to talk to my dad first.

"Hey, Daddy," I say as I round the house and find him at the grill. He looks up and his eyes soften.

"Hey, baby girl," he says.

I make it to his side and look up at him. This man has been my world all my life. He's been there whenever I've needed him. I love my dad.

He cups the side of my face. "I love all of my children, but I remember when you were born. I looked at your face and said to myself, she's going to be a special one. You were stubborn from the beginning with this cute little pout like we all needed to cater to you before we pissed you off."

I laugh and cover his hand. I've always been called the brat in the family. We all know I've been spoiled.

"Divine, I want nothing but the best for you. I'm willing to say when I'm wrong. I've always wanted a man for you that would look at you the way I look at your mother.

"Someone to listen to all those ideas you have, to help you grow them. Someone to understand that sometimes you're just like your daddy and you will get in your own way.

"I think you have found that and more in Omid. Imma kick his ass he ever talks to me like that again, but this time I deserved it. I was old and stubborn. I missed my baby's wedding," he gets choked up. "I should've been there for you. I should've swallowed my pride way before now."

"Daddy, you were there in my heart. You all were."

"Bullshit, little girl. I'll never get that day back. Just like I missed the birth of my little grandbabies. You did good, Divine. Those two are you all over again. If I haven't told you how proud of you I am. I want you to know, baby girl, you've lived up to all my hopes and dreams and then some," he says.

"Thank you, Daddy that means a lot."

"Remember, Divine. I'm always a father first. I'm always going to want to see you happy."

"He makes me happy."

"I got that."

He looks over my shoulder and I turn to follow his gaze. Omid has stepped out of the house holding the twins. He comes over to us.

"Your mother said he won't swing on me if I'm holding the babies," he teases.

"You have to put them down sometime," my father replies with a straight face.

"Daddy."

He cracks a smile. "I'm joking. Hand over my granddaughter. I haven't gotten to hold her today."

Omid hands him Fairuza and my father's face lights up. I move into Omid's side, and he wraps an arm around my waist, while I wrap mine around his. He kisses the top of my head.

"Dr. Omid. Do you like basketball? There's a game coming on and these steaks are almost done," my father says.

"I try to watch when I can. No offense on the steaks. My father and I,—"

"Right, right, I'll remember to go to the Halal butcher next week. You guys coming to the barbeque, right?"

"I'm bringing the rum punch and the potato salad."

"That's my girl." He turns to my daughter and says. "You stick with your mama in the kitchen and learn to make that potato salad."

My heart swells. This is what my family should be like. Omid gives me a gentle squeeze.

"Come on, son-in-law. Let me get to know you. It looks like we'll be keeping you around for a while."

Soon the house is full of my family as they drop in to witness my father welcome Omid in. I couldn't be happier hours later as I stand in the threshold of the living room and watch my father and husband as they each hold a baby talking and shouting at the TV like old friends.

"Now look at that," my mother says.

"Yeah, look at that. Everything I ever wanted. Not when I wanted it, but in divine timing."

"Always in divine timing."

Fit for a Queen

Divine

Seven days. He's throwing me a seven-day wedding. My mind is still blown. The dresses, the venues, the guest list, the menus. I can't believe this is my life.

In hindsight, my little fast ass never should've been online dating and going to meet some boy in the park. I would whip Fair's little ass if she tried something like that and I found out about it. My mother nearly strangled me when I told her our story.

The glares I got for about a week straight said it all. If she wasn't such a fan of Omid's she probably would've throttled me. My mother isn't the only fan of Omid's. My father can't stop talking about his son-in-law the doctor.

"What has you smiling like that?" Marica asks as she walks over to me standing in front of the mirror.

"He kept his promise. This may not be my first time here, but he brought me to Dubai. Do you see all of this?"

"Yeah, I see it." She beams. "I guess we did get that life we dreamed of when we were sixteen."

I turn to look at her. I'm so happy for her. Her little boy is so precious. She couldn't be happier with her family. Although she has aches every now and again, her wrist and leg have healed and she's walking.

"Although visiting and moving to someplace exotic are two different things," I note.

"Girl, please. He bought you a house here and in Shiraz. I sort of got an Island as a birthday gift," she says with a shy smile. "Those have to count for something."

"Okay, I'll give you that." I laugh.

"I'm happy for you. You're glowing."

"That might have something to do with being pregnant," I whisper.

"Maybe this time we can really do this together," she replies and stares at me, biting her lip.

It takes me a second for it to click. When I catch on, I nearly launch myself at her. We embrace and squeal together the way we used to when we were younger.

"How far?"

"About nine weeks."

I do a little happy dance. "This time we're going to have close due dates."

"Looks like it," she says with a beaming smile.

"Look at you." We turn at the sound of my mother's voice. "That dress is breathtaking."

I turn back to the mirror once more. "It is stunning," I reply as I smooth my hands down the blue and gold fabric. It's just the first dress of many but I love it just the same.

"You look like a princess," my mother says.

"She is," Sassa chimes in.

I laugh. I feel like a princess. When Omid said he wanted to do this for our anniversary, I didn't know he wanted to do it this big. I should've known better.

"Omid is going to be speechless when he sees you."

"Have you seen him? How are the twins? Are they driving him crazy?"

"He looks like a proud baba. They're both fine. They adore him."

"I guess that means the only thing missing is me."

Michael Donati

I sit in the shadow, resting on the window sill. He doesn't see us. His jealousy and anger are too blinding for that. It's good that we're finally paying him this visit. It's much overdue if you ask me.

"He's here in Dubai. Why can't you make this happen?" He snarls into the phone. "I don't care about Remi or Ramses. Fuck the Alliance. I want him and his family dead."

He listens to the other end of the phone, nostrils flaring as he's denied his way. He's like a petulant child. I curl my lip back over my teeth.

He's a piece of shit. Selfish, self-centered, arrogant asshole. All the flash and none of the class to go with it.

"No, this cannot wait any longer. I know he knows what I've done. It's me or him. I'm not going to wait another day for him to come for me...Yes, I know I'm talking about a doctor. You don't know my brother. It's all an act. He's as bad as the twins. Do this and I will double the price."

The desperation in his voice seeps through into the air. I can taste his fear. I grin. Omid was right. This fat fuck has lost it.

"Hello? Hello?" he hollers frantically.

It's clear they've had enough of listening to him. Wise choice. I would've hated to have to miss the wedding to pay another visit today.

I flip my pocket watch open. The difference in my brother's style and mine. I like to offer an ambiance for the silence I'm here to bring.

Uri and Val slaughter. Sim and I, we create a short and sweet ending. Now you hear it, then you don't.

"What the hell?" This fat bastard snarls when he hears the sound of Für Elise fill the room from my watch.

I stare at him with a smile on my lips. Like a dance that's timeless, Sim moves in, placing her silencer to his temple. I lift my own gun and together we make him hush. It's swift, neat, and quick. Two to the head. Our way.

I close the watch and stand. The song has ended and time is up. My wedding gift to the groom has been completed. I hold my hand out for Sim's like I've done a hundred times before.

"We have a wedding to get to," I say.

"You have to make the call."

"Yes, I haven't forgotten. Just relishing in the moment a bit."

She grins. "I've been wanting to complete this one for some time. You never go against family."

I turn to her and smile. Those are words we live by. They're the words that have saved us to this day.

Never.

I pull my phone from my pocket and make the call with a peace many won't ever understand. I'm a man that lives happily in the shadows. It's the men who's shadows I enter that should distress. My brother picks up the phone on the second ring. I say all that needs to be said.

"Done."

Omid

I hold my son and daughter in my arms waiting for the call before we'll start the celebration. I have no regrets. When you see a problem it's best to handle it before it handles you. Paiman is lucky he was granted the time he was.

Remi and Ramses had no intention of sparing him a single day. I, on the other hand, wanted to wait. I wanted Paiman to wait and wonder when it would happen. I wanted him to look around every corner stressing about whether or not he was safe.

I wanted him close to insanity when death finally came for him. He came for my sanity when he targeted my wife so I've returned the favor. What kind of big brother would I be if I didn't.

Uri walks over and kisses the top of Fair's head and pinches Fir's cheek. "Un Ur," they sing their version of his name as they bounce in my arms.

He looks me in the eyes. "It's done. Let's get this wedding started."

I nod.

"My son, let's get this celebration started. What are we waiting for?" Baba calls from across the room.

"Nothing. Absolutely nothing."

Divine

Fireworks fill the sky. Gold desserts are being served and laughter surrounds us. This has only been the first day and I'm still in awe of it all.

I look up into my husband's eyes as we dance beneath the stars.

"This," I say to him with a beaming smile.

"This." His eyes sparkle as he looks back at me. "We'll always have this. I love you, Princess Divine Vahid."

"Not as much as I love you, my Prince."

"Weren't you calling me Dr. Feel Good last night?"

I throw my head back and burst with laughter. I love this man. He has been everything I need, whenever I need it, even when I didn't know I needed it.

My life is truly divine.

Blue Collection Character Tree

Legally Bound 1
Bobby Mairettie and Paige Kemble-Mairettie *father and mother of:*
  *Peyton and James Mairettie (*twin boys*)
  *Sydney Mairettie and Maria Lynn Mairettie (*twin girls*)

Legally Bound 2
Marcus Mairettie and Rita Briggs-Mairettie *father and mother of:*
  *Daniel Mairettie
  *Hannah Mairettie

Legally Bound 3
Nathaniel (Nate) Briggs and Pamela (Pam) Kemble-Briggs *father and mother of:*
  *Tiffany and Tracey Briggs (*twin girls*)
  *Nathaniel Briggs Jr.

Legally Bound 4
Jasper Briggs and Marie Mairettie-Briggs *father and mother of:*
  *Clay Briggs

The Mairettie Family
Grandpa Marcello Mairettie and Grandma Marie Ann *father and mother of:*
  *Marcello Mairettie Jr.
  *Andrew Mairettie

*James Mairettie
*Jessie Mairettie
*Lynn Mairettie
*Gianna Mairettie
*James Mairettie and Minnie Mairettie *father and mother of:*
    *Bobby Mairettie
    *Sam Mairettie – (Ellen Kensington-Mairettie, *wife*)
    *Marcus Mairettie
    *Marie Mairettie

The Briggs Family
Thomas Briggs and Raquel Marinos-Briggs (**Deceased**) *father and mother of:*
    *Nathaniel Briggs
    *Rita Briggs

Earl Briggs (Thomas' younger brother) and Caitronia Marinos-Briggs (twin sister of Raquel) *father and mother of:*
    *Kelly Briggs-Fecteau (Alexie Fecteau, *husband*)
    *Jasper Briggs

The Kemble Family
Peyton Kemble and Davina Kemble *father and mother of:*
    *Pamela Kemble
    *Paige Kemble

Other Important *Legally Bound* Characters
Camille (Cam) Mc Wien-Carter (Seth Carter, *soon-to-be ex-husband*) *father and mother of:*
    *Seth Carter Jr.
    *Eddie Carter

*Aiden Carter

Austin Mc Wien (*Camille's father*)

Baroness Olivia Kontos (Baron Kontos' widow; Jasper's ex-lover; Thomas Briggs' new love interest)

Vanessa (Julissa) Smith-Mims (Patrick Mims, *husband,* **Deceased**)

Hush 1
Uri Donati and Valentina Caprisi-Donati *father and mother of:*
  *Vita Khayla Donati
  *Nori Donati
  *Inzo Donati
  *Eva Donati

Hush 2
Luca Donati and Shannon Caprisi-Donati *father and mother of:*
  *Carlo Donati (Introduced in **Ballers 2**)

The Donati Family
Angelo Uri Donati (**Deceased**) and Donatella Manzo-Donati-~~Zuko~~ *father and mother of:*
  *Uri Donati
  *Nico Donati ~~Zuko~~
  *Annabella Donati ~~Zuko~~ (*Nico's twin sister*)
  *Michael Donati – ~~Zuko~~

Nicholas Donati (Angelo Donati's brother) and
Ava Donati *father and mother of:*
    *Luca Donati

The Caprisi Family
Vincent Caprisi and Khayla Grant-Caprisi (**Deceased**) *father and mother of:*
    *Valentina Caprisi
    *Lissette Caprisi (**Deceased**)
    **Shannon Caprisi (*Vincent's daughter*)

Other Important *Hush* Characters
Uncle Valentine Caprisi (*Vincent's brother; head hitter*)

Iman Grant (*Khayla's sister;* **Shannon's mother;* **Deceased**)

Roberto Donati-Zuko (*Donatella's husband;* **Deceased**)
**Posed as Dale the accountant from Legally Bound 3*

Cole 'Brooklyn' O'Brien

DJ

Ballers 1
Bradley Monroe and Tamara Hathaway-Monroe *father and mother of:*
    *Brielle Monroe
    *Ashley Monroe and Ashton Monroe (*twins*)
    *Corey Monroe (*Baby Tam is pregnant
    with at end of **Ballers 1***)

The Monroe Family
Vernon Monroe and Gloria Monroe *father and mother of:*
  *Trevor Monroe (Donna, *soon to be ex-wife)*
  *Bradley Monroe
  *Ann Monroe (*Bradley's twin sister; Tom, husband*)

Trevor Monroe and Donna Monroe *father and mother of:*
  *Jessica Monroe
  *Toby Monroe and Paige Monroe (*twins*)
  *Jonathan Monroe
Tom Rivers and Ann Monroe-Rivers *father and mother of:*
  *George Rivers and Melissa Rivers (*twins*)
  *Amy Rivers

The Hathaway Family
Byron Hathaway and Fiona Hathaway *father and mother of:*
  *Ellerie Hathaway
  *Tamara Hathaway

Other Important *Ballers* Characters
Stacey (Tam's best friend)

Reese (Tam's best friend; Nico's girlfriend in **Ballers 1**)

Alee (Tam's best friend)

Cyrus Pierson (Tam's boss) *father of:*
  *Tommy Pierson
  *Carey Pierson

*Stephanie Pierson

Ballers 2
Nico Donati and Reese Bridges-Donati *father and mother of:*
    *Nico Donati Jr.
    *Lanya Donati
    *Orso Donati
    *Santo Donati
    *Stefano Donati

Other Important *Ballers 2* Characters
Tiberius Roman (Reese's ex-husband)

Symphony (Michael's right-hand)

Brothers Black 1

Wyatt Black and Lanelle (Nellie) Bryant-Black *father and mother of:*
    *Nora Black
    *Evan Black

The Black Family
Joseph Black and Cassidy Black *father and mother of:*
    *Wyatt Black
    *Noah Black
    *Johnathan Black
    *Felix Black
    *Toby Black
    *Braxton Black
    *Ryan Black

The Lockhart Family
Rob Lockhart and Faith Lockhart *father and step-mother of:*
    *Heather Lockhart

Steve Lockhart and Nora Bryant-Lockhart (**Deceased**) *step-father and mother of:*
    *Lanelle (Nellie) Bryant-Black

Chase Lockhart and Jennifer Lockhart *father and mother of:*
    *Rebecca (Bean) Lockhart (Noah's best friend and love interest)

Other Important *Brothers Black 1* **Characters**
Missy (Johnathan's ex-girlfriend, **Deceased**)

Lucy (*Heather's girlfriend*)

Barry Coleman (**Deceased**)

Brothers Black 2
Noah Black and Rebecca (Bean) Lockhart-Black *father and mother of:*
    *Brodie Black
    *Connor Black
    Baby on the way

Other Important *Brothers Black 2* Characters
Joshua (**Deceased**)

Carmen (Nene) Nash (*reporter; niece of Mariah Briggs from Yours Series; Ryan's new crush*)

Logan O'Brien

Brothers Black 3
King Toby Black and Queen Ogeima Feechi (Kamara) Abioye-Black *father and mother of:*
 *Lulu Black
 *TJ Black
 *Baby on the way

Other Important *Brothers Black 3* **Characters**
Missy (Johnathan's ex-girlfriend, ***Deceased***)

Lucy (*Heather's girlfriend*)

Barry Coleman (***Deceased***)

King Elijah Abioye aka Mr. Naidoo

Queen Ada Catherine Naidoo-Abioye

King Kwäzē Naidoo-Abioye

Celeste (Kwäzē's ex-girlfriend)

King Afafa (***Deceased***)

Missy (Johnathan's ex-girlfriend, ***Deceased***)

Lucy (*Heather's girlfriend*)

Barry Coleman (***Deceased***)

Joshua (***Deceased***)

Carmen Nash aka Nene (*Reporter, Mariah Briggs, from Yours Series, Niece, Ryan's new crush*)
Logan O'Brien

Dylan O'Brien

Jamie O'Brien

Cole 'Brooklyn' O'Brien

Uncle Jonah McGowan

Uncle Jack McGowan

Uncle Raymond McGowan

Uncle Ronan McGowan

Carrick McGowan

Malcolm McGowan

Graham McGowan

Jeremiah McGowan

Reilly McGowan

Brothers Black 4
Braxton Black and Heather Lockhart-Black *father and mother of:*
    *Riley Black
    *Rowen Black

Other Important *Brothers Black 4* Characters
    Debbie ~~Lockhart~~ Kline (Rob's ex-wife, Heather's Mother)

    Lucy (*Heather's pretend girlfriend*)

    Amanda Kline (Heather's half-sister)

    Ernest Kline (Heather's Stepfather, *Deceased*)

    Eugene aka Crooked Nose

    Logan O'Brien

    Dylan O'Brien

    Jamie O'Brien

    Cole 'Brooklyn' O'Brien

    Uncle Jonah McGowan

    Uncle Jack McGowan

Uncle Raymond McGowan

Uncle Ronan McGowan

Carrick McGowan

Malcolm McGowan

Graham McGowan

Jeremiah McGowan

Reilly McGowan

Nicholas Lincoln

Sephora Lincoln

Thomas Briggs

Brothers Black 5
Felix Black and Kaye Porter-Black aka Kaye Blaze *father and mother of:*
   *Dashawn Black
   *Second child unannounced

Other Important *Brothers Black 4* **Characters**
Lakia Redding (*Kaye's writer friend*)

Dean (*Kaye's writer friend*)

Hayidah (*Doll for Club Desire*)

Pastor Wayne Porter (*Kaye's father*)

Danesha Porter (*Kaye's mother*)

Danny Porter (**Deceased** *Kaye's brother and Felix's best friend*)

Grandma Reid (*Kaye's grandmother*)

Grandpa Reid (*Kaye's grandfather*)

Alberto Perez (*Felix's best friend*)

Jacob McTavish (*Lead actor in Kaye's movie*)

Mona Richards (**Deceased**, *a fan*)

Logan O'Brien

Dylan O'Brien

Jamie O'Brien

Cole 'Brooklyn' O'Brien

Uncle Ronan McGowan

Carrick McGowan

Yours Series

Nicholas Lincoln and Sephora (Sophi/Soph/Lilla du) Emilsson *father and mother of:*
 *Nicole Lincoln
 *Nadia Lincoln
 *Nicholas Lincoln Jr.

The Lincoln Family

Dean Lincoln and Shelly Lincoln (**Both Deceased**) *father and mother of:*
 *Nicholas Lincoln
 *Rick ~~Carbon~~ Lincoln
 *Gavin ~~Carbon~~ Lincoln

The Emilsson Family

Liam Emilsson (thought to be deceased) and Faraz Emilsson father and mother of:
 *Lucian Emilsson
 *Ettie Emilsson
 *Sephora Emilsson

Lucian Emilsson and Kimberly Ann Clove *father and mother of:*
 *Lilla Emilsson

Other Important *Yours* Characters

Mark Fienberg (Sephora's best friend)

Ivana Graves (Nick's ex-girlfriend; **Deceased**)

Bianca (Liam's mistress; **Missing**)

Winton (Nick's driver and security)

Jillian Carver (Nick's ex-temporary PA; *Deceased*)

Harvey Carver (Jillian's father; Nick's family friend; *Deceased*)

Bailey Wilder (waitress; Mark's girlfriend)

Dylan O'Brien

Nick's Crew
Wyatt Black
Kevin Briggs (Mariah Briggs' husband; Nick's PA)
Craig Hilton
George Ligal
Lucian Emilsson
Andrew Connor (Ettie's husband)

Be Yours Series
Prince Omid Arman Vahid (Dr. O.V-Shah) and Divine Favors
father and mother of:
    *Prince Firuz Arman Vahid
    *Princess Fairuza Araz Vahid

The Vahid Family

Javed Vahid and Hana Vahid (**third wife**) *father and mother of:*
    *Prince Omid Arman Vahid
    *Prince Bazar Vahid
        Padma Vahid *first wife and mother of:*
            *Prince Paiman Vahid
            *Princess Yasmin Vahid

Other Important *Be Yours* **Characters**
Prince Jahan Vahid

Prince Remi Vahid

Prince Ramses Vahid

Sassa Vahid (*First wife of Javed Vahid*)

Marica Thompson (Divine's cousin)

Dr. Nobi

Gretta (Medical Assistant)

Navid (Omid's advisor)

Dada (Divine's best friend)

ACKNOWLEDGMENTS

Yeah, well this was supposed to be a quick write. Ha! The details that went into this one. Thanks to everyone that answered my questions and helped me with completing this book. Ultimately Omid told me exactly what he wanted this book to be. Well, and the other books that were set up in this one. Cough, cough, at least five.

I've learned a lot about myself with this one. It was fun and unexpected. With so much on my plate it really was a process, but one worth going through.

Thank you to all of my readers for your patience and support. Man, if you all could live in my head right now you'd probably run. So many levels and books to all of this. I thank you for allowing me to unfold them all as the characters ask me to. Which sometimes means changing plans and the schedule. Just trust me.

Special thanks to my team. My editor Katrina Fair for always being there to deal with my bazaar hybrid life. This will get better. LOL. To my husband for being my BETA reader, sounding board, and the one always keeping it real with me. Thank you so much to my girls. You guys don't know how much you push me to do more and do better.

Man, let me tell you about God. You guys don't know my life and probably don't care...BUT GOD. I've been walking on water and learning the depths of God on a new level. People I thought I could trust have revealed themselves. I've fallen on my face a few times and had to stand up and remember who I am.

I'm growing and the pains of that are showing themselves sharply. BUT GOD. He has been there every step of the way whispering, guiding, and handing me down like no one else can. I have some days when I just have to stop and give thanks 'cause I know for a fact I couldn't do half of what I do without HIS Divine blessings and Favor. What's on everyone else's plate is not my buiness. It's not my assignment. What God has placed before me is what I have my hands full with and for that I give him all the Glory.

Next! Yeah, Ryan is coming but we may need to talk to Cameron first. My, My, My.

ABOUT THE AUTHOR

Blue Saffire, award-winning, bestselling author of over thirty contemporary romance novels and novellas, writes with the intention to touch the heart and the mind. Blue hooks, weaves, and loops multiple series, keeping you engaged in her worlds. Blue is a hybrid author, writing her own publishing company Perceptive Illusions and for Sourcebooks, as well as Dreamspinners Press as Royal Blue.

Blue and her husband live in a house filled with laughter and creativity, in Long Island, NY. Both working hard to build the Blue brand and cultivate their love for the artists. Creative is their family affair.

Blue holds an MBA in Marketing and Project Management, as well as a MED in Instructional Technology and Curriculum Design. She is also an NLP Master Practitioner.

Wait, there is more to come! You can stay updated with my latest releases, learn more about me, the author, and be a part of contests by subscribing to my newsletter at
www.BlueSaffire.com
If you enjoyed *Doctor Feel Good*, I'd love to hear your thoughts and please feel free to leave a review. And when you do, please let me
know by emailing me TheBlueSaffire@gmail.com or leave a comment on Facebook
https://www.facebook.com/BlueSaffireDiaries or Twitter @TheBlueSaffire

Other books by Blue Saffire
Placed in Best Reading Order
Also available....
Legally Bound

Legally Bound 2: Against the Law

Legally Bound 3: His Law

Perfect for Me

Hush 1: Family Secrets

Ballers: His Game

Brothers Black 1: Wyatt the Heartbreaker

Legally Bound 4: Allegations of Love

Hush 2: Slow Burn

Legally Bound 5.0: Sam

Yours: Losing My Innocence 1

Yours 2: Experience Gained

Yours 3: Life Mastered

Ballers 2: His Final Play

Legally Bound 5.1: Tasha Illegal Dealings

Brothers Black 2: Noah

Legally Bound 5.2: Camille

Legally Bound 5.3 & 5.4 Special Edition

Where the Pieces Fall

Legally Bound 5.5: Legally Unbound

Brothers Black 4: Braxton the Charmer

My Funny Valentine

Broken Soldier

Remember Me

Brothers Black 5: Felix the Brain

A Home for Christmas

Be My Valentine

Coming Soon...
Ballers 3: His Team
Brothers Black 6: Ryan the Joker
Brothers Black 7: Johnathan the Fixer

Blue Saffire Exclusive on the
BlueSaffire.com Site

The Lost Souls MC Series
Forever

Never
Always coming July 2019

The A Million to Blow Series
A Million to Blow
A Million to Stay
A Million Blown Coming soon...

Other books from Evei Lattimore Collection
Books by Blue Saffire
Black Bella 1

Destiny 1: Life Decisions
Destiny 2: Decisions of the Next Generation
Destiny 3 coming soon...

Star